Reckless
LOVE

KG Fletcher

VINCI
BOOKS

By KG Fletcher

The Bennetts of Langston Falls

Faultless Love

Shameless Love

Breathless Love

Reckless Love

Fearless Love

The Stardust Duet

Love's Refrain

Love's Reverie

For Anne
"There are friends, there is family, and then there are friends that become family." ~ Unknown

Vinci Books

vinci-books.com

Published by Vinci Books Ltd in 2026

1

A CIP catalogue record for this book is available from the British Library.
Paperback ISBN: 9781036708191
The EU GPSR authorised representative is Logos Europe, 9 rue Nicolas Poussion, 17000 La Rochelle, France contact@logoseurope.eu

Chapter One

REBECCA BENNETT

The autumn rains came early to Langston Falls. The blustery wetness fell from the sky and pelted the windows, raindrops sounding like copper pennies thrown against the glass.

Tucking her hands into her apron pockets, Becky Bennett sighed and looked out at the deluge. Her older brothers were out in the elements, probably soaked to the skin, rivulets of water dripping from their cowboy hats and mud oozing over the tops of their boots in the fields. At least her father was dry, working away inside his cozy office down the hall. She imagined him wearing his reading glasses and going over the latest winery reports from behind his substantial desk, family photos and keepsakes surrounding him on bookshelves while the family dogs snoozed peacefully near his feet.

But the dreary weather wasn't to blame for her melancholy mood. It was something else. Something Becky couldn't quite put her finger on.

Lately, she'd been moping around, the usual joy she

found in her role on the family Christmas tree farm and winery dulled by the repetitiveness of her daily duties. Sure, she appreciated her small team and their help baking and boxing up treats for the weekly winery tour visitors. They were also a godsend when it came to the annual festivals held at Bennett Farms, most recently, another successful Harvest Hoedown. And providing hearty meals for her brothers, father, and the hired hands was something she was good at. And how could she not be thrilled by the success of her YouTube channel, *The Farmer's Daughter*? It started as a hobby, something fun for her to do while she cooked. She never intended the weekly podcast to become a lucrative job. And wasn't that what it was now? A job?

Becky had everything she'd ever wanted in a legitimate career, especially after partnering with sponsors and using affiliate links which leveled her up to monetization. She couldn't have done it without Elyse Farrell. Elyse was her brother Walt's fiancé and a wiz in the television industry. She hooked Becky up good, and now, money poured into her bank account like the water flowing over Langston Falls. Because of her brand's success, she was now in talks with a publishing company that wanted to publish *The Farmer's Daughter Cookbook* featuring family recipes she shared on her channel.

She was successful and sought after. Monetary success, it seemed, came way too easily for Becky, and she thought maybe she'd peaked too early. She was restless. What else could she possibly attain when she'd already achieved so much in her young life? And why was she so terribly lonely?

Shrugging off the overwhelming thoughts she assumed were the side effect of the dreary weather, she shifted her focus. She looked out over the ample living space in front of the stone fireplace of the Bennett family farmhouse.

Although this was the only home she'd ever known, she liked imagining what she could do with the money she banked.

It'd be so easy to build a place of her own—a private cottage filled with antiques, her cookbook collection, and her mother's heirloom china. A tiny plot of land where she could grow an herb and flower garden and wear big floppy hats and overalls in the summertime without her brothers' relentless teasing. A place with a private bathroom she didn't have to share with her youngest brother, Hank, when he was in town.

But looking around, she realized this was where she belonged. This right here, in this very place, was what happiness looked like. Her daddy working in the next room. Her brothers' boots and hats lined up in the mud room. A quiet moment listening to the rain. A soft cardigan pressed around her shoulders. A sink full of rinsed potatoes ready to be peeled for tonight's supper. The tea kettle on the stovetop and her favorite mug ready to be filled.

Crossing to the appliance, she poured herself the hot beverage and added a generous squeeze from a bright lemon wedge. The legs of the kitchen chair scraped against the ancient wood floors before she sat and held the warm porcelain to her lips, taking tiny sips as heat vapors warmed her cheeks.

Or maybe…

Maybe what she needed was a change of scenery. A small respite away from the testosterone and the big dogs. A break after another successful farm festival and pending book deal. Completely ignoring her social media and YouTube channel sounded amazing. But where would she go?

Becky didn't have an entourage of besties in the small

community of Langston Falls. Most of her high school friends moved away and started their careers and families elsewhere. Now, her friendships were delegated to her brothers' female partners or her virtual friends across multiple social media platforms. How odd to have online friends she'd never met in person?

In fact, one of her favorite internet friends was a sixty-something Southern cook named Alice, who emailed her regularly, the two of them trading recipes and sharing photos of their families. Alice had befriended Becky through her YouTube channel when she was just starting out, and they quickly became online pals.

Maybe Alice's loving countenance and motherly disposition filled the cavernous void in Becky's heart left behind during those years involving her brother's unfortunate incarceration and her mother's death? Or maybe it was the homemade Mississippi mud pie recipe she shared that was a huge hit with all her brothers? Whatever it was, she and Alice had become close over the years, the woman a lifeline in her time of need. Perhaps she should finally make some plans and meet Alice in person? Now there was a thought.

Becky considered herself an old soul. Her job on the farm keeping the hungry help fed, including her brothers and father, was noble and essential. Hers was an admirable vocation, especially with her talents in cooking and baking. Many might deem Becky's career in hospitality as old-fashioned. But over the years, especially after her mother's passing, she'd added modern elements to her world, including her successful YouTube channel and the annual festivals she planned on the farm property.

If the small-town folks saw her bank account now, they might rethink her role as something more like a domestic rock star rather than a laboring cook or party planner. She shouldn't be panicked about book deals, monetization, or farm festivals. She'd spent all this time creating recipes and content, offering little pieces of herself for mass consumer consumption. But what did she have to show for it besides money? A tiny bedroom. A shared bathroom. Millions of strangers following her every move.

Closing her eyes, Becky relished the quiet moment and listened to the sound of the rain. The tightness in her shoulders slowly melted away like butter on a warm biscuit as she relaxed. But her private moment of Zen was interrupted by a loud knock on the back door.

She set her mug on the kitchen table and quickly approached the entrance. A formidable figure stood behind the half-glass door beyond the screen, and she suspected it was a farm worker looking for her father.

"Who in the world?" she muttered to herself. With the door flung open, she gasped.

"Hey, Becky. Sorry to bother you."

Crossing her arms against her bosom, she scowled. On the other side of the door stood family nemesis and archenemy, Glen Kirby—a local bully with a vengeful heart. He held a bushel of apples, his hair and face underneath his cowboy hat splattered with rain. The black slicker he wore was shiny from the elements, the scent of musk and wet earth infiltrating her senses.

"What do you want, Glen?" She stood tall and pulled the cardigan tighter around her shoulders. She wasn't about to welcome him inside.

The way he backed off into a submissive stance because of her unfriendly tone was surprising, his large body hunched over as if he wanted to disappear. He lowered his gaze and mumbled, "Walt said you might want some of these apples. Said I should bring them on up to you before I head out for the day."

"Set them by the door," she barked.

Glen seemed compliant and agreeable, still not looking her in the eye. Nodding, he set the basket on the porch. When he shivered and finally made eye contact with her, his expression held sadness before he offered her a hopeful grin.

"I sure hope you enjoy them. It's peak apple season here in these parts. And I saved some of the best ones just for you."

Becky scowled. She wasn't about to take his clickbait. Glen Kirby had been kissing her ass all spring and summer, trying to weasel his way into some semblance of a friendship. Well, she wasn't having it—any of it, especially with his violent history against her family.

The man severely injured her brother, Teddy, in a barnyard fight just over a year ago, and this past winter, he threatened her other brother, Walt, with a loaded gun. She vowed never to forgive Glen. *Ever.*

Even though everyone else in her family, including Teddy and Walt, had moved on and pardoned Glen for his abhorrent behavior, it didn't mean she had to. And truth be told, she didn't want to. Still, the way Glen stood there soaked to the skin after gifting her with yet another peace offering of ripe apples, she kept her manners. Her mama and daddy didn't raise an impolite daughter, even if she loathed and despised the man standing before her.

"Thank you," she finally mumbled.

Glen's smile tweaked, and he politely took off his hat, holding it against his saturated chest. "You're welcome."

"Who's at the back door in this downpour?" Roy Bennett hollered. Her father came up alongside her and eyed Glen over the threshold. "Glen, what are you doing outside in this mess? Come on in and get dried off."

"Daddy?" Becky cautioned.

Roy pushed the door open wide and waved his hand for Glen to come through. The family dogs, Jaxson and Delia, panted by his legs, uninterested in bolting outside in the rainy weather. The big Labradors gave Glen the once-over with several sniffs and licks, Becky's enemy leaving a water trail across her recently mopped kitchen floors. She growled internally and shut the door with an aggravated thump. Her eyes went wide with horror as she watched her father hand off one of her pretty tea towels to Glen so he could dry off his wet face.

"Not that one," she gruffly remarked, snatching the towel from Glen's hands. Ripping off a few sheets from the paper towel roll, she offered him those. "Here."

Glen nodded and swiped the paper roughly across his face. "I appreciate it."

Becky gritted her teeth and nodded as she unconsciously launched daggers at him from her squinted eyes. At least she wasn't alone with the creep, her father taking over the conversation.

"Rains came early this year," Roy stated.

"Yes, sir."

"You stayin' ahead of the apple harvest?"

"Yes, sir. I still have several varieties we'll harvest in the next month. But it should be a bumper crop this year." Glen combed his wet hair back from his face with thick fingers, the grin on his face annoying.

"That's super. I'm glad for you, son."

Becky listened with her lips pressed into a thin line and folded the tea towel with military precision. Why her father and brothers were so nice to this low-life thug was hard for her to understand. At least she wasn't the one who had to work with him day in and day out. That landed on her brother Walt's shoulders.

The two men had been working nonstop, incorporating Kirby family apples with grape varietals from the Bennett family vineyard. The idea was to develop an apple-infused wine with an extra-unique flavor—a delicious combination of fruits aged in oak barrels until bottled. The idea was more than a good glass of North Georgia wine. It was a true blending of families and an opportunity for Glen to buy back what was rightfully his—the Kirby homestead and apple orchards.

Walt was still the legal owner of the Kirby property but had moved out in late spring, handing the reins back to Glen only after he was released from a drug rehab facility. The man had hit rock bottom, especially after Walt swooped in and bought his family land right out from under him. For Walt, it was an act of revenge for nearly beating their brother, Teddy, to death. But somehow, after everything both families had been through, the two men had miraculously called a truce and worked side by side ever since. They'd grown up together, good friends playing baseball and fishing. Glen was a regular face at Bennett Farms back then, and now, they'd come full circle.

"Well, I best be gettin' on before it's a total washout. Enjoy the apples, Becky."

"Mmmhmm," she mumbled.

"See you around, Glen," Roy said, slapping him across the shoulder.

"See ya, Mr. Bennett."

Becky watched Glen bumble out the door with his pathetic rain-soaked hat perched on his big head. She growled when it was just her and her father standing in the kitchen.

"How can you stand it, Daddy?"

"Stand what?"

"How can you stand that… that *monster* working on our property? I don't trust him."

Roy helped himself to a mug of tea and calmly explained. "Glen is proving himself trustworthy, I promise. He's been through the wringer and has changed his ways."

He pulled out a kitchen chair and sat, cocking his head toward the empty chair beside him. "You need to let go of your grudge and move on. All you're doing is allowing Glen to fill your headspace with negativity."

"But he's done so many terrible things. How can I let it go?" Becky sat next to her father, anxious for his advice.

"You ever hear the saying, 'holding a grudge is like letting someone live rent-free in your head?'"

"Yes."

"That's what you're doing, darlin'. And the only person it's hurting is you. You need to break this vicious cycle and find it in your heart to forgive Glen. Let it go. Your brothers have. Robyn and Elyse have. Heck, even Samantha has changed her tune."

Samantha "Sam" McNeil was her brother James's girl-friend. She was also Teddy's parole officer before he was acquitted of all charges for a crime he didn't commit. Glen Kirby punched Sam in the face on the night of the Harvest Hoedown a year ago after he, Teddy, and Walt got into an awful fistfight in the barn. The terrible memories filled Becky with angst.

"Hey." Her father placed his large hand over hers on the table. "You're my sweet girl. Don't let the past make you bitter. It's time to move on and show some kindness to the man. He's got no one. His mama stayed behind in Macon, and he's living all alone. He works from sunup to sundown and never complains. Walt's told me he has no friends except for his black cat he dotes on."

A pang of sadness hit Becky in the heart. The thought of no friends or family was foreign to her, and she wondered how Glen got through each lonely day without relapsing into his old ways.

"When a man is given a second opportunity in life, it means having a chance to right the wrongs of his past. Believe me, Glen Kirby wants to show us, and the good folks of Langston Falls, what he's capable of."

Staring at the bottom of her empty mug, Becky mulled over her father's words. Maybe he was right? Perhaps she shouldn't continue to be so mean to Glen? What if she made an intentional decision and decided to let go of all her resentment and anger? My God, if Sam could forgive him after the man hit her in the face, surely she could too.

"And what if I do forgive Glen. Then what?" she asked.

"Well, I think you might find a certain kind of peace. That's what I've found. You'll be able to focus on yourself and get on with your life."

"My life," she mumbled, unconvinced.

But maybe her unforgiving heart was the reason for her melancholy mood and not the weather. Maybe her unforgiveness was the root of her loneliness. Still, the act of letting go of her anger would be hard.

Forgiving Glen Kirby would take an act of supernatural strength.

Chapter Two

BECKY

The pastry wheel thumped with each pass Becky made across the chilled dough rolled out on the butcher block counter. Her hands were dusted with flour, her apron smeared with a cloud of white. Humming under her breath, she worked fast, her fingers delicately transferring thin strips of dough over a heaping pie pan full of sliced apples dredged in melted butter, sugar, and cinnamon. She concentrated and repeatedly moved the dough over and under until she had a pretty lattice pattern. Snipping off the edges, she folded the shell's rim back over the strips' border and securely crimped the dough into place.

Satisfied, she took a step back and admired her work. Baking pies was something she'd done her entire life, her mama showing her all the tricks. Homemade crust was the best, and she learned the dough should always be thoroughly chilled before assembling. And lard made the flakiest crust, best if used with sifted flour and cold, cold water.

As a little girl, Becky's mama would set her on a stool in front of the counter, the two of them wearing matching mother-and-daughter aprons. Becky remembered playing with little mounds of leftover dough and turning them into cinnamon pinwheels. Her mama was patient and helped her spread butter on a rolled-out piece, sprinkling it with cinnamon and sugar before they rolled it up and cut it into tiny circles. Becky would stand in front of the oven and watch in awe as her round creations puffed up in the heat, the butter and sweetness oozing out of the flaky folds.

For old-time's sake, Becky rolled out the leftover dough from her pie assembly and constructed a few pinwheels, overcome with missing her mama so badly tears welled in her eyes. The little treats baked way faster than the apple pie, and as she pulled them out, she impatiently took a hot bite, scalding the roof of her mouth.

"*Oooh!*" she exclaimed, rushing over to the sink. She stuck her head under the faucet and took a cool drink from the spigot.

"What in the world are you doing?" her brother, James, asked. There was laughter in his tone.

She wiped her mouth with the back of her hand and rolled her eyes. "I took a bite, and it was too hot."

He eyed the mess of baking tools and dusted counter-tops, his focus landing on the sheet of treats still steaming from the oven. "Are those mama's famous pinwheels?"

"Yes, but they're too hot. You need to let them cool," she remarked, slapping his hand as he reached for one. Her slap didn't deter him.

"God, I loved these." He blew on the perfect circle, crust flakes falling onto the floor.

"Over the sink, Jimmy!" Becky admonished.

Taking a bite, he moaned. "Why do some foods immediately take me back to our childhood?"

"Same."

"It's so good," James spoke with his mouth full as Walt and Teddy clambered in through the mud room. They'd stripped off their raingear, their hair wet, and the air surrounding them sweet and pungent with the scent of lingering precipitation and outdoors.

"What's good?" Walt asked, immediately spying the sweets. "Damn, girl! What are you baking now? It smells so good in here."

Teddy eyed the sheet of pinwheels and grinned. "I love those!"

"Help yourself, boys. I made them for you," she said. But she really made them for herself—and her mama.

Her brothers took over the space, popping the flakey cinnamon treats into their mouths. Becky grinned, the innate feeling of her mother's loving spirit filling the room. Funny how something simple like baked sugary dough could make grown men so happy.

"Is that an apple pie in the oven too?" Walt asked.

The testosterone in the room was overpowering; her brothers' musky odor of pine, sweat, and earth from the fields combined with the sugary scent of the kitchen. She didn't have the heart to tell Walt the pie was off-limits.

"We haven't had pie in ages," James chimed in. The three grown men ogled the oven window, giddy at the possibility.

"Hate to disappoint you guys, but the pie I'm baking is not for y'all."

"What?" Teddy groaned, the disappointment in his voice reminding her of a dejected child.

"Don't worry, I'll make another pie soon. Lord knows I have plenty of apples."

Walt scowled and approached her, his upper lip dusted

with cinnamon and sugar residue from the pinwheels. "Then, who are you making this pie for?"

Becky eyed each of her formidable siblings, wishing her country music singing brother, Hank, was among them. But he was in Nashville with his fiancé recording an album. She knew he'd be just as disappointed as the rest of her brothers. Taking a deep breath, she steadied herself against the counter, ready for an avalanche of questions she was sure to come after her honest confession.

"The pie in the oven is for Glen Kirby."

Male eyebrows shot up, and the brothers looked at one another in disbelief. Walt spoke first.

"Why are you making Glen a pie? To thank him for the apples he brought by yesterday?"

Becky shrugged. "Yes. But I also made it as a sort of—peace offering."

"Peace offering?" James asked.

Becky stood tall and blew back a wisp of hair that had fallen out of her ponytail. "Yes. Since Glen started working with Walt at the winery, I haven't been very nice to him."

Teddy approached her and slipped an arm across her shoulders. "Understandable. There's a lot of not-so-nice history between our families."

"But Glen's a changed man. I can vouch for him," Walt added.

Becky pressed her lips together into a thin line and leaned into Teddy. Looking up into her brother's bearded face, she sighed. "I mean, if you can forgive the man after all the terrible things he did to you, I should be able to forgive him too. The same goes for you, Walt. Right? You work with him every single day." She changed her focus to James. "And the same goes for you and Samantha, Jimmy.

Sam's moved on, and so have you, Daddy, and everyone else. So why can't I?"

James, being the voice of reason, took a step toward her. "I'm proud of you, Becks, for deliberately letting go of your anger and resentment. But I have to tell you. I'm still disappointed."

Becky frowned. "Disappointed? Why?"

He scowled and pointed at the oven. "Because your pie smells so good, I want to eat the whole damn thing!"

They all laughed, her brothers calling dibs on the last pinwheel. But Walt won out, too quick for the rest of them. He sauntered into the living area, licking his fingers, and chewing with glee.

"You snooze, you lose!"

Climbing out of the pickup truck with the peeling red letters of Bennett Farms on the door, Becky trudged up the pebbled pathway to the front door of Glen Kirby's home. It was after supper, and her brothers back home insisted they clean up the family meal so she could deliver the pie to Glen before nightfall. She tried not to make a big deal out of going alone and carefully held the dessert covered with a tight sheet of plastic wrap, her heart thundering beneath her thin sweater.

The air held a faint dampness since the rain moved out, the onset of sunset morphing the mountain skyline with vibrant orange hues beyond the lingering clouds. Standing tall, Becky inhaled deeply and boldly knocked on the door. She waited for a beat and listened with a cocked ear, but no sound came from within. Knocking again, she was startled when she heard footsteps behind her.

"Oh!"

Glen came around the corner of the house and cleared his throat. "I didn't mean to sneak up on you." He was wearing overalls and held a wrench in his hand. She noticed a smudge of grease on his cheek, the big tank of a man eyeing her with caution.

"It's okay." She offered him a tentative smile and came down the porch steps. Displaying the pie in both hands, she offered it to him. "I came by to give you this."

Glen frowned and looked from the pie to her face and back again. When he didn't say anything, she attempted an explanation.

"It's a homemade pie I made with the apples you gave me yesterday. It's my mama's recipe."

Glen's expression softened, and he tucked the wrench into his pocket. His faded red and black flannel shirt under his overalls was ripped at the elbows, the fabric taut against his bulging biceps.

"You didn't have to bake me a pie."

"I… I wanted to. I… needed to." She sighed. "I owe you an apology, Glen. I've been awful to you since you started working with Walt on the farm. Please accept this pie with my sincerest apologies."

Glen's cheeks turned ruddy. Taking the pie from her grasp, he shook his head. "You don't owe me anything, Becky. I'm the one who owes you… everything."

"You need to stop. You've changed your ways and moved on, so you don't owe me a thing, okay?" Their eyes met, something sincere and honest passing between them.

"You have no idea how much I appreciate this, Becky. Apple pie is my absolute favorite."

She studied the man standing before her, his thick fingers

holding the pie as if it were a priceless treasure from a museum. He was a brawny man, solid and strong, half of his face hidden behind a scraggly beard. His hair was clipped short, and his blue-gray eyes held hope as he stared back at her. Becky felt emotional knowing Glen was alone in the world, her small gesture meaningful between them. And even though their two families shared a violent history, she knew it was finally time to call a truce of her own and move on.

"I guess it would be your favorite pie after living on an apple farm your entire life." She shrugged and offered him a forced smile. Walking past him toward the truck, he called out to her.

"Wait," he insisted.

Becky turned around with wide eyes.

"Do you, uh, want to stay and have a piece with me?" His voice warbled with unease.

She didn't answer him and accessed the Kirby compound, awestruck by how tidy everything was. The yard had recently been mowed, and the azalea bushes were perfectly trimmed in front of the ranch-style home. The front door and shutters were painted a deep green, and the windowpanes gleamed like new against the lingering light of day, as if they'd been recently washed. The entire homestead was immaculate among the mature trees, the tips of the leaves starting to turn in the fall season. Becky realized Glen was trying hard to put his life back in order, his home representing how far he'd come.

She offered him a dazzling smile, thankful for the rush of positive feelings. "Maybe next time?"

Glen grinned back with a quick nod. "I'd like that. So, we can be friends now, right?"

Becky puckered her lips to the side and hesitated.

"I promise you won't regret it." He looked lonely and forlorn, standing there holding the pie.

Her answer was fast as she spun in her shoes and entered the vehicle. "Let's just say I won't be so mean to you anymore."

"Works for me."

Backing out of the driveway, she noticed Glen hold up one hand with splayed fingers in a parting gesture. She reciprocated with a little wave, the truck picking up dust as she stepped on the gas.

Her homemade pie delivery had gone well. And she felt relief for having done it.

Relief and, for the first time in a long time—peace.

Chapter Three

GLEN KIRBY

Closing the old storage shed housing his 1960s powder blue pickup truck, Glen wiped his greasy hands on a bandanna and followed the well-worn path to the back door of his home. He'd been tinkering with the vehicle all summer, the truck a junker he salvaged from the Langston Falls wrecker yard. Rebuilding the classic to its former glory was a great diversion to his solitude, the time he spent on the truck filling up the lonely hours of his life with purpose.

But now he had a new purpose—diving into Rebecca Bennett's homemade apple pie. Washing his hands in the kitchen sink with his black cat circling his ankles, he eyed the dessert on the countertop, his mouth watering to taste it. Becky's house call came out of left field, and he was still reeling from her visit. The faint scent of her golden hair lingered in his nostrils, the up-close version of Becky stunning him with legitimate awe.

The only Bennett sister was, and always had been, a beautiful female in his eyes. Back in the day, the Bennett and Kirby boys always hung out. He and Walter were thick as thieves fishing and hiking, throwing bonfire parties, and eating their parents out of house and home. They even played baseball together on the winning high school team, the two known for being hypercompetitive and needing to win at all costs. It wasn't unusual for Glen to hang out at Bennett Farms while they grew up, Becky coming in and out of the still shots in the corners of his mind. With no father figure, Glen often pretended he was one of them, a fifth Bennett brother in their comfortable home.

He remembered Becky always up to something with her sweet mama in the kitchen, the delicious cookies and cupcakes they baked something he looked forward to, especially as a ravenous adolescent. He also considered Becky's brothers overly protective of their only little sister. And why wouldn't they be? She was tiny compared to them, fairy-like with her fair hair and dazzling smile. Thinking back on those innocent days, he smiled.

She'd always been kind to him—until his world went sideways.

Even though Glen was four years older than Becky, he would never forget the summer she morphed from a pretty little girl to a drop-dead-gorgeous woman. It was a few weeks before his brother, Joe, was tragically killed. Becky was about to start high school. Glen had barely graduated and was trying to figure out his role in the family's apple-farming business. He had a secret side gig he was pretty good at back then—selling weed. It was illegal in Georgia, and if his single mother ever found out, he'd surely be kicked out of the house. But Glen was a clever young man with a cocky attitude, sure of how he handled himself and his entrepreneurial ways.

Before the new school year started, Becky showed up at a party in the back pastures on the Kirby land. Glen was already toasty from passing a joint around with some of his regular druggie friends around a bonfire and was shocked to see her there, especially as a young up-and-coming high school freshman. Staring at her from across the flames, he watched her try a beer with the girl she came with, her nose wrinkling with displeasure at the taste.

Surrounded by a pungent cloud of bonfire and marijuana smoke, Glen couldn't take his eyes off Becky Bennett. The way the flickering flames threw shadows across her rosy cheeks. How her big doe eyes crinkled every time she giggled, and the way her blonde hair fell over her shoulders in golden waves. Gone was the little-girl version of Rebecca Bennett he grew up with, all flat-chested with gangly legs. In her place was a beautiful, buxom young woman with curves for days.

She'd offered him a timid wave, and his heart blipped with possibility for a split second. But Glen was no fool. He knew there wasn't a chance in hell her older brothers would ever approve of someone like him asking her out on an official date. First of all, she was way too young, only fifteen. And secondly, her brothers knew about his involvement with his illegal side hustle. Besides, Becky was way out of his league; he could never compete for her beauty and popularity in the small town. According to the high school kids, he was a stoner—a freak. Still, back then, he fantasized about the possibility of hooking up with a future homecoming queen.

Fast-forward to today, and he was just as smitten. Only now, he was older, wiser, and totally sober. For grown-up Becky to give him the time of day, let alone an entire pie, was an absolute miracle.

"I've got something special for you too, Garth," he said to his renamed cat. Pulling a carton of milk from the refrigerator, he poured some into a saucer and set it on the kitchen floor. The cat made a noise in his throat and dove right in.

Glen chuckled and plated a generous slice of pie for himself, not even bothering to sit at the kitchen table. With his lips curled over the fork in his first bite, he moaned with pleasure. The flaky crust dusted with cinnamon and sugar melted in his mouth, and the filling was tart with just the right amount of sweetness, the apples grown on his land firm, not mushy from the baking process. He'd never tasted anything so damn good in his entire life. Not even his own mother had ever made a pie this good.

Lifting the milk carton to his lips, he took a hefty gulp before indulging in another piece. He hadn't made supper anyway, the apple pie turning into his main course. Taking his time, he walked from the kitchen into the open living space and stared out the back window overlooking the orchard fence line while he ate another huge slice.

He was a lucky son-of-a-bitch, getting a second chance and living his life back on his family's land again. Swallowing hard, he remembered how he came close to losing it all last winter. He'd convinced himself there was absolutely nothing to live for. Closing his eyes, he remembered the night everything came to a head, the conversation he'd had with Walt Bennett changing the trajectory of his life forever...

"Do you remember how you got here?" Walt asked.

Glen slowly angled his head to where he looked right at Walt in surrender, realizing he'd woken up at Bennett Farms. He'd literally hit rock bottom. "I... I don't remember shit." His voice was scratchy and hoarse.

Walt nodded. "You came back to your house during a snowstorm."

"My house?"

"Yes. I was there with my girlfriend, Elyse. You threatened us with a gun."

Glen's face paled, and his bearded jaw hung open as he tried to remember.

"It is your house, Glen. I'm living there temporarily until we can make arrangements to get you moved back in."

Glen blinked at him, and his forehead wrinkled with confusion. "What the fuck are you talking about?"

"I shouldn't have bought your house and land, Glen. It rightfully belongs to you and your mother. It's your inheritance. What I did was wrong and... and I'm so sorry."

Glen continued to stare at him as if he had two heads.

"I know you're tired and coming down from whatever drugs are in your system. And furthermore, I know you're confused, and you don't know which way to turn." Walt reached for his arm and squeezed. "But I'm here to help you now. You need help, Glen."

He stared at Walt's hand gripping his arm, his eyes brimming with tears. "Why?" he croaked. "Why do you want to help me after everything I've done to you and your family?"

"Because now I understand. I don't blame you for your actions anymore. I understand your motivation." He spoke his next words calmly—evenly.

"You miss Joe—you miss your only brother."

"Yes." His voice was a strangled whisper as he tried to keep it together. He pressed his eyes shut, causing a stream of tears to trickle down his hairy, ashen face.

"And you miss your home. I'm so fucking sorry for taking that away from you. I'm sorry for everything that's happened between our two families."

Glen jerked his arm free and swiped at his face, his features contorting with pain. "Joe was everything to me."

"I know, Glen. I know." Walt swiped a tissue from a box on the *bedside table and handed it off to him. "My brothers and sister are everything to me too."*

Glen scrubbed the tissue under his nose, openly weeping. "And when you bought our house and land, I couldn't take it anymore…"

Walt moved closer. "Is that why you started doing drugs?"

"Yes."

"Why did you come back during the snowstorm? To fight me? To… kill me?" Walt waited for an answer with bated breath.

A torrent of tears spilled down Glen's cheeks as he shook his head. "No."

It took him a full minute before the unfathomable words came out of his mouth.

"I wanted to kill myself…"

Glen blinked rapidly as he came down from the horrible memory. Thanks to Walt and his family, he'd come a long way since last winter. His rehabilitation and ongoing AA meetings gave him a second chance at a fresh start. He still had years to go with buying back his property, but Walt told him to take his time. It seemed time was the only thing going for him as of late. At least he was back home, carefully tending to his house and land. And he was thankful for the bumper crop of apples that would monetarily move him closer toward his goal. Having a beautiful woman drop off a decadent homemade apple pie wasn't too shabby, either.

Garth hopped onto the back of the sofa nearest Glen and licked his paws as if satisfied with the milk. Running his free hand over the animal's sable fur, he grinned.

"Aren't we a couple of lucky fellas, huh, Garth?" The cat's purr was audible. "I agree," he chuckled.

Lucky was an understatement.

Chapter Four

BECKY

Becky stood in front of the live fir tree in the corner of the Langston Petals flower shop. The pine branches decorated with twinkle lights and ornaments advertising the Bennett Christmas Tree Farm year-round always made her smile. Since the successful Harvest Hoedown was over, it was time to start planning for the annual Christmas Tree Festival, the weeks between the two events flying by like Santa in his sleigh.

Becky enjoyed working with Charlotte Ross, the owner of the flower shop. She was a wiz at creating the perfect shabby chic centerpieces for all the annual festivals they'd held at the farm. Teddy's wife, Robyn, worked at the shop for years before she passed the bar exam and became a lawyer. Even though Robyn and her brother still lived in Langston Falls, Becky missed her presence in the shop; her help and suggestions always welcome when it came to festival planning. But Charlotte was amazing too.

Breathing in the sweet aroma of flowers, Becky took her time. She perused the gloriously happy space taking in the display cases holding a variety of cut bouquets wrapped in cellophane and buckets of single flowers. The shop also showcased Charlotte's curated collection of items, including potted plants, artwork, pottery, and jewelry. Charlotte was a visionary floral designer crafting ambitious arrangements with various textures and fragrant blooms. She'd already started decorating for the fall season with garlands of autumn leaves strung across the front windows and orange and white pumpkins in all shapes and sizes peppered throughout the store.

"Here we are," Charlotte announced, coming from the back room.

Becky smiled and ambled toward the checkout counter, where Charlotte opened a file folder and extracted a spreadsheet.

"Last year, you ordered twenty-five large poinsettias and fifteen smaller ones, all in classic red. Do you want to keep or change the order this year?"

Becky nodded. "I want to change it up. Can we do half red and half white? The red ones were hard to notice against the barn, so I think having a few white ones will make them pop more."

"I agree," Charlotte smiled, taking notes. "I'm glad you're ordering early. I can't tell you how many businesses wait until the last minute and then get mad when my suppliers are out of stock."

Becky leaned her forearms on the high top of the counter. "You know me. Once one festival ends, I'm jumping headfirst into the next one."

Charlotte turned the paper around for Becky to sign. "Well, don't work too hard, young lady. You need to enjoy the holidays and not just work through them."

Signing off on the order with a flourish, Becky giggled.

"Yes, ma'am. Funny you would say that. I'm actually thinking about taking some time off and traveling."

"Really?" Charlotte sounded surprised. "Where might you go?"

"I'm thinking about Florida."

Charlotte closed the file and came from around the counter. "Florida is lovely this time of year. You should totally go."

The two women slowly walked through the store as the front door opened with a ding announcing a customer.

"I'm seriously considering it if I can get all my ducks in a row."

"You're Becky Bennett. If anyone can get their ducks in a row, it's you." The two women hugged and said their farewells.

Outside, Becky took her time and roamed the sidewalks of downtown Langston Falls at her leisure. The sun was bright, and the air cooler since the deluge of rain had passed through over the last week. The peak autumn season of color was still a couple of weeks away, nearer Halloween.

Fishing her sunglasses out of her purse, she slipped them over her eyes and stopped in her tracks when she noticed Glen Kirby coming straight toward her. The grin on his face was apparent, and she immediately noticed he'd trimmed his beard, making his face appear thinner without all the shaggy hair.

"Hey, Becky."

"Hey. I like what you've got going on here." She made a hand motion in front of her face.

He laughed and ran a hand down his jawline. "Yeah, well, when you start finding snacks in your beard, it's time for a trim."

His comment made her laugh out loud.

"By the way, thanks again for your pie. It was incredible. I ate the whole damn thing in two days."

"You did not."

"Did too. Can't you tell?" He patted his belly with splayed fingers.

They were stopped on the sidewalk between the local bookstore and the neighboring coffeehouse, a favorite of Becky's because of their signature chai tea. She curiously asked, "What brings you into town today?"

"I was about to ask you the same thing," he replied.

Becky pointed behind her toward Langston Petals. "I was putting in a Christmas order at the flower shop."

"Already? It's not even Halloween."

"Well, you can never be too early with an order nowadays. The annual Christmas Tree Festival will be here before you know it."

"I guess so." Glen shoved his hands into his front jeans pockets making his biceps bulge from underneath his flannel button-down shirt. He was a formidable man reminding her of a lumberjack. All that was missing were the steel-toe boots and a rumbling chainsaw in his hands.

"So... what are you doing in town?" she asked again.

"Oh. I was, uh... well, I had a meeting."

"What kind of meeting?"

Glen adjusted his cowboy hat with noticeable unease.

"I'm sorry I'm being nosey. It's really none of my business—"

"No," he interrupted. "It's okay. I was attending a meeting at the rehab center. I go a few times a week. I'm officially eight months sober today."

Becky wasn't sure if it was the humbled tone of Glen's voice or the genuine smile he offered as he stood a little taller, admitting his eight-month feat. Pride immediately bubbled up inside her, happy for Glen and what he was doing to purposefully move his life forward in a positive direction.

"Wow. That's... that's amazing. Congratulations."

Glen bashfully looked at the sidewalk. "Yeah, well, it's hard sometimes, especially living alone. But I'm getting there. One day at a time, right?"

Becky nodded. "Absolutely."

Her eyes darted to the giant picture window of the coffeehouse, an immediate idea coming to mind, surprising her. "Let me buy you a coffee, my treat." Before he could decline her offer, she grabbed him by the arm and pulled him toward the double doors.

"Becky, you don't have to do this."

"I want to. Please. This is a huge milestone you don't have to celebrate alone."

Several minutes later, the waiter dropped off her chai tea and a jumbo white chocolate mocha with extra whip for Glen. Becky held her porcelain mug into the air and locked eyes with him.

"Cheers to your hard work."

"Cheers," he repeated. "And thank you for this. I don't think a woman has ever bought me a drink before. Well, a non-alcoholic drink."

Becky giggled and savored her first sip of tea, the blend of cloves and other spices, a beautiful balance of smooth and spicy. When Glen lowered his mug to the table after his first taste, her eyes went wide at the sight of him. The whiskers above his mouth were covered in thick, white cream. She pressed her lips together to thwart off a bout of giggles. He looked ridiculous.

"What?" Glen innocently asked. With his solid fore-arms on the table, he leaned forward and whispered, "Do

I have something on my face?" He was teasing her for sure.

"Uhh, yes, you do. It's all over your whiskers." She made a circular motion in front of her mouth.

Glen grabbed a paper napkin from the dispenser and swiped it across his mouth in a crinkle of paper, his hearty laugh inducing a mega-watt smile. She had to admit, she liked seeing Glen genuinely happy.

"My brother and I used to do this at the dinner table when our mom served us anything with whipped cream. We'd see who could get her to laugh first without laughing ourselves. Of course, I always won. I could keep a straight face forever." He picked up his coffee and took another sip.

Becky's smile faltered, the mere mention of Glen's deceased brother conjuring up all kinds of post-traumatic flashbacks. He must have noticed because he immediately backtracked.

"I'm sorry. I didn't mean to bring up Joe. Dang it, why can't I keep my big mouth shut?"

Careful with her choice of words, Becky spoke calmly. Evenly. "It's okay. You have a happy memory. I can envision you and Joe back in the day with food all over your faces making your mama laugh." She smiled. "Thanks for sharing with me."

He swallowed and nodded. "I don't think I've thought about those memories in years. Thanks for reminding me with the coffee drink."

"You're welcome. Is your coffee good?"

"It's delicious. You want to try it?" How he was trying to please her caused a pang of empathy to shoot straight to her heart.

Becky hesitated, trying to keep her wits about her. "Sure."

Glen slid the drink across the table, and she brought it up to her mouth to take a sip. The chocolate-infused coffee was decadent, like a dessert, the whipped cream just the right touch to make it extra creamy.

"Mmm."

"I told ya."

"I might have to order this the next time." She pushed the coffee back to him, licking the foam from her upper lip.

"Well, next time, I'm buying."

Becky's eyes went wide. Was he being sly and asking her out? "Oh, really?"

"Yeah, if you'll let me. We are friends now, right? And a friend can buy another friend a treat when there's something to celebrate. You said it yourself."

"And what would we be celebrating that would cause you to want to buy me a treat, Glen?"

His features softened in the ambient coffeehouse lighting, his gaze focused on her face.

"We'd celebrate you being the nicest woman in Langston Falls."

Chapter Five

GLEN

Glen shook his head and grumbled under his breath.

"We'd celebrate you being the nicest woman in Langston Falls."

Seriously? What a jack-ass thing to say. He'd lobbed plenty of one-liners at women over the years, but they were usually filled with sexual innuendos and spoken to the local bar whores and tramps in town when he was out on the prowl in an intoxicated, horny state. For him to launch one of those lame lines to none other than gorgeous Becky Bennett was a crappy attempt at a sincere compliment.

"What a nice thing to say," she replied. There was no deadpan stare or eye roll, her sunny smile intact.

"Oh." Surprised, he back-peddled with an explanation. "Well, it's true. You're the only woman in these parts who will give me the time of day."

"Why do you think that is, Glen?"

He shrugged, swirling the straw in his coffee drink in lazy circles. "Because of my past. Because of who I used to be." Locking eyes with her from across the table, he kept his voice low. "I'm not that guy anymore, Becky. I was in the dark for way too long. But I'm out of it now. I'm a changed man. Sobriety has changed me for the better."

Becky tilted her head and offered a weak smile. "Tell me how it's changed you."

Glen cleared his throat, intentional with his words. "The thought of getting sober was overwhelming at first. I had to remember why I wanted to do it. I wanted my life back. I wanted a better future without drugs or alcohol messing things up. I wanted a deeper... more satisfying existence."

Taking a quick sip of his java, he shifted in his seat, thankful Becky was a good listener. It felt good to open up to her and tell her his truth.

"Right away, I started to feel better emotionally and physically. Heck, I've lost almost thirty pounds."

"I can tell. From the looks of you right now, it was a good decision. You're a handsome fella, Glen."

Dumbstruck by her comment, he felt a surge of heat travel up the back of his neck. No one but his mama had ever complimented him on his looks. "Thanks, Becky."

He fumbled with his drink causing it to slosh and spill on the table. He was all thumbs, the two of them grabbing napkins from the dispenser and cleaning up the mess he made. She didn't seem flustered at all, her cheery disposition noticeable in her voice.

"Tell me more."

Wiping his hands with a dry napkin, he continued. "Substance abuse numbed all my senses over the years. When it was all out of my system, my thoughts became clearer, and my day-to-day life turned more vivid if that makes any sense."

"Makes total sense."

"Through rehab, I've learned new skills and how to cope with my emotions and feelings." His eyes flicked to hers with chagrin. "Sounds kind of crazy, I know. But for some reason, it worked for me."

"It worked because you were finally open to receiving help. And you had a lot of folks, including my family, cheering you on." She reached across the table and pressed her hand over his flannel-covered forearm.

When she gently squeezed, her touch sent an electrical current through his entire body.

His voice vaporized in his throat as he nodded, his gaze fixated on her dainty hand, her fingernails painted with the slightest hint of pale pink. The shade reminded him of his mother's peony bushes. Or the sky right before the sun hit the Langston River at sunset.

"You're still young, Glen. For you to seek treatment and get sober is life changing. I can see the dramatic transformation in you since last winter." She removed her hand from his arm and sat back in the cozy booth, the absence of her touch disappointing.

"It's been slow going, though," his voice rumbled. "Some days, it's real hard, especially being all alone out in the country."

"I can imagine."

"But I've got Garth to keep me company."

"Garth?" She grinned. "You kept his name? You know, Walt named him Garth, don't you?"

"I know," Glen chuckled. "Garth is a whole lot better than what his name was before."

"What was it?"

Glen shook his head. "It was a dumb name. I'm too embarrassed to tell you."

"Come on," she insisted.

He licked his lips. "Don't judge me."

"I won't."

Glen inhaled a deep breath. "Jabba The Butt."

"What?" Becky giggled.

"Yep." His shoulders shook with laughter. "Jabba The Butt. Butt for short. I was a huge *Star Wars* fan back in the day, okay? I thought it sounded cool."

"It sounds terrible. Poor Garth."

"I know, right? Walt's name is way better. Garth suits him."

"I agree. And for what it's worth, I'm glad you and Walt are friends again."

Glen paused for a beat, snapshots of his youth with Walter Bennett coming to mind. There was a time he might've even considered Walt his best friend. They were joined at the hip, playing baseball, fishing, and being hyperactive boys.

"You know, it's weird when I think about my past. I was so cocky back then, even before everything horrible happened. Through rehab, I've learned how to handle my emotions and not say some of the stupid things I used to say —things I didn't mean or act in ways that negatively impacted my relationships with others."

Becky nodded again.

"It's an incredible feeling to have the… fog lift. I literally feel like a brand-new person. I can think again, read a book, remember my mama's birthday, and engage in an intelligent conversation like we're doing right now. I have *ideas* again. I'm not just looping terrible thoughts on autopilot in my brain anymore. It's been liberating."

"What kind of ideas do you have, Glen?"

He inhaled sharply. "Well, I recently tried a few yoga classes at the rehab center, and I took a CPR class at the local fire station because, why not? And I'm restoring an old Chevy truck in my shed. She's gonna be a beauty when I'm done. Getting my hands dirty has been fun, and working on the truck keeps me occupied when I'm not working on the farm. And the apple-infused wine Walt and I are trying to come up with has kept us busy. I know it's probably not the smartest thing to do because I no longer drink. But I know we're on to something special. Working with your brother has been cathartic, and there's something cool about bringing our two families together. The history, the land, the mountainous bounty the good Lord has bestowed on us."

His words induced a full grin from Becky. "Spoken like a true sommelier. I think it's a great pairing. And I think with your new attitude, y'all will come up with something our customers will love."

"You do?" Her comment surprised him.

Pushing her empty cup to the wayside, she nodded. "Yes, I do. I admit, at first, I was totally against the idea of you working with my family. And there's no point in rehashing the reasons why—"

"It's because you hated me and what I did," he interrupted, pinning her with his stare. "Becky, I'm so sorry for all of it. You have to know I wasn't in my right mind after Joe died, and that's not an excuse; it's a fact. But I hope you can somehow forgive me for every single thing I did to make you hate me."

"I didn't hate you, Glen. I was afraid of you."

He groaned with displeasure, his voice hoarse with mortification. "Even worse."

"Hear me out," she requested.

Glen hung his head and nodded.

"Our families go way back. I mean, you were always at our house. We all grew up together, and then a terrible tragedy struck. But look at us now." She lowered her head to make eye contact. "Look at me, Glen."

Flicking his eyes to hers, he was struck by the beauty and compassion in her smile.

"You've chosen a better path. You're open to seeing what else this life has to offer. You have more self-esteem and humility. You're trying new things. Your eyes are bright, you've lost weight, and your complexion is healthy. Even if you don't notice, I do. You're right—you are *not* the same person you were before. Give yourself a little self-love, okay? Your world has completely transformed in the last eight months because of your optimism and perseverance. I know it hasn't been easy, and it's probably been unpleasant. But you need to remember you are *not* alone. You have an opportunity to own your home and land again. You have a good job where you're using your creative mind to concoct a delicious wine using the harvest from your trees and our grapes. You have Walt, my other brothers, and my dad cheering you on from the sidelines."

Her words resonated deeply with him. "And what about you, Becky? Are you on those sidelines cheering for me too?" He wanted her to say it. He needed her to say it.

She lowered her gaze and fiddled with her fingers in her lap, her silent pause causing him to hold his breath. When she finally looked up at him with wide eyes, her voice was barely a whisper among the coffeehouse clatter.

"Of course, I am. That's what friends are for."

His face burned with a blush, and he was sure his skin was the color of a Honeycrisp apple. He pressed his lips together to keep them from unfurling into the biggest shit-eating grin.

"I'll toast to that," he held what was left of his coffee drink into the air. Becky reciprocated, clinking her empty porcelain mug against his. Tossing back the coffee in one gulp, he knew he had residual cream all over his whiskers again. Entwining his fingers together on the table, he acted nonchalant before he summoned the waiter with a theatrical wave for their check. Bits of cream dripped from his face as Becky snort-laughed out loud.

"Oh, man. Do I have something on my face again?" He rolled his eyes and grabbed a napkin as she giggled at his silly antics.

It felt good making her laugh. Damn good.

Chapter Six

BECKY

Becky turned off her ring light on the kitchen island and tidied up. Remnants of today's creation lay spread out on the surface, her eerie twist on the traditional candy apple a delicious Halloween treat for her YouTube viewers. She had plenty of leftover apples since Glen dropped off an entire bushel over a week ago. And her fans loved easy recipes, especially ones with a holiday theme. Since Halloween was less than two weeks away, she thought this would be the perfect time to experiment and film a seasonal episode.

After thoroughly washing and drying the apples, she placed them on a baking sheet and poked each piece of fruit with knobby sticks she'd collected from the farm property, whittled, and cleaned. She mixed a combination of sugar, water, and corn syrup over the stove and patiently waited for the temperature to rise until it reached the hard-crack mark at 310 degrees. She added black food coloring to the mixture, some cinnamon flavoring, and swiped the apples through the candy, shaking off any excess and placing them on wax paper. When she finished, she had over a dozen candy apples she dubbed "poison candy apples." The finished product was a hoot, the menacing black orbs sure to make her brothers and the farm hands do a double take when she handed them out.

Hanging her apron on a peg by the refrigerator, she opened the back door wide and carried the tray of spooky treats outside. She carefully descended the stairs leading to the big red barn where a few wine-tasting guests stood at high-top tables sipping samples. She confidently strode inside underneath the Edison-style lights strung through the rafters.

Walt stood on the other side of a long counter, giving instructions to one of the winery workers. As Becky came toward him, he stopped talking and furrowed his brow.

"What the—"

"Would you care for a poison candy apple?" She grinned and presented the tray with a gleam in her eye. "Of course, they're not really poisonous. I just made them look spooky. Do you wanna try one?"

Walt guffawed. "No thanks. They look rotten."

Becky slid the tray onto the counter and rested her hands on her hips. "They're not rotten, Walt. They taste just like a candy apple. I used real sticks and added black food coloring to the candy to make them look sinister. Fun idea, right?"

"If you say so." He ignored her and focused on a clipboard, unimpressed.

Glen came around the corner of the workroom and immediately greeted her. "Hey, Becky. How's it going?"

She relaxed and smiled back at him. "Good. I was trying to get my brother to taste one of my poison apples."

Glen's eyebrows shot up in surprise as he took in the tray of apples pierced with sticks and covered in black candy. The look on his face was comical, as if he genuinely believed she was trying to poison everyone.

"They're not really poisonous. I made them look spooky, is all. Do you want one? I used the rest of your apples, so you know it will be good."

Glen lightened up with a deep chuckle. "You had me going there for a minute. Don't mind if I do."

"Don't do it, Glen. They probably taste as bad as they look," Walt warned, glancing up from his clipboard.

Glen sniffed the treat with his big hand wrapped around the knobby stick. "No, they won't. These look… cool, especially for a Halloween party. And if my apples are behind all this black candy, you better believe it will be delicious." He chomped down on the treat, taking a huge bite. "Mmmmhmmm!"

Becky boldly thrust her chin in the air, pleased by Glen's wholehearted reaction toward her treat. "See, Walt?"

Swinging the apple by the stick, Glen gestured toward her brother, talking with his mouth full. "Don't knock it till you try it, buddy. It's good."

Walt made a sour face and shook his head. "Yuck. No thanks."

Becky watched her brother disappear into the workroom, leaving her and Glen alone with the tray of black candy apples between them. "I'm going to leave these with you. Can you put the tray in the break room for the workers? Hopefully, they won't be as turned off as Walt was."

"Will do." Glen licked his lips and set the treat on a Bennett Farms Winery napkin. "You look… nice today."

Becky felt her cheeks heat with a blush, compliments a rarity living and working with a bunch of farmers. "Thank you. I wear a little more makeup on filming days." She flicked her golden hair over her shoulders. "I was shooting a

Halloween-themed episode for my YouTube channel, hence the 'poison apples.'" She gestured air quotes with her fingers.

"Cool. Any other creepy creations on the menu for today?"

"Oh, yes. Walt's going to be so disappointed at dinner tonight. I made a meatloaf monster with gory tomato sauce. It has sliced olive eyes and celery stick legs. It's horrific." She giggled with pleasure.

A half-smile curled across Glen's lips, and she could practically feel the drag of his gaze over the fullness of her mouth. "Sounds like you're having a fun day."

Becky stood a little taller, aware of the burly man from across the counter, his spiced scent of earth and ripe cinnamon-infused fruit making the air around her feel warmer with visceral memories of autumn bonfires in their youth.

"I'm having a great day. How about you?"

"Can't complain. Especially after receiving a sweet treat like this." He picked up his apple and took another big bite, his lips turning dark from the candy shell.

"Let me try it," she said, reaching across the counter.

Glen handed off the stick, and she bit through the candy shell into the fruit. The ripe apple was juicy, and the candy held a hint of cinnamon extract she'd added at the last minute to the batch of boiling sugar. The taste reminded her of childhood, Halloween's past when she dressed as a princess or Miss America, her late mother handing out candy apples to her and her brothers instead of store-bought fun-size candy bars. Becky loved the treat, but her brothers, not so much.

"Mmm," she moaned, passing the stick back to Glen. "Tastes like Halloween to me."

"Speaking of Halloween..." Glen placed the apple back on the napkin. "Do you have any plans?"

Becky licked residual sugar from her bottom lip, sure her mouth was Goth and dark like Glen's from the black food coloring she used on the candy apple. She shook her head. "Not really. Sometimes I'll go into town and watch the kids trick-or-treat from store to store to see all the cute costumes. Other than that, we don't really do much around here. It's a lot between August and mid-October, harvesting acres of wine grapes and celebrating during the Harvest Hoedown. We're all pretty spent and need a break before the Christmas tree season starts."

"I know what you mean. I'm in full apple-harvest season too. I've got pickers in the fields as we speak."

The two ambled toward the barn entrance with the long counter scrolling between them. When the surface ended, Glen came around the wooden structure and easily walked beside Becky.

"When the vines start turning gold, and the leaves change color in the North Georgia Mountains, I always know we're almost at the end of the harvest season," she said.

"Yep." Glen stopped on the pebbled path leading to the main house.

The midday sun was bright, beams of light filtering through the puffy clouds in the sky. Becky squinted, looking up at Glen and holding a hand over her eyes to fend off the glare.

"I meant to ask. Why didn't you come to the Harvest Hoedown this year? Hank and his fiancé, Ella Mae Miller, performed and drew in the biggest crowd we've ever had. You would've loved it."

Glen averted her gaze, his hat shadowing his face as he

shoved his hands into his denim pockets. "It wouldn't have been right for me to be there after what happened a year ago."

"Oh."

Becky nodded with understanding, the one-year anniversary memory of the horrible night sure to haunt her for years to come. It was the night Glen and her brothers Walt and Teddy got into a huge barn fight. The same night Glen punched her brother James' girlfriend, Samantha, who was only trying to break up the fight. And later, Glen and two others nearly beat Teddy to death in the holding cell at the county jail, sending him to the hospital where doctors put him into an induced coma. The awful memories crashed into her like a tsunami, and she suddenly didn't feel like talking to Glen Kirby anymore.

"Well, I'll see you around. Don't forget to take those apples to the break room—"

"Hold on," he interrupted, grabbing her by the wrist.

Becky jerked her head to where she looked right at him. Immediate stress heightened her senses, urging her to take flight. Blood roared in her ears as he tightened his grip—not enough to hurt, but enough to remind her how he could overpower her if he wanted. Glen had once taken down her huge mountain man of a brother; he could easily do it with her.

Their eyes locked, and the roaring intensified. Beneath Glen's dark eyes, she glimpsed a spark of heat that startled her. A fracture started low in her belly, the warmth rolling through the rest of her, spreading slow and delicious like honey. Yanking herself free, she stepped back, surprised by her visceral reaction.

"I'm sorry, Glen. You're right. It was probably a good idea you didn't come to the Harvest Hoedown this year. I don't know what I was thinking asking such a dumb question."

"It's not a dumb question. Please believe me when I say this to you, Becky. I wish I could go back and change what went down that night. I wish none of it ever happened."

Becky studied him silently for a moment. Thinking about the past had her all worked up, and whatever heat was brewing between them confused her. She needed to regain her composure.

Changing the subject, she asked, "So what about you? What are you doing for Halloween?"

Glen tipped his cowboy hat and pinned her with his stare. "I was hoping we could go into town together. We could... grab a bite and watch the kids in their costumes— as friends," he reassured. "Will you think about it? Please? Sitting at home alone on one of my favorite holidays isn't too appealing. Having a friend to share a fun night out with sounds much better, don't you think?"

Becky's initial reaction was to decline his invitation. Even though he asked her as a friend, she knew good and well it was a backdoor invite to a first date. But her and Glen Kirby—on a *date*? The thought was downright shocking. And besides, it would never work. There was no way her family would ever allow her to be associated with Glen as more than a friend. But maybe they could casually... run into each other?

"Hmmm... as friends? Maybe. But I'd have to meet you in town if I decide to go." She inhaled deeply through her nose. "I'll think about it and let you know how my schedule pans out."

A wolfish grin took over his entire face as he tipped his hat, his eyes never leaving hers. "I look forward to hearing from you then."

Chapter Seven

GLEN

Bouncing on the cracked leather seat in his work truck, Glen drove across the graveled back roads toward town while resting his forearm on the rolled-down window. The air was clean and crisp, and the fall colors of the North Georgia Mountains swept down the mountainsides from high elevation to low, the turning of yellow birch, sugar maple, sweetgum, and hickory trees vibrant. Autumn in Langston Falls was both a beautiful and busy time of the year, the annual show of seasonal colors attracting huge numbers of sightseers, especially around Halloween.

Wearing a perfectly pressed long-sleeved dress shirt, dark denim, and his dressy black cowboy hat and boots, Glen was excited to meet Becky Bennett at their designated spot in front of the coffeehouse downtown. She'd finally agreed to meet him for a Halloween supper, insisting this wasn't a date but a meeting of two friends on a fun holiday outing.

Secretly, Glen pretended this *was* their first official date, something he'd dreamt about for years during his youth. To have Becky on his arm was like winning the freakin' lottery, the beautiful woman doing funny things to his insides when he was around her.

The truck went from gravel to paved road, the smooth ride into town uneventful, except for the traffic. Cars were lined up along the roadside overlooks, with folks taking in the stunning mountain views. Glen never really paid much attention to the changing of the leaves in his hometown. Now completely sober, he realized it was a much-antici-pated Georgia tradition he enjoyed. Leaf peepers came out of the woodwork heading out on hikes to catch the beauty of autumn, or they'd lazily pull up to the roadside overlooks and roll down their windows to capture the views without leaving their cars.

Because it was Halloween, hometown folks and tourists were out in droves dressed in ridiculous costumes. Food trucks were spread out, and businesses set up tables in front of their storefronts, handing out candy and other treats. Kids scampered through town carrying jack-o-lantern buckets, pawning candy from the locals, the town decorated with autumn-themed flags and twinkle lights twisted around black lampposts. Vying for a space in the back alley near the coffeehouse, Glen easily parked and turned off the truck engine. Gripping the steering wheel, he intentionally inhaled a few deep breaths.

He was nervous.

Since his brother Joe was killed, he struggled to talk to people in his hometown. It always felt like everyone was looking right at him, judging him, or feeling sorry for him. He knew some of his angst was in his head, but some of it was true, especially after the highly publicized trial and then his fall from grace last winter, almost overdosing in front of

Walt. Everyone in this town knew everybody's business, especially his.

Fast forward, and this was a once-in-a-lifetime chance for him to prove himself worthy of Becky's company, and he wasn't about to blow it. He genuinely liked her. But he also knew they had to be careful because she was adamant her brothers and father not find out about their secretive meeting. He couldn't blame her. Even though he knew he was forgiven, how would she ever forget how he was once the destructive enemy of the Bennett clan? Still, he wanted to prove himself and dive deeper into their new friendship.

Stepping out of the truck, the air was heavy with country music from the local bar and the scent of popcorn, thick with tension and excitement, nerves and elation. Between the rumbling of traffic and his pounding heart, he was feeling it all. The town hummed with a happy, colorful buzz inducing a genuine feeling of contentment. But when he spotted Becky standing in front of the coffeehouse, he frowned, the pendulum of his emotions taking a hard swing into panic mode.

"Am I late?" he lamented.

Her angelic smile immediately put him at ease. "No. I'm early."

Glen breathed a sigh of relief and took off his hat with a nod, giving her the once-over. She wore a long rust-colored maxi dress, cowboy boots, and a faded denim jean jacket with gold embroidery on the front pockets. Her blonde hair was pinned back at the sides with a ring of tiny daisies circling her head.

"What?" she asked, bursting his bubble. A slight breeze pushed her scent right under his nose, hints of rosemary and lemons infiltrating his senses. It was heavenly, and he fended off the urge to tuck his nose near her ear where he could breathe it in with pleasure.

"You look beautiful, Becky."

She avoided his gaze and clutched her hands in front of her dress in a bashful stance. "Thank you. You don't look half bad yourself."

Parking his hat back on his head, he gestured with his hand for her to start walking ahead. "Shall we?"

"We shall."

They ambled up and down the sidewalks parallel to Main Street, taking in the street party in full force. Glen loved the way she paid attention to every detail, pointing out the various costumed children and entire families in matching themes catching her eye. They stopped at the local diner and feasted on grilled burgers and milkshakes, their continued conversation effortless and easy. After supper, they decided to check out the local church grounds, where a mini carnival was set up with fun games and kiddie rides.

"Okay, hold up," he said animatedly, rubbing his palms together with glee.

"What?"

"They've got a baseball game set up right over there." He pointed to the white and red checkered tent where several wooden stools held three aluminum milk jugs in a triangular formation.

"Step right up, step right up. Strike the jugs off the stool, and you'll win a prize!" The elderly game host announced, theatrically over-enunciating his words. "You look like a solid player, Big Boy. How about it?"

Glen picked up one of the rubber baseballs and squeezed it tight in his grip. This game would be so easy to win, and he might impress Becky with his ninety-mile-an-hour curve ball left over from his glory days playing in high school.

"See a prize you might like to have, Daisy Girl?" He pointed to the array of cheap stuffed animals hanging from the tent poles.

Becky sidled up to Glen and squeezed his bicep. Pointing to a unicorn with a rainbow-striped horn and pink mane, she whispered for only him to hear, "That one, right there."

A sly smile unfurled from his lips, and he nodded. He didn't know whether it was the heat from her delicate hand pressed against his arm or the subtle scent of her sweet essence wafting under his nose again that had him digging into his wallet and stepping up to the tent with gusto.

"How much?"

The host smirked. "Five dollars for three throws."

"Five dollars?" Becky countered. "Those stuffed animals aren't even worth two."

"Five dollars to play, ma'am. All proceeds go to the Baptist Church Boy Scout summer camp."

Glen shoved a five-dollar bill into the man's hand. "There you go."

The host slid a flipped-over Frisbee holding three balls toward him and moved out of the way. Glen unbuttoned his shirt at the wrists and pushed the fabric up his forearms, ready to show off and win Becky the unicorn in one pitch.

"Go on, Glen. You got this," she cheered from the sidelines.

Glen focused on the center of the milk jug configuration and took a deep, cleansing breath. He was aware of Becky nearby, her hands pressed against her mouth in a praying position. Stretching his neck from side to side, he planted his boots in a familiar stance and pulled his arm back in a wind-up before he let go of the rubber baseball with force. The ball whizzed through the air and narrowly missed the top jug, hitting the back of the canvas tent with a pronounced thud. The sound reminded him of a catcher's mitt popping in a stadium after a strikeout.

"Strike one!" The game host hollered with glee.

Glen scowled and blew out a hot breath. What the fuck? He hadn't made contact with the jugs? How embarrassing. Becky came up alongside him and took his hat off his head, placing it on her own over the ringlet of flowers.

"Maybe the shadow from your hat was messing with you. Try again. I know you can do it."

The hope in her eyes was apparent, and he'd be damned if he didn't win her the freaking stuffed unicorn. He nodded and waited for her to get out of the way before he concentrated and got in his pitching stance again.

Winding up his arm, he relaxed and loosened his tight grip on the ball at the last minute, launching the rubber like a rocket aimed at the aluminum jugs. The minute the ball struck the metal, a sharp crack pinged the air. It was like a ten-pin strike in a bowling alley. Becky jumped up and down, squealing and clapping her hands with delight.

Glen's nostrils flared as he stared at the now empty stool, void of metal jugs. He still had it.

"Pay up, mister. My lady would like the unicorn with the rainbow horn, please."

The host unpinned the stuffed animal from the tent pole and handed it to Becky. "Nice job. My radar clocked you at ninety-two miles per hour. Impressive." He picked up a contraption and showed Glen the reading.

Becky leaned in to see, patting Glen on the back. "Wow. Way to go, Glen."

He couldn't help himself and puffed his chest out with a bit of bravado. "Glad I could support the Boy Scouts of America."

"You still have one more pitch left. Want to go again?" The host held up the last rubber ball.

"Nah, I'm good. Mission accomplished." He rolled his sleeves back over his wrists and buttoned them. Glancing at Becky, he smiled. The backdrop of the sky at dusk held brush strokes of bright orange as she cradled the cheap stuffed unicorn to her chest. His cowboy hat hung low on her head, shadowing her face. But he could tell she was all smiles underneath.

"Where to now? You see any other games you might want to play?" he asked. They walked between the carnival tents, several little kids running between them in high-pitched giggles and laughter.

The two moseyed through the carnival as Becky handed his cowboy hat off to him. "Not really. Let's keep walking and talking. I'm having the best time tonight."

Glen shifted the hat on his head and nodded. "Me too."

Their eyes met, and he swore she batted her eyelashes at him. Pausing near the pony corral where adorable little ones wearing Halloween costumes were lined up for a ride, Becky gasped.

"Oh, no."

Glen scowled. "What is it?"

She motioned with her head toward the gathering crowd. Craning his neck, he could make out Becky's brother, James, and his girlfriend, Samantha, coming their way.

"Let me do all the talking, okay?" Becky insisted. Worry etched her pretty features, and she appeared anxious.

Glen noticed how she moved farther away from him, keeping her distance. His earlier happiness faded with each intentional step she took.

"Okay."

Chapter Eight

BECKY

Becky plastered a sunny smile on her face and welcomed James and Samantha with hugs. When she glanced in Glen's direction to offer some kind of half-truth greeting, he was gone—vanished into thin air.

"What are you doing out here all by yourself? You could've ridden into town with us," James scolded.

Becky waved him off, scanning the area for any sign of Glen. "I've been running into so many people I know tonight. I'm fine."

Samantha pointed to the brightly colored unicorn in her arms. "Where did you win your prize? It's cute."

"Oh, well… I was over at the baseball tent and—"

"Is that Glen Kirby?" Samantha didn't give Becky a chance to finish her sentence, her eyes going wide with recognition as she pointed over her shoulder and interrupted. "Wow. I hardly recognized him for being so dressed up. And has he lost weight?"

Becky turned around slowly and noticed Glen talking to a couple near the fence posts of the pony coral, his hearty chuckle echoing into the night. The threesome acted like old friends, the couple's toddler daughter dressed in a bright pink ballerina costume planted on the man's hip. Becky watched Glen palm the little girl's back and lean low to say something to her. The gentleness in his actions was precious.

"Earth to Becks," James said.

"Uh… yeah, looks like him."

Samantha tugged James's arm, pulling him toward Glen. "Come on. I have something I want to say to him."

James didn't resist, and Becky followed behind, unsure of what Sam was doing. The woman was tiny compared to Glen, and for the briefest moment, she was transported back to the horrible night of the barnyard brawl, images of Sam's sinister black eye haunting her. Shaking off her tumultuous thoughts, she steeled herself for a confrontation.

"Hey, Glen," Sam greeted.

Glen bid the couple goodbye and turned around, his smile immediately replaced with a poker face. Steely eyes. Blank and impassive. "Hey… Ms. McNeil. Hey, James. Becky…"

"Hey, Glen," Becky replied. She was following his lead, her heart hammering beneath her jean jacket.

"What's up, Glen?" James echoed. "Are you having fun tonight?"

"Uh, sure. How about y'all?"

Samantha wrapped her arm around James's bicep and looked up at him. "Sure, we are. Would you like to join us? We were about to head over to the pub. There's a live band playing tonight."

Glen shot a look from Sam to Becky and back again. "Oh, well… thanks, but I, uh. I don't drink anymore."

"He's going on nine months sober," Becky announced,

her voice tinged with pride. All eyes landed on her, and she felt herself blush. Immediately, she backpedaled. "Glen told me the other day when he delivered some apples to the main house."

"Yes, I did. Thanks to the Bennett family, I'm almost nine months sober," Glen added. He stood closer to Becky as if in protection mode. She hugged the unicorn to her chest, her thoughts reckless, wishing she could wrap her arm around his, ready to defend him in front of her brother and Sam if he needed her. What in the world?

"That's remarkable, Glen. Congratulations. I'm proud of you," Sam offered.

"Me too, Glen. You can still join us at the pub if you want. We'll be outside listening to the band. They'll have non-alcoholic options, I'm sure."

Glen stared right at Becky as if waiting for her permission.

"Yes," she smiled. "Come join us, Glen. It'll be... fun."

His mood instantly perked up, sparks of life reappearing in his eyes. "Cool."

The foursome strode through the crowds toward the pub, where the sounds of live music filtered through the night air, the band dialing up classic rock hits. Finding a spot near an empty high-top table positioned in the grass, they circled around and waited for a server who came over to them within seconds.

As James asked what beer specials were on tap for the evening, Becky laid the unicorn beside Glen. He picked it up and smirked. "Where'd you get this from?"

Becky shot him a warning look with raised eyebrows. He knew good and well where she got it from. Boy, he was really going all out trying to keep their budding friendship under wraps and acting like they hadn't been spending the entire evening together. Still, she played along.

"I won it at one of the carnival games. You know, the one where you have to throw a baseball?"

"Good job." There was a twinkle in his eye, and she playfully punched him in the hip under the table.

They put in their drink orders and bobbed their heads to a familiar Eagles oldie, James, striking up a conversation.

"Walt says y'all are super-close to finding the perfect blend for the wine you're creating. Must be exciting."

"It is," Glen replied. "We're experimenting with all the different grape and apple varieties, trying to come up with the best combination."

"If you don't mind me asking, how will you know which combo tastes the best if you don't drink alcohol anymore?" Samantha asked.

James huffed. "Sam, I really don't think it's any of our business. The man said he was sober. I don't think there's any risk of him falling off the wagon because of a little wine tasting."

Surprised by her brother's admonishment toward Sam, Becky kept her mouth shut and watched the couple publicly disagree.

"You're wrong, James. Addicts can't do anything in moderation."

"Sure, they can," James countered. "Especially if they've been through treatment."

"Nope. Wrong again. I've seen it happen over and over. An alcoholic will go on a spree or a bender and usually not stop until a consequence jolts them back to reality."

Becky couldn't take it anymore. "Y'all need to stop talking about Glen like he's not here. It's rude."

"It's okay, Becky," Glen reassured. Facing Sam, he said, "I don't think you have anything to worry about with me, Miss McNeil. I have no intentions of ever drinking or using again."

"You say that now, but the statistics are not in your favor, Glen—"

"Okay, enough of this negative talk, Sam," James interrupted with a furrowed brow. He was usually so even-keel and accommodating—a peacemaker with a heart for diplomacy. But Sam pushed his buttons for some odd reason, and he wasn't having it tonight.

"Poor Glen here is trying to enjoy himself on a night off, and Becks is right—you're talking about him like he's not even here. It's Halloween. Lighten up."

Becky noticed Sam glare at her brother before she offered Glen an apology. "I'm sorry, Glen. I just want you to succeed. We all do."

He nodded. "I appreciate it very much. I promise I won't let you down."

The server brought out their drinks, beers for James and Sam and sparkling water for Becky and Glen. Becky wasn't a big drinker anyway, so her order wasn't unusual. The band slowed things down, and Becky overheard Sam ask her brother to dance. Maybe she was trying to smooth things over?

"Please excuse us," James said, taking Samantha by the hand.

"Don't step on her toes," Becky chided, trying to add some humor to the dark cloud hovering over the couple. When they were out of earshot, she turned to Glen and whispered, "What the hell is up with Sam tonight?"

Glen took a sip of his water, undeterred. "It doesn't bother me. She sees a ton of shit in her job in law enforcement. Seeing me up close and personal again is unsettling for her. She's just trying to show me who's boss, and I let her. It's all good."

Becky rested her chin in her hand with her elbow on the table, taking in Glen's profile. The man was handsome in a rough and tough way. But he wasn't a villain anymore. His actions gaining help to end his addictive behavior proved he wasn't an evil or vengeful person. He was an ordinary man trying to find his way in life after a series of unfortunate events got him off track. But underneath Glen's tough exterior, she knew Samantha had probably struck a nerve. Could he abstain from alcohol and drugs for the rest of his life, especially while working at a winery? Only time would tell. If having a friend could help him in his journey, she realized she wanted to be there for him.

"You want to dance?" she asked out of the blue.

He jerked his head and eyed her with confusion, his dark eyes pinning her with his stare. "You think it's wise?"

"It's fine. I wouldn't have asked if I thought it was wrong."

The strong column of Glen's throat moved when he swallowed hard. "I'd love to dance with you, Becky."

With gentleness, he offered his hand, and she took it. The calm, chivalrous, respectful side of Glen was the man James, Sam, and others hadn't really experienced. Becky wasn't sure why Glen opted to show this side of himself to her, but she knew she had to handle him with care. And it wasn't because of his past anger issues and addiction but because she knew he was far more sensitive than he let on. His wounds ran deep, and he'd patched them with a tough persona and smug attitude that didn't match the gentle giant she was getting to know.

Swaying to the music in the crowd of tipsy dancers,

Glen's hand pressed against her lower back, and he was intentionally leaving a few inches between them as if to appease her overprotective brother and his cop girlfriend, who curiously glanced their way more than once. Becky looked up at him with complete ease and smiled. His dance moves were rigid and awkward, but she knew he was trying, and that's all that mattered.

"I had a great time with you tonight," she said. "And you deserve an Oscar. You're a good actor. Thanks for going along with my story so my brother didn't think we were here together. In hindsight, it was kind of stupid and childish of me to ask you to do such a thing. I'm sorry."

His features turned soft in the romantic haze of criss-crossing twinkle lights strung through the trees above the makeshift dance space. As he smiled down at her, his voice rumbled with a reply.

"There's nothing to be sorry for. Tonight has been the best night I've had in years. Thanks for meeting me."

"Thanks for dinner and for winning me my unicorn."

"Thanks for asking me to dance." He nodded his head in the direction of James and Samantha. "But I'm not so sure we've gotten away with anything yet. Your brother and Sam are trying hard not to make it obvious they're keeping tabs on me. You sure you should be dancing with the enemy out in public?"

Becky shifted closer to Glen and tilted her head back to gaze at him. "You're not the enemy. And I'm a grown-ass woman. I can dance with whomever I want."

Glen chuckled, the deep sound resonating through her body. "Good answer." He stepped back from their dance pose and lifted her hand high into the air.

"Do a little twirl for me, Daisy Girl. Make it count. Might as well put on a little show."

Becky beamed, enjoying the little nickname Glen kept calling her. She lifted one side of her skirt with her free hand and twirled underneath his arm like she'd never twirled before.

Chapter Nine

GLEN

Halloween gave way to November, and life on the Kirby apple farm became hectic with the last harvest of the year. Glen had been so busy on his property he'd barely had time to work with Walt on their wine creation or tinker on the old junker sitting in his shed. Of course, he made it into town once or twice a week to attend regular meetings at the rehab facility, thankful for the counselors and the band of misfits he'd befriended over the last few months. But he was antsy to find some free time to make a trip to Bennett Farms and track Becky down. To lay eyes on her beauty and offer a polite hello.

She was probably just as busy, feeding the hungry crew and filming episodes for her YouTube channel, *The Farmer's Daughter*. On the restless nights Glen was so dog-tired sleep evaded him, he often watched Becky's show from his phone as he lay in bed. Her sunny smile and natural charm soothed him, and inevitably, seeing her calmed his spirit, allowing him to eventually fall fast asleep.

Glen often thought about their magical evening together

the night of Halloween, his mind branded with images of her rust-colored dress and halo of flowers surrounding her golden hair. The way her womanly curves felt in his arms as they danced under the moonlight and the look of longing in her eyes when they'd said their goodbyes. Of course, he wasn't about to try to ask her out in front of James and Sam, even though he wanted to.

They would never understand the friendship they shared. Ever.

But it was more than a friend connection. There was a certain spark when they were around each other—a fluttering of butterflies, clammy palms, a thundering heart, and an inability to focus on anything but her. The thought of seeing her again made his heart skip a beat, his nerves inhibiting his once ravenous appetite. His body did all the talking while his mind listened, and he was sure Becky felt something too. Unfortunately, whatever they had brewing beneath the surface would have to wait until after harvest season.

By this time, autumn was dialed all the way up, the crisp yellows and sultry oranges of the leaves blanketing the mountains in jaw-dropping splendor. Traipsing along the well-worn paths of the orchard, Glen breathed in the delicate perfume of apples, the branches of each tall, sturdy tree spread wide as if boldly displaying their bounty with pride. The ripe fruit almost glowed, the party of colors, nature and order, beauty and reward, remarkable proof of the circle of life starting from tiny seeds blessed with mud and rain.

The Kirby farm had been producing fruit for over half a century with only modest care involved, usually in pruning and fertilization. The trees did well in the cooler climate of the North Georgia Mountains, the seasonal changes key for the growth cycle. The trees would flower and fruit during the warmer months, while the long, cold dormant period was for the growth cycle. Glen learned as a young boy how to protect the trees with natural insecticide early in the growing season, leading to a bountiful harvest most years when the weather was kind. Thank God, this was one such year.

Glen was content for the first time in a long time. He was settled back into his home, looking forward to a lucrative harvest propelling him closer to owning his property. And partnering with Walt and being on the cusp of their new apple-infused wine with a preliminary launch date set for next spring had Glen in a good place with his vocation and mental health. If only he had someone special to share it with.

Closing the back gate of the orchard, Glen continued toward his house and noticed Walt's truck parked in the driveway. Confused, he pulled out his cell phone from his back pocket and checked to make sure he hadn't missed a call from him. There was none.

"Hey, man. What's up?" Glen greeted.

Walt sat on the lowered lift gate of the truck, his booted legs dangling in the air. "Hey. I haven't seen you in a week. I know you're knee-deep in harvest, but I wanted to swing by and check in on you instead of calling. How's it going?"

Glen rubbed the back of his neck, unaccustomed to anyone but his mother or maybe his counselor checking on his well being. "It's going great. It's a bumper crop this year, so I've had to hire extra help."

"That's good news. The weather gods have been kind to all of us farmers this year."

"Yeah. I'm grateful."

"Me too." Walt hopped off the truck and planted his

hands on his hips. "I also came by in person to ask you something. And you don't have to give me an answer right away, but I'd like for you to at least think about it."

"Okay?" Glen furrowed his brow and focused on Walt's face.

"Elyse and I have set a date for our wedding. We want it to be on New Year's Eve in Atlanta. Long story, but it's the anniversary of when we started our journey together as a couple."

"Cool. Congratulations."

"Thanks. We're trying to get as much planning done before Thanksgiving and Christmas, so we don't drive our families bonkers with wedding stuff, including my bachelor party. My dad and brothers want to take me to Nashville. Makes sense because Hank's living there now, and I've never really experienced Nash-Vegas in all its honky-tonk glory."

Walt grinned, and Glen felt a familiar pang of jealousy shoot straight to his heart, wishing he still had his brother Joe in his life. Never mind he didn't have a father either, his deadbeat dad abandoning them before Glen knew any better.

"Sounds fun. When are y'all heading out?"

Walt shut the back end of his truck. "We're driving up there on Thursday for a long weekend. We'll be back on Sunday night. So, here's my question, and if you're too busy with everything you've got going on, I'll totally understand."

"What is it?"

"I was hoping you might be able to stop by the farm over the weekend and check in on Becks."

Glen felt heat surge across his cheeks at the mere mention of Walt's sister's family nickname. Was it obvious?

"Sure," he coughed. "I mean… I can check in on her. No problem."

Walt nodded. "Great. I wouldn't want to intrude on your weekend plans, but Sam and Robyn will be in Atlanta, and Elyse is in Kansas City visiting her folks. They're having an early Thanksgiving celebration and shopping for her wedding dress."

A warm feeling settled over Glen, the need to be needed a sense of significance, rooting him in a cause beyond himself. Belonging and purpose had eluded him for years. To feel important in the eyes of Walt and his family was a fundamental desire rocking him to his core. This was a no-brainer, no matter how busy or tired he was during harvest season.

Walt palmed Glen's shoulder and squeezed before he sauntered to the driver's side door of his truck and opened it. "I appreciate you, Glen. When I get back, we need to nail down a wine combination. And, of course, you're invited to my wedding in Atlanta on New Year's Eve. I'll have more details soon. It'll be here before we know it."

Glen numbly nodded, his thoughts still parked on Becky and the opportunity to see her again. The sound of the truck engine roared to life as Walt leaned his arm across the open window, startling Glen out of his daze.

"I'm looking forward to it, Walt. And don't worry about a thing while you're gone. Have fun."

"I will. I trust you, Glen. I want you to know that."

Glen swallowed a lump in his throat and nodded vigorously. "You can trust me with anything, including your sister."

Walt gave Glen the side-eye. "Now, don't be getting any ideas where my little sister is concerned, ya hear?"

He forced a laugh. "You think I have a death wish?"

This time, it was Walt's turn to laugh. "See you later, bro."

Glen threw his hand up in a wave. "See ya. Don't have too much fun in Nashville."

Walt waved his hand out the truck window and sped up the driveway kicking up dust.

Energized, Glen hopped up the front steps of his house and entered with gusto, his mind reeling with thoughts of Becky Bennett.

———

Glen's house smelled wonderful as he got out of the shower, the scent of apples baking in his oven reminding him of childhood. He'd found the recipe scribbled on an index card tucked inside a rusted metal box, a keepsake from his grandmother. Glen was not a baker, but this recipe was foolproof and easy, an integral part of his apple-farming family over the years. Brown sugar and cinnamon oatmeal packets baked inside a few cored apples in individual foil boats was easy enough. The hardest part was cutting in a few pats of real butter into the mixture so it would turn nice and bubbly while baking.

After buttoning up a clean flannel shirt in dark blue and green stripes, he ran his fingers through his short hair and headed for the kitchen, ready to open the oven door to reveal his masterpiece. But his happy mood turned sour when he opened the oven to a wisp of smoke and noticed the tops of the baked apples charred and blackened.

"Dammit," he lamented. Shoving his hand into a baking mitt, he pulled the tray out. Eyeing his creation with a furrowed brow, he realized all was not lost. Taking a spoon, he flicked off the top layer of fried, sizzling goo and was relieved to find the creamy center bubbling and intact. If Becky Bennett could make him a homemade pie, he could reciprocate with a tray of baked apples when he showed up on her doorstep to check in on her, even if they were a bit on the well-done side.

His kitchen was a disaster zone, remnants of apple and oatmeal strewn about on the countertop. But he'd deal with the mess later. Right now, the only thing on his mind was heading over to Bennett Farms and laying eyes on his daisy girl again.

He thought he could wait until the weekend, but knowing the Bennett boys and their father were on their way to Nashville gave him the green light to proceed with his plan. After all, Walt specifically asked him to check in on his sister while they were gone. And even though it had only been a few hours, a promise was a promise.

Right?

Chapter Ten

BECKY

The big dogs barked, warning Becky someone was on the property.

She hated the late fall season when the sun dropped below the horizon before five o'clock, the impending dark night tricking her senses into thinking it was later than it was.

"Get back, Jaxson," she scolded the energetic sable dog. Delia obediently hung back, sitting on her yellow haunches, Jaxson joining her.

Becky flicked on the light and was surprised to see Glen Kirby coming up the front porch steps. And he was carrying a large tray covered with tin foil.

"What in the world?" She opened the door before he had a chance to ring the bell, his eyes going wide at the sight of her. Jaxson scampered out onto the porch, tail wildly wagging.

"Becky—hey! How are you?"

"I'm fine, Glen. What are you doing here?"

The man was hatless, his large body covered in a dark pea coat to fend off the evening chill.

"Oh. Well, I, uh… I came by to check on you since your family went out of town."

Becky gave him the side-eye. "Is that so?" Folding her arms across her chest, she messed with him. "Checking in on the helpless female all by her lonesome? Are you going to go around and check all the windows and doors to make sure they're locked tight, so I won't be taken in the night?"

Glen's face morphed with confusion. "What? No, that's not it at all. I know you can manage by yourself." He stood a little taller and presented his shiny tin foil creation to her. "I also wanted to give you this."

Curious, Becky took a step closer. "What is it?" As she lifted the foil's edge for a peek, he jerked the tray, making her squeal.

"Baked apples," he chuckled.

Taken aback, her eyes flicked to his. Glen baked something for her?

"Now, don't be getting too excited. It's a fool-proof recipe using instant oatmeal packets and butter. But you put them into some of our apples fresh off the farm, and they morph into something magically delicious."

Becky licked her lips, humbled by Glen's thoughtfulness. "Where are my manners? Won't you please come inside? Make yourself at home while I put on a pot of tea, and we can dig right in." She took the tray from his hands and headed toward the kitchen. "Make sure Jaxson comes back inside. The last time he was out after dusk, he had a run-in with a skunk. It took me an entire week to air out the downstairs."

Glen whistled and shucked off his coat, hanging it on the hall tree. "Wow. Must've been horrible."

Becky set the tray on the island and busied herself, filling the tea kettle at the sink. "Thank God we caught it early. Poor Jaxson had to sleep in a storage shed before we let him back inside. We opened all the windows, ran the fans, and I boiled big pots of vinegar on the stove."

"Vinegar?" Glen asked, standing next to the island.

"Yes. And believe me, vinegar smells terrible. But not as terrible as a skunk." She turned around, giving him the once-over. Funny, she was glad to have a visitor. Happy the house wasn't so achingly quiet since her family left for Nashville. Glad it was Glen.

Rubbing her hands together, she approached the foil-covered sheet on the island. "Now, let's see what you've created."

Glen planted one hand on his hip and rubbed his other hand across the back of his neck. "I'm sorry it's not very pretty. I might've had the oven on too hot."

Becky nodded and carefully removed the tin foil revealing six baked apples in gooey rows of two. The outside of the fruit was shriveled from the baking process, and the tops held a few charred remnants of oatmeal pieces. Still, the fragrant aroma of sugar and cinnamon wafted under her nose as she breathed the scent in.

"Mmmm. Smells heavenly."

"My mama always said Mutsu apples are best for baking. They have firmer flesh and are less tart. The structure holds up when you cook them. They're very similar to the Golden Delicious variety."

Becky plated two apples and handed one off to Glen.

"Ma learned this trick from my grandma. She wasn't the best baker, hence the instant oatmeal packets inside. But this was more of a convenience, especially being a single mom. Joe and I loved these just the same."

Becky nodded with empathy. "How can you go wrong with oatmeal mixed with cinnamon, sugar, and a little butter? Especially stuffed into an organic apple from Kirby Farms?"

Glen's reaction was priceless, his features beaming with pride.

Before she took her first bite, she tilted her head and pinned him with a genuine smile. "Thank you for this, Glen. What a sweet and thoughtful surprise on a Thursday night."

"You're welcome, Becky."

Their eyes lingered for a beat before she blushed and focused on the apple. Spooning a big bite, she chewed slowly, taking in all the flavors. What Glen lacked in presentation, he more than made up for in taste. The dessert was delicious.

"Wow!" she exclaimed with her mouth full. "This is amazing."

Glen nodded with approval. "I know, right? So easy too."

Setting her plate down, she ripped off a paper towel and pressed it to her mouth. "It's one hundred percent your apples. They're baked perfectly. So what, the inside mixture got a little crispy on top? If you want to know the truth, I think the smokiness gives it more flavor. What counts is the middle—what's on the inside."

Glen mimicked her and set his plate down. He ripped off a paper towel and swiped it across his whiskered mouth, his eyes never leaving hers. "Coming from a master baker, that's the best compliment I've ever gotten."

They finished their apples, and because it was still early, Becky suggested they play a game of cards at the kitchen table. Their conversation was effortless and having her own space and company away from her meddling brothers and overprotective father felt good. It was just her and her new and improved old family friend, Glen, for a few precious hours.

For once, she didn't have to serve a herd of testosterone or clean up after them. She could pretend she was the lady of the house and leisurely do whatever she wanted without questions or comments. Her time with Glen was freeing and, dare she say—fun!

Stifling a yawn in the later hour, she apologized. "I'm sorry, Glen. I was up at the butt-crack of dawn seeing the boys off today."

Glen immediately gathered the playing cards and tucked them inside the box. "No worries. Thanks for letting me hang out with you. This has been... nice."

She studied him from across the table. The way his arm muscles flexed in his movements, causing the flannel of his shirt to pull taut across his biceps. The tinge of red in his whiskers from under the kitchen pendant light hanging over the table. His cheery disposition emoting a happy vibe in her presence. The blue in his smoky gray eyes more pronounced. Becky liked hanging out with Glen Kirby. And she wanted to do it again.

"You wanna come over tomorrow? I can make us a nice supper. Nothing fancy. Afterward, we could play another game of cards. Keep each other company?"

Glen's shoulders relaxed as his eyes held hers. And it was then she saw something in them akin to joy.

"I'd like to very much, Becky."

She pushed her chair away from the table and stood. "Well then, it's settled. Why don't you come over before sunset? Think you can get away by then?"

"Of course."

They ambled toward the front door. "We won't eat too early, but I'll make us a little charcuterie, and we can watch the sunset off the back porch. It really is the best seat in the house in these parts."

They stopped at the door, and Glen shrugged on his coat. "I love a good sunset." When he turned around to face her, she felt unmistakable heat emanating from his body being in such close proximity to him.

"Me too." Her voice was but a whisper and she could practically feel the drag of his gaze slide over the hollow of her throat. Instinctively, she lifted her hand to her neck, the idle thought of Glen Kirby being more than a good friend messing with her reverie.

Glen had been part of her family for many, many years. Before his brother Joe died. Before tragedy struck both of their families. He'd been familiar and brotherly. He was Golden Delicious apples during the fall harvest. He was river fishing in the sticky summer heat. He was baseball games in high school, with both him and Walt hitting home runs, throwing constant strikeouts, and schmoozing for the fans. He was smelly socks and giant boots parked in the mud room when he hung out at Bennett Farms, devouring all the cookies and cupcakes as fast as she and her mother could bake them.

Her relationship with Glen was the closest thing to family aside from her parents and brothers. Was it possible to rekindle the kind of relationship they shared in the past? Or was what they had something new and improved in their adulthood—something they needed to unpack carefully. Delicately.

"I'll see you tomorrow then," Becky said, opening the front door. She was dumbstruck when he opened his arms wide, indicating he wanted a hug.

Swallowing hard, she shuffled into his embrace and breathed in his manly scent, cheek pressed into the itchy fabric of his coat. She felt his lips press into the top of her head, his voice low and mumbled.

"See you tomorrow."

They lingered a moment longer in the hug before Glen pulled back. Raising his hand, the tips of his fingers dragged across her cheek, sending ripples of pleasure to her core.

"Don't forget to lock the door behind me."

"I won't." Staring up at him, his rough edges seemed a little blurred, the image of Glen Kirby standing before her a towering vision of masculinity and predatory focus. He gave her a final look, a half-smile curved underneath his beard. She was certain there was a secret hidden behind the whiskers on his face. And she found herself more than willing to discover what it was.

"Thanks again for the delicious apple dessert. Good night, Glen."

His grin said it all. "Sweet dreams, Daisy Girl."

Chapter Eleven

BECKY

Becky drove the Bennett Farms pickup truck on Main Street through downtown Langston Falls and noticed the heavily decorated lampposts and large swags of evergreen overhead, crisscrossing the road. It wasn't even Thanksgiving yet, and the whole town was decked out in Christmas décor. She was nowhere near ready for the holiday season, the annual Christmas Tree Festival on the farm still weeks away.

Once the boys returned from Walt's bachelor party weekend in Nashville, she knew things would kick into high gear with Thanksgiving, the annual festival, and all the holiday preparations surrounding the season. But she was old-school and preferred Christmas decorations after Turkey Day. Regardless, life went on despite her preference, and life on the farm rarely had any downtime.

She decided to take advantage of her little weekend break from the boys and headed into town for a shopping spree. Only, this wasn't Christmas shopping. This was personal shopping. Becky wasn't the kind of girl who needed or wanted much in her life. The only thing she was obsessed with were high-quality, organic ingredients for all the recipes she shared online and beautiful flower arrangements and decorations for the annual festivals she painstakingly planned. Other than that, she rarely spent money on herself.

Perusing the window displays of the local shops, she tucked her chin into the folds of her heavy coat. A cold front had come through in the clear night, the plunging temperatures depositing a thick frost on everything by daybreak. The vineyards and Christmas tree farm looked like something out of Narnia, with frosty edges and frozen branches against the backdrop of the misty North Georgia Mountains. She made a mental note to bring in a few more logs for the fireplace to fend off the chill.

Becky welcomed the warmth of a charming clothing boutique as she opened the solid door. A few customers lazily combed through the dress racks and rows of pretty sweaters and scarves. She wasn't much of a shopper but still a woman who appreciated pretty things. Shopping for clothes was usually out of necessity, not for fun. Thick socks, solid work boots, and thermal underwear during the Christmas tree season. Maybe a new apron or sundress during spring and summer, especially while filming her show.

She'd never owned a proper evening gown, not that she ever needed one. But there was a time she borrowed a gown from Teddy's wife, Robyn. The plunging red dress she'd worn on New Year's Eve in Atlanta almost a year ago came to mind, and she wanted to capture the feeling again but in a more dressed-down version. Feminine. Classy. Gorgeous.

"Looking for anything in particular?" a middle-aged employee asked.

Becky unbuttoned her coat and sighed. "I have no idea. Something... pretty? But comfortable."

"What's the occasion?"

"Dinner at home." She laughed. "I just want to look nice and not wear the same old blue jeans and sweatshirt." She followed the woman to the rear of the shop.

"These items came in the other day. I haven't even had a chance to put the price tags on them yet. And by the way, my name is Lisa. I'm the owner."

Becky ran her hand across the soft sweater fabric, the crimson color perfect for the season, and her complexion. "Hey, Lisa. It's nice to meet you. My name is Becky."

"Well, Becky, the sweater you're admiring paired with some cute velvet leggings and boots would be awfully pretty on you. If you'd like, I can select a few things and put them in a dressing room."

Becky nodded. "Yes, please."

Her afternoon turned into a fashion show trying on several outfits with the help of Lisa and her impeccable taste. By the time Becky left the boutique, she had four bags filled with numerous items, including soft cashmere sweaters, fashionable leggings, a long skirt, and two pairs of stylish boots. She even accessorized with a few semi-sheer metallic scarves, bracelets, and earrings. It turned out shopping was fun now that she had plenty of money in the bank. And she was thrilled by her choices, the clothes flattering and feminine on her curvy, buxom frame. Robyn would take one look at her and want to borrow her new clothes for sure.

With her bags deposited on the front floorboard of the truck, Becky ducked into the coffeehouse and ordered a chai tea to go. As she waited in line, she absentmindedly peeked over at the booth she and Glen had shared not too long ago. Visions of his burly figure wrapped in flannel and his whiskers covered in cream came to mind, and she had to stifle a big grin. Thinking about him coming to the farm for supper had her all worked up and indecisive about what to wear and what to serve.

Earlier in the morning, as the frost pressed against the windows in shimmering crystal patterns reminding her of delicate snowflakes, she baked a loaf of homemade bread. The quiet calm of the new day held endless possibilities, and she was ready to dive in, her nimble fingers kneading and punching the bread dough before sunrise. Two Cornish game hens were rinsed and patted dry, the cornbread stuffing with simple aromatic herbs ready to be spooned into the small cavities, the tiny drumsticks tied together with butcher twine. She planned on serving the hens with steamed broccoli and glazed baby carrots, the meal substantial for a man of Glen's stature yet healthy. A meal served on her mother's heirloom china among the romantic glow of two ivory tapered candles in brass holders. Add the warmth of a roaring fire and homemade bread slathered with real butter, and this was sure to be a cozy night in.

Becky had it all planned, most of her food prep finished before she headed into town. The only thing left was to assemble a charcuterie board with fruit, meats, and cheeses. Oh, and dessert. There must always be dessert. Stopping by the local market on her way home, she picked up the few remaining items on her list and put them in a red plastic basket she carried over her arm.

Eyeing the ice cream aisle, she had a flashback of a summer long ago when Glen joined her family for a cookout after a baseball game. Her mother had made a family favorite—peanut butter ice cream pie. And she recalled Glen mentioning peanut butter desserts were his favorite. God, how long ago was that? And why did she remember this out of the blue? She couldn't have been in high school if the boys had just finished a baseball game. But somehow, she remembered the look on Glen's adolescent face was one of pure bliss. Peanut butter had a way of making her happy too.

The ingredients were simple: vanilla ice cream, graham cracker crust, cashews, peanut butter, honey, and fudge topping. With her groceries laid out on the conveyer belt, she scrolled her portions and made a mental check by each item before she panicked for a beat.

What was she going to serve Glen to drink?

Whenever she hosted a dinner guest, opening a few bottles of Bennett Farms wine was a no-brainer. But Glen was sober and didn't drink anymore. And she wasn't about to imbibe in front of him. That would be cruel. Would water suffice? Or maybe iced tea, but it was winter, and she only made iced tea during the warmer seasons.

Flummoxed, she asked the cashier to hold on for a moment and dashed to the water and soda aisle, where she grabbed a few bottles of club soda and carbonated mineral water. Knowing she had a big bowl of bright lemons sitting on the counter back home, she thought a generous squeeze of citrus in store-bought water was a better drink option than regular old tap water, right?

"Looks like someone is having a little party," the female cashier winked from behind the register, happily ringing Becky up.

She felt her cheeks heat and avoided the woman's gaze. "I have a dinner guest coming over. Nothing fancy."

The cashier, whose nametag read "Flo," cleared her

throat and cocked a thin eyebrow while holding up an expensive block of smoked gouda and a wheel of brie in her hands. Becky's groceries were definitely fancy. The pricey nuts, organic honey, grapes, raspberries, and Italian meats and cheeses were definitely decadent choices.

She stammered, "Only the best."

"May I make one more suggestion, honey?" Flo's southern drawl was endearing.

"Umm… sure?"

"You need a couple of bottles of wine from aisle three." She pointed in the direction of the aisle. "I suggest a bottle of the Bennett Farms Mountain White and a second bottle of the Red Barn Blend, that way your guest will have a choice. And wine goes great with meat and cheese."

Becky pressed her lips together to thwart off a grin and nodded. "Great suggestions. And I already have both back home," she nodded, taking her credit card out of her wallet. It always surprised her when she found out her family's wines were available in some of the grocery stores in the region.

Flo was pleased. "Well, enjoy your Fri-yay. Get it? Fri-YAY!" Her laugh was deep and robust, making her big chest heave.

Becky laughed and gathered her bags. "Happy Fri-yay to you too. Thanks."

Back at the farm, Becky struggled to carry all her bags into the house in one trip. The big dogs sniffed the pink-striped boutique bags full of clothes she'd dropped on the floor as she put the perishables, including the ice cream, into the refrigerator. She only had to set the table and put together the ice cream pie before she showered and got ready.

The sweet, yeasty aroma of homemade bread lingered

in the kitchen as she pulled two plates from the china cabinet against the wall. Running her fingers across the delicate gold edges, she closed her eyes and thought of her mother. Lillian Bennett took pride in serving her family and friends with added touches of beauty, and Becky took right after her.

Her mother once told her life was short—use the fine china and sterling silver. Light the candles. Eat the cake, or in this case, the pie. She wanted Becky to understand every day you're alive was a special occasion. Every second, every breath, a gift from God.

Opening her eyes, Becky sniffled back hot tears threatening to surface. Taking a deep breath, she soldiered on and set her pretty table, the chargers and plates, glasses, and cutlery settings directly across from each other. The dishes gleamed in the light, ready to be filled with Cornish game hens, steamed vegetables, and warm buttered bread. The silver glinted on top of fabric napkins in a soft rose pattern, passed down from two generations. Roses were a theme in her family, her great-great-grandmother Rose Bennett her namesake. Rose was Becky's middle name.

With her hands on her hips, she took a step back and marveled at the simple aesthetic of the table. She was grateful to be able to express herself in such a beautiful way, the heirloom items tying her to the past, a tradition starting with her ancestors.

After her mother died, if Becky had a terrible day, she'd often drink from an antique crystal glass or serve pizza on one of the china plates while in sweats. This perplexed her brothers, and they'd tease her saying she was acting like an English aristocrat. But she learned from her mother to treat herself like a person worth special treatment. It was a form of self-care on a hard day. And the finer things in her life passed down from her mother shone the brightest when she chose to share them with others.

And tonight, she chose to share them with Glen Kirby.

Chapter Twelve

GLEN

Glen knew he was pushing it, trying to make a trip into town before heading over to Becky's place. But he didn't want to arrive empty-handed. He wanted to bring her a little gift to express his gratitude for becoming his friend. And he knew just the gift—daisies, for his daisy girl.

The entire town of Langston Falls was decked out with Christmas decorations, the twinkle lights strung around the lampposts and across the street winking at him in the late day. Boy, someone in town was undoubtedly ahead of their game.

Glen's shined boots clomped across the sidewalk as he hurried toward Langston Petals, the pretty flower shop a staple in the community where Ted Bennett's wife, Robyn, used to work. Holding the door open for an elderly man, Glen admired the large bouquet of red roses wrapped in brown paper as he exited. Were the flowers for his wife? Or maybe they were for his date, the man equally nervous as Glen.

But this wasn't an actual date. This was dinner with a friend. At least, that's what he kept reminding himself.

"Hello, how may I help you?"

Glen focused on the woman, her nametag covered by a strand of her auburn hair.

"I, uh…" He looked around, overwhelmed by the sights and sweet smells. His eyes landed on a Fraser Fir tree in the corner lit up with Christmas lights advertising Bennett Farms Christmas tree farm. The scent of pine immediately calmed him.

"I'd like a bouquet of daisies, please. The little white and yellow kind if you have them," he requested with self-assurance.

The woman tilted her head and frowned. "I'm so sorry, but those are out of season, and I don't have them in stock in the store right now. But I can order some from my supplier and have them delivered?"

Glen's heart fell to his knees. Wouldn't you know it? He was in the wrong season.

"Or I can show you some lovely gerbera daisies leftover from a party arrangement I'm working on. Would you like to take a peek?"

"Uh, sure. Why not?"

Glen followed the lady into a back workshop room. Left-over snippets of thorns and green leaves were scattered across a large counter. He eyed the creation in the center and smiled, the layered and lush piece dramatic with orange roses, yellow lilies, sunflowers, and sizeable red gerbera daisies.

"Wow," he uttered.

The woman gathered a few wayward flowers in her hands and made a mini bouquet in seconds. "How about something like this? I know it's not what you wanted, but the seasonal colors are bright and happy. This particular gerbera daisy in deep red is one of my favorites. I use it in all my November arrangements."

Glen eyed the handful of flowers. An orange rose, a sunflower, and a sprig of greenery intertwined with two red gerbera daisies. It was perfect.

"Yes, this is beautiful. I'll take it."

The two returned to the showroom, and Glen reached for his wallet. She waved him off and handed over the bouquet she'd wrapped efficiently in brown paper.

"On the house today." She smiled.

Glen did a double-take, unaccustomed to such kindness. But then again, he'd never had a reason to frequent a store like this before.

"Are you sure, ma'am? I have the money."

"Of course. I'm sorry I didn't have what you wanted in stock. But come back in the spring, and this place will be filled with yellow and white daisies, I promise."

Glen tipped his hat. "I'll definitely be back. Thank you very much."

He was careful laying the flowers on the front seat of his truck, anxious to get this show on the road. Speeding past barbed wire on fence posts, he could make out the entrance of Bennett Farms in the distance. Driving under the curve of the custom, heavy-gauge steel letters, he passed a few tall Georgia pines, his heart racing like the truck motor rumbling up the hill. Checking his reflection in the rearview mirror, he slid his fingers down his beard one last time before he exited the vehicle with flowers in hand, careful not to crumple the brown paper in a death grip.

Jaxson and Delia barked from inside the main house as he ascended the steps. Before he could knock on the substantial front door, Becky greeted him with a whoosh of femininity. The woman was drop-dead gorgeous wearing a sultry dark red sweater dipping off one shoulder, the color reminding him of the gerbera daisies in his hand. Every curve of her legs and ample bootie were outlined in black velvet leggings, her zip-up suede ankle boots fashionable in a low heel. Her wrists jangled with several bracelets, and her long hair hung in big waves over her shoulders.

"Hey, Glen. I'm so happy you're here." She waved him inside and patted his shoulder, her touch sending a shock-wave through his system. "I know it's chilly outside, but I've got everything on the back porch, so leave your coat on. Oh, and I've put some big blankets out there too, so we can drape them over our legs if we get cold. The weather is cooperating with clear skies, so I know it will be a gorgeous sunset in the next half hour."

Glen was humored by her high-pitched tone and speed of conversation. Was she nervous too?

"Hold on, Becky. Here." He awkwardly presented her with the flowers, holding them in front of him like a torch.

Her mouth formed the shape of an "O" as she took the gift from him. "Oh, Glen. These are beautiful." The paper crumpled when she held them against her chest. "And look! The daisies match my sweater. What a thoughtful gift. Flowers are my favorite. These will be perfect for our table centerpiece."

She motioned toward the dining room, the table already set for dinner. Glen took off his hat and held it at his stomach, watching Becky rearrange the flowers in a vase she pulled from a cabinet. Inhaling a deep breath through his nose, he eyed the table setting of beautiful fine china, crystal, and candles. The romantic setup beckoned him to sit with her and dine for hours. She was the thoughtful one.

"Becky, you didn't have to go to all this trouble."

"It's no trouble at all. We use these dishes all the time." She offered him a reassuring smile and set the flowers in the center of the table. They looked like they always belonged there.

"Now, let me get my coat on, and we can go outside and enjoy the sunset with a little charcuterie."

Glen nodded and followed her into the mudroom. She struggled for a beat to get her arms into her thick coat.

Plopping his hat back on his head, he said, "Here, let me help."

"Thank you."

Her golden hair was wedged between the coat and her sweater, and he tenderly swept his hand underneath, grazing her nape with his fingers and lifting her tresses gently. He watched her hair fall like an angel's wing against the dark fabric.

"There you go." Her golden locks felt like fine silk to his touch, the aroma of sweet flowery shampoo permeating the tiny room.

She turned and looked at him with big doe eyes, the slight blush on the apples of her cheeks noticeable. Avoiding his gaze, she opened the back door, which led to the sprawling rear porch where several rocking chairs were lined up, facing the majestic North Georgia Mountains beyond the vineyard and Christmas tree fields. The horizon at this time of the day was breathtaking.

Jaxson and Delia playfully cantered down the hill, Becky offering him a beverage with a thick lemon wedge perched on the rim of the glass.

"I hope you like club soda. I wasn't sure what you'd want to drink, and I didn't want to serve you boring old tap water."

"This is great. I love club soda." Glen took the glass

from her, overcome by her attention to detail, remembering he didn't drink alcohol anymore.

His comment induced a beaming smile from Becky, and she held up a similar glass, clinking it with his. Taking a sip, he eyed the large outdoor table, overwhelmed by the spread in front of him. She'd gone to a lot of trouble artfully arranging a variety of meats, cheeses, fruit, and nuts on a thick board. Little cocktail napkins with a fall leaf motif were placed nearby, the color scheme matching the flowers he gifted her.

"Help yourself."

Glen picked up a cashew and popped it into his mouth. "This looks like art, Becky."

"Food art," she giggled. "I know I put out too much, but I enjoy doing it."

They nibbled for a few minutes, Glen enjoying the spread and sampling a little of everything. When he had his fill, his deep voice rumbled, "So…."

"So?

Their eyes met, and something humble and sincere passed between them. Glen set his glass on the table and took off his hat.

"You've gone above and beyond, Becky. I mean, look at all this." He waved his hand over the charcuterie board filled with abundant food. There was no way they could eat it all in one night. "I don't know why you went to so much trouble tonight for a guy like me."

The space between her brows furrowed. "A guy like you? You mean, my friend?" Her smile tipped into something beautiful, like the shifting shades of sunset painting the sky in large swaths of warm colors as far as the eye could see. It was a smile he never wanted to forget.

He grinned back at her before marveling at the expanse

of Bennett Farms, where the vineyards were turning gold, and the pine trees rolled up the mountainside like a thick, green blanket. He could imagine leading her through the rows and rows of trees as the sun set, holding her hand, the air around them quiet enough to hear how their boots crunched along the hard ground. Where pine branches swayed, and they were the only two people for miles and miles. He wanted this sunset with her to last forever.

Glen could feel Becky Bennett filling the empty space in his heart slowly, sweetly, with her pretty smile, generosity, and friendly conversation. And somehow, without her even knowing it, she was the one leading him—back to himself.

Chapter Thirteen

BECKY

Becky glanced at Glen and then back at the sky. She wanted to remember this version of him in her mind, not the drug-addicted bully who hurt her brothers. The happier version with the colors of the heavens splayed vibrant across his face, hat held to his chest. Eyes bright and glowing with sobriety, his free hand running down his whiskers as he took in the wonder and beauty of nature.

She also marveled at how much she enjoyed hanging out with him. Everything up until now felt like putting on shoes that were the wrong size. But when she was around him, she felt free to be herself. Free to wiggle her toes. She kept waiting for this feeling to disappear, but it wasn't. It was only intensifying. What did it all mean?

Staring at the horizon morphing with a collision of violet and indigo, she nibbled on a cracker, taking it all in. The air around them stilled, and the silence was cavernous. Looking at Glen's profile again, she noticed his reverent expression as if he were staring at the face of God.

"It's pretty, isn't it?" she said, humbled by his honest reaction. Before she let him respond, she dared to ask him a personal question. "Glen, do you experience moments like this completely different since you're sober now? Or does it really matter? Is this the same old sunset you've always seen?"

He paused for a beat and swallowed, his Adam's apple bobbing in his throat. "This is the prettiest sunset I've ever laid eyes on."

His comment made her beam with pride, knowing she was the one who had shown him something special. And thank goodness Mother Nature came through for her, the November skyline like something out of a priceless watercolor painting or picture-perfect postcard.

Somewhat relieved, she sat in one of the rockers, the temperature dipping with the fading sunlight. "Glen? Where is the last place you felt happy?"

She waited with bated breath and watched him leave his hat on the table and amble to the rocker next to hers. Easing his large body onto the seat, he lifted his face toward the last glow of sunlight before it completely disappeared behind the mountain peak, his face shadowed and hard to read.

"Right here. Right now." His voice rumbled low, his comment making her blush. "What about you? Where is the last place you felt happy?" he asked.

It came to her instantly, but it wasn't a place. It was memorable moments—with him.

"Thick cream in your whiskers," she giggled. "Baseballs thrown at metal milk cans. Dancing underneath the Halloween moon. The scent of baked apples covered in foil. The colors of the sunset in a cloudless sky where the mountain peaks reach for the heavens." Becky rolled her shoulders back and breathed in the first deep breath she'd taken in what felt like months, her poetic words falling from her lips.

"And I guess you could say it's the same for me too, Glen. I feel happy right here. Right now."

He angled his head and stopped rocking. Looking at her from his chair, incredulousness was written all over his quiet face. "Seriously?" he asked, his voice raw and hushed.

She turned her focus toward the fading horizon, a little surprised by her detailed confession, unable to look him in the eye. Her pulse buzzed like bees under glass. "Mmhmm."

The quiet thumping of the curved rockers moving forward and backward on thick wooden porch planks filled the silence as the big dogs scampered toward them, huffing and puffing from their frolic in the pine tree forest. Jaxson approached Glen and rested his panting muzzle on his knee. He stroked the animal's dark fur, a slight smile burgeoning across his lips.

"If I forget to tell you, this has been the best night of my entire life."

Becky stifled a nervous giggle. The evening had barely begun. They hadn't even had dinner yet.

She intentionally turned in her rocker and boldly looked at him, head leaned back against the curved, horizontal slats of the chair. The temperature plummeted as the sky morphed from sherbet colors to a canvas of midnight blue with a smattering of stars. Her words came out in a puff of vapor when her hot breath hit the cold air.

"Same."

Becky guffawed with wild abandon, freely expressing herself in front of Glen, his story from the past reminding her of an innocent time in their lives not too long ago. Gazing into his eyes from across the dining room table, she saw history.

"You don't remember your mama's reaction?" he chuckled. "She was mad as a hornet when she had to call the local fire department to rescue us from the mud."

Becky wiped laughing tears from her eyes and nodded. Glen had just finished retelling the story about how he and her brother, Walt, had become trapped in one of the back fields of the farm. They were utterly stuck after daring each other to jump over a vast gulley of mud left behind after a deluge of rain.

The boys were still in elementary school, the large sloggers they'd borrowed from the mudroom entirely too large for their youthful feet. Walt went in first, immediately getting his boots stuck in the mire, his white-socked foot popping out of the boot and oozing deep into the thick sludge after he lost his balance. He reached toward Glen for help, and when their hands clasped, Walt pulled too hard, and Glen ended up face-planting in the mud, his body spread eagle like a snow angel.

Teddy, James, and Hank discovered them after hearing their cries for help from across the fields, the three brothers slinging a thick hemp rope across the pit, urging them to grab hold and hang on. But it was no use. The mud was too thick, and their strength waned from floundering up to their waists in the bog. They looked like horror creatures from a southern swamp movie.

"I remember the sirens and Daddy leading the firemen along the back access road parallel to the fields. I was so scared for y'all. But when I finally laid eyes on you and Walt covered head to toe in mud, I had to laugh," Becky giggled.

"Mama used a garden hose and sprayed y'all down. Walt wailed like a girl because the water was so cold."

Glen chuckled at the memory. "I swear, I had mud remnants in crevices I didn't even know existed. If it hadn't been for your mama calling the fire department, we might still be stuck in the pit."

Becky sighed and rested her chin in her hand, elbow propped on the dining room table among the aftermath of their meal. Pools of melted ice cream and peanut butter were left behind on dessert plates, and candles flickered romantically, hazy orbs of light bouncing off crystal.

Glen leisurely leaned back in his chair and eyed her from across the table. "What's next for you, besides the Christmas Tree Festival and Walt's New Year's Eve wedding in Atlanta? Anything happening with your cooking show on YouTube? I saw you've gained a ton of new followers."

"You watch my show?" she asked.

"I try to. I usually watch on my phone before I go to sleep. But then, I get so hungry from all the food you make, I have to get back up and have a little snack to tide me over till morning."

Pleased by Glen's support, she smiled. "Sorry about that." Bashfully, she dipped her head. "I don't know, Glen. I'm thinking about taking a little breather soon."

"Oh? Why? Are you getting burned out?" The space between his brows furrowed with concern.

"Maybe? I don't know. Elyse hooked me up with all these partnerships and sponsors. But I feel like no matter how much time I spend creating content and interacting with strangers, it's still never enough."

"What do you mean?"

Becky struggled to find the words to explain what she was feeling. "I feel like the public consumes me like a product, if that makes any sense. I've given away little pieces of myself for the last year, and what do I have to show for it? Complete strangers following my every move on all my social media platforms. More money than I know what to do with and a sense of dread trying to do and be everything everyone wants me to be. I'm tired, Glen. I think it's time for me to take a break." The words she hadn't said to anyone else slipped from her mouth in a slow exhale.

"You should take a break," he agreed.

"I know, right? This entire thing started as a fun hobby, and now it's snowballed into a career. I have success, a book deal, and hundreds of thousands of followers. I'm doing something I love while caring for my family simultaneously, yet I'm terribly discontented and...." She paused.

"And, what?"

"And... lonely."

Glen's eyes locked with hers. "I'm sorry you're lonely, Daisy Girl."

Beneath those dark pools of history, she glimpsed a spark of something that sent heat rolling through her stomach again. She wasn't totally discontented all the time, especially tonight.

It was nice experiencing the sunset with him. It was nice coming back inside with the scent of Cornish game hens in the oven and the dining room table glistening with pretty things. The big dogs lounging on their beds by the crackling fire, and Glen's boots parked in the mudroom. Seeing him relax was nice, his expression lighting up with genuine surprise at the sight of the dinner spread, especially the peanut butter ice cream pie. It was nice laughing and sharing family stories, his eyes flashing with childlike mirth. She remembered how she grew up feeling a certain kinship with Glen. He was like a fifth brother to her all those years. But now it was something different. More profound.

Becky liked spending time with Glen Kirby. She liked seeing flickers of his true self come to the surface. The ones he did his best to hide underneath his gruff, often stand-offish exterior. She liked how sobriety agreed with him.

Good Lord. She liked *him*.

Chapter Fourteen

GLEN

The evening with Becky Bennett played repeatedly in Glen's mind as he lay in bed. Never in his life had a woman catered to him like she did.

From the back porch spread watching the sunset to the sit-down dinner with real linen napkins, fancy dishes, and the backdrop of a roaring fire. He'd felt like a king, spoiled and pampered. And how could he forget their easy conversation and hug goodbye as they stood by the front door?

Becky humorously stuck her hand out to shake his, reiterating how much she enjoyed their time together. Clasping his thick fingers around hers, he pulled her forward into his arms, hugging her with gentle gratefulness. With her cheek pressed against his shoulder, he could smell flowers and Langston Falls, hear childhood laughter from long ago and see her morph from pretty little girl to drop-dead gorgeous woman.

When he was with Becky, his loneliness dissolved.

They'd come full circle. And even though he pined for a kiss under the light of a million stars, he was grateful for the hug. For the closeness to her womanly figure, her sweet breath grazing his ear before she pecked his cheek with her warm lips and bid him goodnight.

Knowing her family wouldn't be back for another full day and night, he casually asked her to stop by his place if she could find the time.

"I need to practice taking a break. I think I can make it happen," she'd said.

"Then it's settled. My place. Five o'clock. And come hungry."

"Oh?" Her eyebrow cocked with pleasure. "You gonna make me some more of those baked apples again?" She playfully poked him in the ribs.

"Maybe," he teased, grabbing her index finger and squeezing. "Wear some comfortable shoes too. I want to show you something."

"I look forward to it." Something in her eyes conveyed she meant it too. "Good night, Glen."

"Good night, Daisy Girl."

The full moon lit the backcountry roads, the night air crisp and exhilarating, his mood buoyant. He was experiencing a natural high like no other. The feeling was unparalleled to alcohol or drugs, and he didn't think he could ever come down from the rush. Now, as he lay in bed with Garth curled up and purring in the crook of his neck, he rested his head against his bent arm and stared at the shadows on the ceiling.

Stroking his cat, he thought about how far he'd come and wondered where the universe was taking him next. Did his path include a pretty farmer's daughter who wore daisies in her hair? A woman who treated everyone she met with absolute loving kindness?

He'd been so close to kissing Becky. Damn close.

On the back porch, with sunset colors highlighting her gorgeous face. After dinner, her hands immersed in soapy water as they stood side by side and washed the delicate dishes. At the front door, with his chest an inch away from hers, pink highlighting her cheeks. He'd wanted to kiss her so badly. But he wanted the moment to be right.

And worrying about Walt and the rest of her family was another consideration. They'd never approve of a guy like him wooing the only Bennett female in the family, especially with his violent history. And don't forget, he was in the process of buying back his home and land from Walt. He couldn't screw this up.

Becky was completely off-limits in their eyes; he was sure of it. And he would never ask her to settle or compromise. A girl like Becky Bennett deserved anything and everything in this world, even if it meant she could never be his.

Still, Glen would walk a million miles over broken glass to have just one chance with her. *One.* But he knew it didn't matter how many days, months, or years he stayed sober or how many times he apologized and asked for forgiveness— his wicked past would always come back to haunt him. And he was sure the Bennett men would never give him their blessing.

Drifting off into a fitful sleep, his dreams were filled with scattered pictures of his life when he was blameless and young. Before Joe was killed and Teddy was beaten. Before Mrs. Bennett passed away from cancer and the family was still whole. When Becky was just a girl, watching him and her brothers act like fools on the farm, visions of baseballs and mud, cupcakes and daisy chains dancing like sugar plums in his slumbering head.

Grill smoke wafted into Glen's face as he took off the cover and poked the meat sizzling on the charred grate, his grandfather's famous ribs almost ready for the last coating of sauce.

It felt odd cooking outside without a beer or a cocktail in his hand, his subconscious ticking with memories of how he used to enjoy a cookout. He was usually shit-faced, running back and forth from the family room to the backyard while watching an Atlanta Braves baseball game on TV. An iced-down cooler full of alcoholic beverages conveniently located by the grill. Empty beer cans scattered in the yard. Pissing in the grass with a thick stogie hanging from his lips.

Today, he was totally sober, a pink can of flavored sparkling water in his grip—pomegranate, to be exact. Eyeing the aluminum decorated in pastel-colored branding, he wondered who the hell came up with the delicious drink?

Becky was due to arrive in a few minutes, and he rushed to slather the last of the barbecue sauce on the meat, accidentally flicking some across his face in his rush.

"Dammit," he uttered. At least his clothes were protected by an apron, the stains from cookouts past forever ingrained in the fabric. Before he could remove the covering with bold lettering humorously spelling out, "*I'll Feed All You Fuckers,*" he heard a honk from his driveway.

"Shit," he lamented. Using tongs, he lifted the rack of ribs off the grill and set them in a large tin pan, covering them with foil. "She's early again," he muttered. But he was glad and a little bit shocked she actually showed up.

The wide grin on his face spread warmth throughout his entire body. Wiping his hands across the apron, he jogged around the house and watched her exit the truck. And then he remembered the foul language written on his apron and struggled to untie the knot at the small of his back.

"Hey there," she greeted. A plate covered in foil was in her hands as she gave him the once over and squinted. "Does your apron say 'farmers'?"

Glen palmed the word "fuckers" and shook his head. "I'm sorry. This is from my rowdy days. I wasn't paying any attention. Whatcha got there?" He flipped the top part of the apron over his head to hide the evidence of the salty language.

"Deviled eggs," she smiled. "I know you said come hungry, but I never go anywhere without bringing something to share. I hope you don't mind."

"I don't mind at all." He fucking *loved* deviled eggs.

Becky wore dark denim jeans flared at the ankles and showing the tips of her cowboy boots. Her hair was tied back with a black ribbon matching her puffy coat, and her eyes were bright as if she'd slept well. Or maybe she was happy to see him?

Balancing the plate in one hand, she reached toward his face and swiped her finger across his cheek. "You've got something on your face," she said.

Glen rolled his eyes and dragged his hand across his skin, remembering the barbecue sauce splattering. "It's sauce."

Becky sniffed her finger before sticking it into her mouth, sucking off the dollop of wayward sauce between her lush lips. Glen was gobsmacked.

"Brown sugar?" she asked.

Glen realized his mouth hung open like an idiot. Pressing his lips together, he nodded like a bobblehead doll. "Uhh… yup. I cheat though. I buy store-bought sauce and doctor it up a little so it tastes homemade."

"Nothing wrong with that. I often do the same thing in my kitchen to save time." The two ambled into the backyard, where smoke drifted into the bright blue sky. "What kind of meat?"

"Ribs," he replied. "I hope you like ribs."

"More like *love* ribs," she laughed.

"They've been cooking all day. I need to finish them up in the oven wrapped in foil." They walked to the back of his house, and he held the door open for her with his free hand. Once inside, he gestured toward the plate in her hands and said, "Here, let me take those eggs for you."

"Thanks. If we're not eating for a while, these need to go in the fridge."

Becky handed off the deviled eggs, and he proceeded to the kitchen, where he slid the plate on the counter before shoving the loaded tin pan of ribs into the preheated oven. Remnants of his attempt at coleslaw were piled in the farmhouse sink with no extra time to clean up.

"This is it. This is home." With the eggs in the fridge, he finally got his apron off, bunched it up, and tossed it on the counter. He watched her peruse the family room and take in the items on the built-in bookshelves on either side of the stone fireplace and wondered what she was thinking.

Glen didn't have much. But what was most important to him was on full display. A few farming almanacs and biographies. Framed pictures of him with his mom and brother, Joe. A signed baseball from Atlanta Braves Hall of Famer, Hank Aaron. An American flag in a display case, the keepsake commemorating the funeral of his grandfather, who was a military veteran. And a row of collectible die-cast trucks and cars in various colors.

"You collect toy cars?" Becky asked, her eyes flicking to his.

"Not on purpose. Most of those are from when I was a boy. I was fascinated with anything with an engine, so my ma made it her mission to start me a collection. There was a car or a truck in my stocking every Christmas for many years."

Becky picked up a powder blue truck resembling the junker he was working on in his shed. She smiled, careful with the piece as she eyed it from side to side. "I think it's wonderful your mama started you a collection. It's such a fun way to reconnect with your childhood."

"What about you? Do you collect anything?"

Becky carefully placed the truck back on the shelving. "I had a big dollhouse while growing up. Over the years, I collected handmade furniture and a little family until I was too old and lost interest. It's sitting in the attic with a furniture pad protecting it. I'm hoping I can pass it on to my daughter or maybe a granddaughter someday."

Glen could imagine Becky as a sweet little girl, sprawled on her stomach and using her imagination while playing with her dollhouse. And why wouldn't Becky have a daughter someday to pass her collection to?

She'd make a great mama. The thought made him smile.

Garth meowed, Becky's attention immediately diverting to the floor where the black cat circled her legs. "Hi, Garth," she sing-songed.

Passing her coat off to Glen, she knelt and scooped the cat in her arms. He was humored watching them rub noses, Garth making purring and half-meows in his throat.

"He's so sweet. I remember when Walt and I found him in the backyard the night he moved in." Her eyes went wide at her unintentional blunder, and she immediately apologized. "I'm sorry, Glen. I didn't mean to bring up a bad memory."

Glen's mouth twitched, and he avoided her forlorn gaze. "It's okay."

Becky set Garth on the sofa and grabbed Glen by the wrist before he could move away. His eyes ran the length of her arm up to her pretty face, her expression holding concern.

"I mean it. I'm sorry."

Glen shrugged and played it off like it didn't bother him. But it did. It bothered him a lot. Once again, he would never be completely free from his past, moments like this ruined by a few unintentional words during a conversation. He needed to find a way to let it roll off his back.

"It's all good, Becky." He decided to change the subject. "The ribs are gonna take another half hour or so. Can I show you something outside while we wait?"

Becky offered him a tentative smile and took her coat from his hands, shrugging it back on. "Sure."

They traipsed through the backyard, past the smoking grill toward the storage shed near the fence line. The sweet scent of apples permeated the air, the sky turned cloudy, and the temperature taking a dip. Glen was used to the elements, the thermal undershirt he wore beneath his flannel keeping him warm. Still, he'd have to wear a coat if things got any colder.

Grabbing the rusted handle of the sliding door, Glen opened the unit amidst the high-pitch squeal of hardware, revealing the 1960s powder-blue Chevy pickup truck parked inside.

"Oh, wow!" Becky exclaimed. "This is the truck you said you're restoring, right? It looks exactly like the miniature truck on your bookshelf inside."

Glen beamed with pride and watched her approach the old vehicle with curiosity. She ran her hand over the beveled-edged hood.

"She's gonna be a beauty when I'm done. I like getting my hands dirty, and working on the truck keeps me busy when I'm not working on the farm."

Becky's eyebrows lifted. "Your truck is a she?"

Glen chuckled. "Of course."

"I'm jealous," Becky teased.

Chapter Fifteen

BECKY

"Does she have a name?" Becky asked.

Glen shook his head. "Not yet. She's not fully functional. It'll come to me when the time is right." He approached the door and gallantly opened it for her. "Have a seat and check out the interior. These trucks were the first to comfortably hold three adults up front."

Becky came around his big frame and ducked her head under his arm to get in. "Don't mind if I do." She sat on the leather seat, swiveling her legs inside.

Glen shut the door, and she rested her arm across the open window, feeling like she'd entered a time machine sending her back to the rural 1960s. She watched Glen amble around the front of the cab and enter through the driver's side door, slamming it shut. Gripping the steering wheel, he nodded with satisfaction.

"This is an honest, solid old truck."

"Tell me more about her, Glen." She liked seeing his face light up. Liked the way his eyes glistened and how his voice rumbled with pleasure. She liked seeing Glen happy.

"Well, this particular model has a longer wheelbase, perfect for farmers back in the day. And I love the style of the hood. The manufacturer at the time was intentional with the design, allowing the driver more visibility to see up to ten feet more of the road than other truck models."

Becky craned her neck and surveyed the area beyond the giant front windshield across the hood, trying to track with him. "Go on."

Glen turned in his seat to look at her. "You sure you're interested in old truck talk? I'm not boring you?"

She demurely angled her head and shook it. "Not at all. Tell me more. Tell me what you love about this old truck."

Running a hand through his hair, Glen chuckled again. "Well, I think the egg-crate style front grill is cool. I had to send off for the original part online. And the twin I-beam suspension, which was very rugged back in the day, made for a smoother ride. Much better than the solid axle."

"Oh, yes. The solid axle was crap."

Glen's eyes flicked to hers, his smile smug. Their teasing banter was flirty, and she was having fun with him.

He laughed. "None of this makes any sense to you, does it?"

"Kind of? Sort of?" Now it was her turn to laugh. "Not really. Let's go back to the part where you called the truck a 'she.'"

Glen explained. "I guess when guys refer to their vehicles as 'her' or 'she,' it continues the tradition of ships. You know, when boats were given female names to calm powerful water goddesses... for safety reasons or something."

"Aha. Safety reasons. I never thought of it that way. Or..."

"Or?" He pinned her with his stare.

"Or you could say it's because this truck takes all your money and must be tended and coddled with a gentle hand, therefore perceived as feminine."

Glen whistled through his teeth and completely shifted his body to face her, his denim backside making a squeaky fart sound against the leather seat. He didn't seem to notice.

"Now come on. Isn't what you're saying a bit... sexist? I'm surprised. Maybe it's more simple. Maybe it's me investing my time and effort into something special to keep my hands and mind occupied. Like—" He paused as if trying to find the right words. "Like... a significant other?"

"You're comparing your truck to a significant other?" She laughed.

Glen's complexion turned beet red. "Yeah, that doesn't make much sense either." He forced a laugh, joining her titters until the sound dissipated.

"You know I'm just kidding with you. We're just playing around." She reached out and touched his arm. "Right?"

He focused on the front dashboard. "Sure. I know."

"I think it's great what you're doing. And you're right. She's going to be a beauty when you're all done with her. As the saying goes, 'everything old is new again.'"

A slight half-smile tugged at his lips beneath his whiskers. "Yeah." His long arm draped across the back of the bench seat, his jean-clad legs spread wide.

Becky placed her open hand in the space between them in a truce, thankful when Glen gently pressed his hand into hers. They were quiet, studying their fingers laced together. She didn't know if it was their childhood connection, the toy vehicles on his shelves, Glen's handprints all over the antique truck, or her time away from everything she'd deemed important. But she felt little pieces of herself sliding back into place when she was around him. She was more settled into her contentment. Freer to joke around and laugh out loud. More intentional with her words and actions.

The rugged man sitting next to her, with his brown sugar scent of barbecue sauce mixed with the recent rain and fragrant apples, hung in the air. Sitting there and holding his hand in the truck's interior made her feel warm, with visceral flashes of winter and hot cider on cold nights. The feeling was something beautiful and bold, haunting her in the unexpected moment. The smell of Glen Kirby would forever live in her thoughts, tucked away with her mother's apple pie and wild daisies in her hair.

A wolfish grin took over his face, and he squeezed her hand before letting go. "You hungry? The ribs should be ready by now."

"Sure. I'm hungry." Heat curled through her stomach, hers a different kind of hunger. Shocked by the realization, she remained rigid in the seat, her eyes tracing Glen coming around the front of the truck again. He opened her door and offered his hand to help her out. Clutching his thick, calloused fingers, she squeezed.

They were in the middle of a delicate dance where the true meaning of what they said and did was somewhere beyond words. They were heading into uncharted territory, without a ship named after a water goddess, without pickup truck high beams to light their way. What they had was fragile and somewhat dangerous brewing beneath the surface. Becky knew she needed to proceed slowly and with caution.

"Glen?"

He closed the door of the old junker with care. "Yeah?"

"Can I be the first to go for a ride when you're finished with her?"

He came across as positively giddy, something honest and heartfelt passing between them. His nostrils flared with virility.

"I wouldn't have it any other way."

With her hands immersed in soapy suds, Becky asked, "Was there snow in the forecast? Looks like snow clouds out there to me." She motioned with her head out the kitchen window over the sink as she finished washing the last of the dishes.

Glen came up beside her, setting a large baggie of left-over ribs on the counter for her to take home. When he peered outside, he made a low sound in his throat. "Hmmm. It does look a little gloomy out there. Let me check my weather app on my phone."

Becky washed away the residual bubbles and wiped her hands on a kitchen towel, surprised when Glen harrumphed.

"What is it?"

"Snow flurries expected. And it's already dropped to thirty degrees outside. I hadn't even noticed."

"I hadn't either. I was so engrossed enjoying your delicious ribs."

Glen smiled and tucked his phone and hands into his front jeans pockets, making his flannel shirt taut against his bulging biceps. "I'm glad you enjoyed them. It was a labor of love."

Her cheeks heated with a blush. "Well, I appreciate you going to all the trouble. And thanks for the leftovers to take home. I'll have to hide them from my brothers before they come home tomorrow." Her words hung in the air like a black cloud, the reality of their situation coming to a head.

Her father and brothers were headed home the next day from Nashville, she and Glen's secluded, private world of flirty meals and friendly, uninhibited conversations coming to a close. But it was inevitable, wasn't it?

They both knew they were in a willing suspension of disbelief, examining something impossible in their reality for the sake of enjoyment. And she knew they could never be anything more than friends. So why was she flirting with the idea of something more? Why was she tap-dancing around heartache, knowing they were never meant to be?

It was time to acknowledge the existence of their sober reality, whether he liked it or not. As her brother, Walt, often quoted, it was time to "take the bull by the horns."

"What happens tomorrow, Glen?" Her voice was hushed, tinged with sadness.

He shook his head and stared at the floor in defeat. He must've been thinking the same thing. "I don't know."

"Do you think about me like I think about you?" she said in a rush of words. "Because I've been thinking about you since the rainy day you brought me those apples." A secret part of her unlocked, unleashing an avalanche of honesty.

The look on his face appeared pained, tense with unease. "Of course, I think about you."

"Well then, why haven't you kissed me?" She stood taller, chin thrust into the air. She wanted to know. She *needed* to know. They'd had plenty of opportunities away from prying eyes and listening ears. Maybe her fantasy was one-sided after all?

"I'm waiting for the right moment."

Scowling, Becky folded her arms across her chest. "Well,

I hate to be the bearer of bad news, but we don't have many moments left before my family gets home."

Glen moved toward her in a flash, his hands gripping her upper arms with intensity. His eyes were wild and wide, his voice scratched with pure desire. Shocked, she stared at his broody features mere inches from hers, the heat from his body surrounding her with thick warmth.

"Becky, I'm waiting for the right moment because... once I kiss you, there won't be any turning back for me. And I won't pursue anybody else for the rest of my life. I'm not gonna fall for anyone but you. I'm not gonna care about a goddamn thing but you and your happiness. I'm waiting for the right moment, Becky, because when I kiss you, it's gonna be the most important kiss of my entire life." The strong column of his throat moved in a heavy swallow.

"And I just want to make sure I get it right."

She stared at him, the wish in her voice full of longing. "You'll never get it right if you don't try."

Chapter Sixteen

GLEN

Glen's muscles vibrated with the urge to punch his fist through a wall. He wanted to flip the kitchen table and smash plates against the floor. Scream in agony at the top of his lungs.

Forcing himself to sit on the sofa, he interlocked his fingers together and rested them on his head, eyes closed, while he pushed intentional breaths through his nose. In and out. In and out, like his anger management class taught him in rehab.

Becky was gone; her words lodged in his chest like arrows.

"You'll never get it right if you don't try."

She'd stood in his kitchen, vulnerable and open to the possibility they could connect on a deeper level. She was a goddess standing there—a girl asking a boy to kiss her. And what did he do? He froze. He stood there like a fool and watched her sunny smile fade, her face pinched with disappointment as she grabbed her coat and boots and left without saying goodbye, her sniffles indicating he'd made her cry.

He was a fucking fool.

Glen wasn't angry at Becky. No. He was angry because of their situation. He didn't want to need her. Because he knew in his gut he couldn't have her.

His desire for Becky felt like it was manifesting in real time when she asked him point blank if he thought about her. Of course, he thought about her—every waking hour of every damn day. Even at night, in his lonely solitude, she visited him in his dreams.

He'd always felt a magnetic pull toward Becky, and he'd finally been man enough to admit it. But it was worse now because tonight, he didn't do anything about it. She was standing in his kitchen, offering herself on a silver platter, and he did nothing. The bases were loaded, and a grand slam was inevitable. But instead, he struck out.

Shifting his anger to something positive, he thought about how nice the evening had been with her. In the shed, sitting in his old junker and joking around. Holding her hand, her skin warm and her touch, a gentle pressure of reassurance his feelings weren't one-sided. Coming back into the house with ribs in the oven and deviled eggs on her pretty plate with tiny pink roses lining the edge. Garth lounging across the sofa, and Becky's cowboy boots discarded by the door. It was nice eating another meal together, her eyes lighting up at the first taste of his famous ribs he'd made just for her. Washing dishes like an average couple, lavender soap suds floating among the ping of laughter in the air.

But they weren't an average couple. What they shared was anything but ordinary.

Rubbing his palms across his face until he saw stars, he hoisted his body up into a standing position and looked around. A tidal wave of negative emotions overwhelmed him again, and he couldn't think straight, unable to remember his newfound coping mechanisms and strategies he'd learned in rehab.

He pondered the logistics of calming himself with one drink. Just one. It'd be so easy to drive into town and sit at the bar, hands curled around a beer bottle. No harm in one beer, right? A beer wasn't even in the same ballpark as hardcore drugs. Or he could swing by the liquor store near the highway incognito and buy a small bottle of whiskey and disappear into the night. No one would be the wiser. If he could calm the negative chatter in his head with his craving, he promised himself he'd stop after this one time.

But he knew he was only one drink away from the devil. If he started with one, one would lead to two. Two would be a gateway for more than just booze. And then there'd be more self-sabotage. More self-loathing. Complete self-hatred. Had he learned nothing from being in therapy all these months? And the worst part was knowing if he crossed this line, he'd lose any chance with Becky—forever.

Glen knew he was stronger than his addiction and an impending relapse. Struggling to get his phone out of his pocket, he fired it up, found his sponsor's number, and called him. Ken Lambert was a facilitator in his weekly meetings, someone he felt safe discussing his ongoing recovery and struggles with. He answered on the second ring.

"Hello, this is Ken."

Glen swallowed hard, the grip on his phone intensifying. "Hey, Ken. This is, uh, Glen. Glen Kirby from our meetings?"

"Hi, Glen. How are you?"

"Umm, well…"

"What's going on? Are you having a moment?"

"You could say that." He gripped the ledge of the fireplace mantel and decided to be brutally honest. "I want to get in my truck, go to the local bar, and get shit-faced. I assume this is a normal part of the process, right?"

"It's expected, Glen. In recovery, it's commonplace to entertain the cravings of your past, especially if you're having a mentally challenging day."

"So, what should I do? I mean, I'm not *really* going to get in my truck and go to a bar." He forced a laugh. "But I am thinking about it." He hung onto Ken's every word, hoping the intense feeling might pass.

"You're doing the right thing by calling me. This is a healthy approach, Glen. You must address this moment without fear or denial and let it pass. In instances like this, time is your best friend."

"Time?" His voice cracked.

"Yes. Distract yourself. Give yourself a set amount of time before you do anything. You'll find the urge will pass, allowing your rational thinking to retake control instead of your craving."

Ken made it sound so easy. But he was right. A distraction might help.

"I'm proud of you for reaching out. You've interrupted this stage of relapse going into motion. And I'm not saying relapse for you was imminent. In many cases, recognizing the warning signs early enough can prevent a relapse from happening, which is what you've done."

Glen ran his hand through his hair and finally exhaled the breath he'd been holding, a feeling of relief replacing his earlier anger and angst. "The urge was so strong, like a vice-grip."

"I know, Glen. But you need to remember there is so much value in your sobriety. Don't forget how strong you really are. You are worthy of success. You're worthy of good health and love."

The word "love" struck a nerve with Glen. Was he worthy of love after all the terrible things he'd done? Could he dare to dream love was in the cards for him? Could he open up his heart and love Becky?

"Will you be okay tonight?" Ken asked. "Is there anyone you can hang out with? A hobby you can focus on until you're feeling better? You know, a distraction?"

Becky's beautiful face immediately came to mind. She embodied love with her big heart, especially after she befriended him. He never wanted to return to those lonely feelings of hurt and disappointment when he hit rock bottom. When heartbreak cracked him wide open.

He realized he was ready to release the false notions of what it meant to love and be loved. First off, he needed to let go and love himself more fully. Trust himself. Believe he was worthy like Ken said. In their weekly meetings, he'd learned to practice self-forgiveness, which made him see self-judgment only hindered his recovery. It made him smaller, enslaved to hurt and anger. It was all making sense now.

"Umm, yeah. I have a friend in town I can call on. I'm sorry for bothering you tonight."

"You're not bothering me, Glen. I'm here for you 24/7, okay? That's what a sponsor is for. Call me later if you still need to talk."

"Thanks, Ken. Good night."

"Good night. And Glen?"

"Yeah?"

"You've got this."

Glen ended the call, thankful for his sponsor's support through this rough spot, his feelings of frustration and craving waning. His gaze scrolled the family room into the kitchen, where he spotted the ribs he'd packed up for Becky sitting on the counter. Immediately, he took it as a sign and knew what he had to do. This was his chance, a slight window of opportunity for a do-over, and he was taking it.

Pulling on his boots, his heart thrummed a low, steady rhythm. Standing, he imagined himself waiting for the pitch in a baseball game. With clenched fists, he held an imaginary bat over his shoulder and paused for a beat. Swinging his arms out in from of him, he hit an imaginary baseball. And in his mind, he envisioned the ball soaring high into the sky, the home run knocked straight into the stands to the crowd's roar.

The windshield wipers on Glen's truck thumped back and forth, clearing the wet sleet from his vision. The temperature had taken a nosedive, the local weather forecast predicting snow flurries later in the night. It was mid-evening, which gave him plenty of time to visit Becky before the impending snow, his excuse sitting on the front seat of his truck in a plastic bag. At least, that's what he kept telling himself. But it was more than forgotten ribs left on the counter. He and Becky needed to have a heart-to-heart conversation. Glen needed to acknowledge his feelings and set her straight.

"You'll never get it right if you don't try."

Her last words to him echoed in his mind. She hit the

nail on the head. What if he never tried? What if he left things the way they were and put Becky on a high shelf in his mind, compartmentalizing his fears and his desires when it came to her? It would be impossible for him to *not* think about what might have been.

Pulling over on the side of the road before the turn under the curve of the custom Bennett Farms sign, he put his truck in park and listened to the rhythmic patter of freezing rain hit the metal truck roof. In the distance, he could make out the main house on the hill, soft light filtering out of the windows and the faint scent of a wood fire in the air. He imagined Becky sitting in front of the hearth with the big dogs snoozing on their beds, flames creating a halo of gold around her fair hair.

Glen realized every sober waking moment, every single vision of his past and future, had Becky in it. Everything he wanted was shrunk to the size of her beautiful face. He thought about her 24/7. It was as if she'd hijacked his brain.

Looking back, he remembered where it all began—the night of the bonfire when she was an incoming high school freshman. He was sitting near the fire when she joined the party. She wore a purple shirt, tight blue jeans, and cowboy boots. He could remember where they were in the field and who was sitting next to him, a million stars scattered across the night sky. And as she smiled at him from across the flames, his peripheral vision diminished, and it wasn't because of the weed he'd been smoking. He remembered thinking he must have her in his life. It was physiological.

But when the party ended, and he was clear-headed, he knew it would never work. Years passed, and through all his tumultuously agonizing fuckups, it was a miracle he found his way again. And here he was, sitting in his truck, burdened by the same feelings of his youth, and struck with an enormous need. Becky Bennett had reentered his life like a shooting star, blazing and piercing the center of his heart.

She was right. He had to try.

Tonight was the most important night of his life.

Chapter Seventeen

BECKY

"Yes, Daddy, I know where the extra gas cans are in the barn," Becky replied.

Roy sighed on the other end of the phone line. "Well, just in case you lose power, you've got plenty of fuel for the generator. But I don't think that'll be the case. There's only a slight chance for snow accumulation in Georgia. It's worse here in Tennessee."

Becky leaned her head back against the couch. "So, what's the plan? Are you going to wait it out? Or are you going to try and beat the storm home?"

"The storm is coming in fast, darlin'. Weatherman says Nashville is getting walloped with a few feet of snow over the next twenty-four hours. Tomorrow, it will depend on whether or not they've shut down the Interstate over Monteagle. It's already pretty dicey with all the sleet, and black ice is dangerous, especially with all the truckers on the road. They're advising folks to stay home."

"Walt will probably be thrilled to have another night celebrating in Nashville. Are y'all having fun?"

Roy chuckled. "We're havin' a ball. Remind me to tell you about the hot wings Hank dared us to try at Hattie B's."

"Tell me now, Daddy," she giggled, imagining her father trying to keep up with her brothers' frat-boy shenanigans.

"Of course, they ordered the 'shut the cluck up!' heat-level version. Teddy got a bloody nose. Jimmy threw up. And Walt got the hiccups so bad we had to pick up a jar of peanut butter at the nearest convenience store. He carried the jar around all night into every bar and honky-tonk we entered until those hiccups ran out of steam." Roy's hearty laugh was infectious.

"Y'all are silly. But I'm glad you're having a good time."

"It's been great. But we miss you, darlin'."

"I miss you too."

"Don't go to any trouble fixing supper tomorrow. I'm gonna make the call and say we'll see you on Monday after the weather clears out. Better safe than sorry."

"Okay. I'll check in with you. I love you."

"Love you too, darlin'. Stay warm."

"I will."

The line went dead, and Becky set her phone on the side table. Snuggling under a soft blanket, she stared at the flames in the fireplace and listened to the crackle and pop of burning wood. She didn't feel like reading or watching TV, and her appetite had been non-existent since she came home from Glen's. Remembering the ribs she'd left on his counter made her sad, her abrupt departure leaving her empty-handed and cross.

What was wrong with Glen anyway? She'd practically thrown herself at the burly man, more than ready for a kiss, and he'd left her hanging. Becky knew he was being cautious, scared of her brothers' reactions if they ever found out. Scared of what he might be feeling in his clear-headed state of mind.

Scared of the possibility of something—*more.*

The ball was in his court, and she'd left it there, hoping he might come to his senses. But what would that look like? If they decided to date, they'd have to sneak around at first, the repercussions of springing it on everyone sure to mess up the upcoming holidays. They'd need to let them down easy. Gently. Show them it wasn't any big deal.

Or maybe she should rip the band-aid off fast, have a stern conversation with her father and brothers outright, and tell them to mind their own business. But that wasn't fair, especially after everything her brother Teddy and both families had been through. Unfortunately, Glen went through years of using and abusing drugs and alcohol. Becky was sure if he'd been clean, he wouldn't have resorted to such violent behavior toward her family after his brother, Joe, was accidentally killed. Things would've been different if Glen hadn't been an addict. How she wished they could let bygones be bygones and live their lives how they wanted to.

"Hypocrite," she mumbled under her breath. And who was she to talk? She was the last one holding the bygones— the last one in the family to forgive Glen, and now it was coming back to bite her in the ass.

Jaxson lifted his head from the doggie bed and growled.

"What is it, boy?"

Both dogs popped up and rushed to the front door, barking incessantly. A cold chill ran the length of Becky's spine. Throwing the blanket off her lap, she grabbed the fireplace poker and tip-toed to the front window, easing the edge of the curtains back to take a peek.

Speak of the devil.

Glen Kirby was clambering up the front porch steps, his thick coat and cowboy hat recognizable.

Flicking on the porch light, she smoothed her hair back from her face, her ponytail lopsided from lying on the couch. She knew she looked tired, her new shirt wrinkled with one of the sleeves half-rolled and the other caught at her elbow. She was unraveled, Glen's surprise visit making her uneasy. But a familiar feeling took over—a fracture low in her belly spreading sweet and smooth like honey.

Maybe this was Glen trying?

Swinging the front door open, she eyed him with edginess and gripped the fireplace poker tighter. The big dogs bumped her legs and scrambled across the porch out into the yard.

"Whoa," he uttered, pointing at the rustic weapon. "You gonna stab me? Or were you about to poke the fire?"

"Huh?" Her brow furrowed before she registered what he'd said. She eyed the poker and loosened her grip. "Oh. I'm sorry. Yes, I was about to poke the fire. Come on in, Glen."

But he remained stoic in his stance, offering a half-smile curled across his lips.

"It's cold. Get inside," she scolded, rubbing her free hand against her opposite arm.

He licked his bottom lip, his eyes scrolling the curve of her face and tangle of hair falling out of her ponytail against her shoulders. Leaning against the doorjamb, she stared back at him, the front porch lights emitting a hazy glow around his large figure.

"You have a coat on, Glen. I don't. But if you want to stand there and stare at me shivering in the doorway, I'll give you two minutes. After that, I'm closing up shop and locking myself inside. Do you understand?" Her body trembled, not from the cold but from the adrenaline pumping through her veins. Her ultimatum hung in the air like the icy rain falling from the dark sky.

Glen stepped toward her and gently removed the poker from her hand, leaning it carefully against the wall. Taking off his hat, he whipped it inside the foyer like a Frisbee, shocking her.

"Wha... What are you doing?" she whispered, confused by his actions.

A hot vapor of breath floated across her face as he spoke, his thumb tracing the swell of her cheek.

"I'm trying."

She wanted to bottle this moment up with his rugged face mere inches from hers, the sounds of winter all around them. Tree branches scratching at the windows, and the scent of burning wood in the air. Porch boards creaking with his booted feet pressed against the welcome mat. The gentle pressure of his hands holding her face.

Her skin tingled the instant his whiskers grazed her skin, his full lips pressing against hers. At first, Glen was tentative. But then, as if something powerful overtook the man, he devoured her mouth with a searing kiss that set fire to every molecule in her body. His tongue swept between her lips. Teasing. Tasting.

From the moment Becky forgave Glen, every time they were around each other as new friends was incredible. But tonight? Tonight was something different. Tonight was their first kiss, eager and reckless, driven by anguish as much as desire. Even though she knew it was their first magical kiss, it felt like their last. It felt like goodbye. And what if it was?

Pulling back from their lip-lock, she tucked her nose below his ear where it was warm. His skin smelled musky with a hint of sweetness, and she dragged her face down until she could press a kiss to the hairy line of his throat. When she pulled back, she watched him blink open his bedroom eyes. They were shining with tears but smiling.

"Did I get it right?" he asked.

Becky nodded quickly, her heart aching with urgency and euphoria. He was more than her friend, the realization striking her core. He was forgiveness and second chances. He was homemade apple pie fresh out of the oven. He was colorful sunsets and whipped cream on whiskers. He was pickup trucks and old-fashioned handholding sitting on the front seat, the scent of smoked meat lingering in the air. He was rainbow unicorns and apple-infused wine percolating in oak barrels in the big red barn.

Glen Kirby was more than a boy kissing a girl. He was incomparable. He was—*special*.

Bringing her fingers to her lips, the swoony feeling washed over her as the sleet beyond the porch posts turned into big fat snowflakes. The crisp air hushed, and she held her breath. The snow fluttered from the sky with grace and elegance, dusting the earth.

"It's snowing," she whispered in awe. She wasn't cold anymore, desire burning and coursing through her blood.

"Let's get you inside. Your hands are like ice, Becky."

In a daze, she allowed Glen to escort her inside as he summoned the big dogs from the yard with a shrill whistle. The warmth from the fire was a welcome reprieve, and she watched him put the poker back in its rightful place on the hearth. She watched him take off his coat, shuck his boots off by the door, and speak to the dogs and pat their heads. She watched him amble toward her, his animal magnetism lighting her libido on fire.

"Can you stay?" she boldly asked.

Glen stopped in his tracks. "I can for a little while."

Becky shook her head. "That's not what I meant." She swallowed hard and held her own. "Can you stay the night?"

"But I thought—"

"They won't be back until Monday," she interrupted, not giving him an explanation.

But no explanation was needed. He pressed his teeth into his bottom lip and shook his head. His expression turned apologetic.

"I can't, Daisy Girl."

Chapter Eighteen

GLEN

Glen was dying on the inside, knowing he had a chance to spend the night with Becky. But his subconscious wouldn't let up, tickling his memory with all the bad shit he'd done to her family over the years. For him to swoop into the Bennett home and take advantage of the situation while Walt and the others were out of town wouldn't be right. He'd definitely be playing with fire, and he knew he'd get burned.

Because he was in a better headspace, he had his morals and wanted more than anything to do right by Becky and her family. If it meant putting his desires on the back burner, so be it. This was the only way until he could have a heart-to-heart with Walt.

"I don't understand," Becky lamented. She twisted her hands in front of her, the glow from the crackling fire surrounding her in an orb of warmth and yearning.

Glen cleared his throat and strode toward her with arms open wide. She shuffled into his embrace and clung to him. They stood there for several seconds, Becky's hands gently stroking his back.

He knew he loved her, but he couldn't say the words.

He didn't want "I love you" to feel like the emotional equivalent of drunk sex—reckless, overeager, and hangover-inducing. But not saying the words when he wanted to depressed him. His strategy was to achieve some insane arbitrary "appropriate" benchmark before he dove in head-first. He needed to speak with Walt. He needed to convince the entire Bennett clan he wasn't up to no good or had an ulterior motive when it came to Becky. But if the goal was to be truthful, vaguely sane, and sober, when would the right time to say "I love you" come?

His voice was low and thick, splintering with emotion. "You know I'm falling for you, don't you, Daisy Girl?"

She waited for a beat before she sighed and pressed her cheek against his chest. "I'm falling for you too."

Glen wanted to weep with joy and held her tighter in his arms. Knowing they were on the same page meant every-thing to him, which only solidified his carefulness in their situation.

"I'm asking you to stay the night," she rasped. "I want to sleep with you, Glen. We might not have another chance until the new year. I'll make your coffee with extra whip in the morning, and I promise I won't say a damn word about cream in your whiskers. We'll hold hands, sit by the fire, and share funny stories. I'll even make you another apple pie if you want."

Glen blinked at the pressure building behind his eyes and untangled his arms from around her body, her sweet plea overwhelming him. "Let's sit down so I can explain myself, okay?"

Her eyes were wide and dark looking up at him, her sad expression annihilating his strength.

Sitting side by side, he held her hand and twisted his

body to face her. "When I hit rock bottom, Walt was right there and begged me not to give up. He urged me to dig for the deep-rooted forgiveness I needed to pull myself away from certain death. He gave me my farm back. He gave me a second chance by working with me to develop a wine flavor so I could make enough money to buy my property outright. He kept a roof over my head and food on my table.

And most importantly, he said if I accepted responsibility for my wrongdoings, and if I embraced the part of my soul that was ugly by 'taking the bull by the horns' as he called it, I'd become a man of some humility and my life would take on new meaning. And I did all those things, Becky, and it worked. All he asked in return was for me to stay honest and pay it forward in some way."

Glen watched a lone tear make a path down Becky's face. Using the pad of his thumb, he gently wiped it away and pressed his hand against her cheek. "As much as I want to stay with you and love on you all night long... I can't."

"I understand," she muttered, turning away from his gaze.

"But do you?" He tipped her chin with his fingers so they were eye to eye. "I want to be with you, Becky. I do. But we've got to go about this the right way. I owe it to you. I owe it to your family." He was as honest as he'd ever been in his entire life. "I love your family. Walt is like a brother to me. And I can't...," he paused, overcome with emotion, and choked on the words.

"You can't, what?" she asked, pinning him with her stare.

"I can't... lose another brother." His lower lip trembled as he fought to keep it together, hot tears erupting and stinging his eyes.

"Oh, Glen." Becky threw her arms around him in a hug. "It's obvious, Walt and everyone else has forgiven you. You've put in the hard work to gain everybody's trust again. I think you're a very brave and honest man," she whispered in his ear.

"The bad stuff is easier to hold on to."

"Let go and… stay. I don't want you to be lonely tonight," she confessed. "Being alone and out in the country by yourself. I hate thinking of you lonely."

"I have Garth," he grinned, pulling back from her.

"It's not the same, and you know it."

"I know."

Holding her hand again, he didn't know if it was the childhood memories, the snow falling softly outside, the romantic fire flickering, the quality time he'd spent with Becky, or how far he'd come from the dark space he used to live in. But he felt like all the pieces of his puzzle were finally sliding into place. Had Becky Bennett been the missing piece in his life all along? They weren't quite there yet, not the perfect fit. But he was trying and being as honest as possible to get it right.

They were quiet, and he studied their fingers laced together.

"You left the ribs I bagged up for you on my kitchen counter. They're on the front seat of my truck."

Becky nodded, her voice tinged with humor. "So the ribs are the real reason you came over, huh? To drop them off?"

Glen chuckled. "It was a good excuse, right? But you know full well I came over here to give you more than ribs."

The earnest longing on her face had him breathless like he'd stayed underwater for too long, desperate for a clean breath. Combing his fingers into the side of her hair, he stared at her mouth and urged her forward, melding his lips with hers again. Kissing Becky felt euphoric, like a release. If he wasn't being so dang honest, he knew they'd be in a compromising position exploring each other under a deep sea of blankets. Holding back was not going to be easy.

In fact, nothing in Glen's life had ever come easy for him. His ma always told him, "God ain't a wishin' well." He learned things in life the hard way, with no father figure guiding him. The big lessons he'd learned, the ones that mattered the most, came from heartbreak and age.

"Mmmm," Becky moaned in his mouth.

Glen was lost in the ecstasy of her kiss, his entire body tingling with want. With his dick strained against his denim, he willed himself not to cross the precarious imaginary line floating between them. It would be so easy to gather Becky into his arms and carry her upstairs. To slowly unbutton her shirt and undress her, leisurely taking in her naked beauty. But being sober and clear-headed allowed his moral compass to work overtime, and he wasn't about to ruin what he had with Becky by giving in to his hot-blooded desire.

Unlocking his lips from hers, he buried his head into the crevice of her neck and sighed. "Damn, Daisy Girl. You're making this hard for me."

Her fingers stroked his hair, making him woozy with lust. "I'm not. I promise."

Glen eased himself back and was mesmerized by her glistening lower lip. The bright pink was sensual, as if the color had been stolen from the perfect flower blooming in spring. Quickly, he spread his legs and patted the spot on the couch before him. Her brown eyes were dark and sexy, her expression holding genuine affection.

"You want me to sit between your legs?" There was an aura of caution in her tone.

Glen was intentional with his actions, entirely controlling his lust and desire. "Sit on the floor and relax. I'm really good at shoulder massages."

"Oh. I like the sound of that."

He grabbed a throw pillow and dropped it on the braided rug. The second she sat between his legs, he caged her in, pressing his jean-clad thighs against her arms. She curled her hands together in her lap, legs outstretched with toes pointing toward the flames beyond the hearth. Every time he exhaled, his breath caressed her golden hair. He felt like her protector, her bodyguard, confident in his movements.

Brushing her silky ponytail away from her neck, he moved his mouth next to her ear and tenderly kissed her skin; in shock he had this much freedom with her. He had the sudden urge to tip her head back against his leg and hold her in place to better ravage her neck with more kisses, but he kept his cool.

"You're always safe with me," he stated, trying to convince himself what he was saying was true.

Was she safe with him? Could he contain his primal instinct to have his way with her here and now? It would be so easy, cloistered in their little world, safe and tucked away from everyone for a few precious hours. He made a path with his nose from her ear to her cheek, then back again. Her sweet skin was intoxicating.

"Now, close your eyes and relax."

Moving his hands to her shoulders, he gently kneaded her muscles, causing her head to fall forward and an unmistakable moan to emit from her mouth. He pressed his thighs more firmly against her arms. He was panting, pushing the boundaries with liberty to touch her. Inebriated. Aching

"Does it feel good?" His words came out in a sexy

rumble, his hard-as-steel erection throbbing between his legs.

"Oh, yes," she moaned.

Glen vibrated with desire, determined to stay in control. His fingers unhinged from her shoulders, and he slowly stroked up and down her arms leaning his chin near the shell of her ear, his warm breath skating across her skin. She tilted her neck to give him access to her creamy throat. The second she did, his lips continued a trail of tiny kisses. And he smelled her hair continuously, the aroma reminding him of sweet flowers and summer sun.

Wrapping his arms around her, he hugged her with every ounce of restrained sexual passion he could muster. He was caught up in her spell, and if he wasn't careful, he was about to nosedive into dangerous territory.

"Have you ever made love in front of a fire?"

Glen froze.

"I mean, I know you're not ready to because you want to talk to my brother. But… I was just curious. Have you?" she asked, her breathing turned ragged.

Glen wanted to shout he was ready now. Instead, he made sure not to make any sudden, risky movements. He pressed his mouth to her hair and whispered, "I haven't. What about you?"

"No. But it would be awfully romantic, don't you think?"

"Mmmhmm." Glen stared at the flickering flames and imagined the two of them stretched out across a blanket, Becky's naked body radiant in the light.

"Can we pretend?"

Glen frowned. "Pretend? I'm not sure I'm following you."

"Since we can't do it for real, maybe we could… talk

about it? You know, pretend we just got home and go from there."

"Okay." Glen allowed himself to let go and imagine, if only for a moment, they were a legitimate couple free to explore their sexual desires together. With his arms draped over her shoulders, he was pleased when she laced her fingers through his and squeezed.

"Let's pretend… we've just returned from having dinner in town," he started, making things up as he went along. "Maybe we want each other so badly we don't make it to your bedroom upstairs. Maybe we collapse right here in front of the hearth and… and… light our fires."

"Light our fires?" She laughed.

Good God, what in the hell was he saying? He was nothing but a bumbling idiot. *Light our fires?* Geez.

"I'm sorry," he groaned. "I'm not any good at pretending."

Becky giggled and shifted between his legs, turning her body around to face him. "Sure you are. I like how you started the scene." Flicking her eyes up to his, the sight of her gazing up at him on her knees was almost too much to handle. "What happens next?"

"You tell me."

The air stilled around him, his heart thundering so hard he was sure she could hear it. It took every ounce of willpower he had not to hoist her over his shoulder cave-man-style and carry her upstairs so he could have his way with her.

"I see you sitting there exactly as you are now," she said.

"You do? And what are you doing?

"Well—" There was a long pause before she continued, her eyes fixated on his. "I'm on the floor like I am now. And you're sitting there with your jeans… down around your ankles." Her eyes scrolled slowly from his face down to his crotch. "Can you picture it?"

He gasped, the ache between his legs intensifying with each word coming out of her lush mouth. Who knew Becky Bennett could be so… *naughty*?

"We'd have the house all to ourselves while I…," she paused, her cheeks ripening with color.

Glen reached out and caressed her face with trembling fingers, enthralled by her attempt at dirty talk. What the actual *fuck*?

"While you, what, Daisy Girl?"

Her wry smile spread slow and sexy across her face, her head dipping with sudden shyness. "You know."

"Is that what you imagine when you think about the two of us together in front of the fire with no one else around?"

"Yes." Her response stopped him in his tracks.

That one tiny word held a billion consequences.

Glen tucked an errant strand of hair over her ear and reverently caressed her cheek. Becky was practically dragging him into the forbidden danger zone. Her gaze held unmistakable lust and determination. But there was trust there too, which made it ten times harder for him to cross a line with her.

"I want to give you pleasure too, Becky. I do." He leaned forward and pressed his forehead against hers, not used to the intense feelings running rampant through his being.

"I know. And I know you're scared, Glen. I am too."

The truth was out in the open. She must've sensed his hesitation or seen something beneath his bearded expression. Once again, he was being as honest and open as he'd ever been in his entire life.

He wanted her. But they were on a precarious path, the

unknown pinching his heart with agony. Love was a cautionary tale—and he was bound and determined to get it right.

Boldly, she reached for his zipper, her hands grazing his denim crotch. Grabbing her by the wrists, he stopped her.

"Becky... *please*."

"Please, what? We don't have to have sex. We can do everything else but have sex. It'll be okay. No one will know. It's just you and me, Glen. We're safe here. It's okay."

He was in physical pain, his dick straining for release. Still holding her wrists, he stood and brought her up with him, caging her in his arms. Part of him was desperate to hold back and do right by Becky, but the other half felt like she might disappear right before his eyes if he didn't hurry. His voice was gruff, his words changing the trajectory of the evening.

"If we do this, we're doing it my way."

Chapter Nineteen

BECKY

Becky nodded quickly, her arms imprisoned against Glen's chest as he held her tight. His predatory focus was a bit intimidating yet oddly a turn-on. She was desperate to touch him, her heart pounding and feeling too small for her chest, making it hard to breathe. Or maybe it was how he held her snug, trapped against his solid heat.

Fire burned in her center as she stared at him. His dark eyes. His hairy face. His broad shoulders and muscular arms. Those hands gripping her like he owned her. She'd never been with anyone like him.

The last time she was intimate with a guy was right after high school graduation. He was a skinny, awkward college boy who didn't know what he was doing. Not anything like the mature man holding her in his arms now. Glen was a real man, strong and rugged. Everything about him exuded masculinity, from his tall stature and commanding presence to his palms that fit the entire width of her thigh. Yes, she noticed. How his fingers flexed and stroked, the tips calloused and gritty like sandpaper when he touched her cheek.

"Come with me," he said.

Wide-eyed and winded, she gripped his hand and thought he was about to lead her upstairs to her bedroom and have his way with her. But he stopped short of the kitchen table and pulled out a chair.

"Sit," he commanded.

Tentative, Becky did as she was told, unsure of what Glen was doing. When he grabbed the tea kettle off the stove and moved to the sink to fill it, she scowled.

"What are you doing?"

His back was toward her, the sound of water hitting the bare metal and plugging the silent void. "I'm filling the kettle."

"Why?" Her mouth hung open, trying to figure him out.

He threw her a sideways glance before putting the kettle on the stove and turning it on. Grabbing the seatback of the chair at the opposite end of the table, he flipped it around and sat with his arms folded across the top.

"We needed a time out."

"Glen—"

"No, Becky," he interrupted. "I'm not gonna be the reason you have to lie to your family when they ask you what's going on."

Now she was confused. "What are you talking about? They don't know anything about us, I swear."

"They're gonna notice your dreamy eyes when you're not looking. They're gonna ask what you did while they were gone. And what are you going to tell them, huh? That you gave Glen Kirby a blow job in front of the fireplace?"

Becky gasped and immediately pressed her lips together. They were silent for a beat before both of them burst out laughing. Glen's face turned ruddy, the low rumble of his chuckle putting her at ease.

"I'm sorry for being so crass. But I'm in a situation I never imagined I'd find myself in. I'm falling for you, Becky, and losing you is not an option. Sex needs to be off the table for now, including oral sex. All of it—the things that always made me feel closer to a woman. You deserve something better than the usual bar-to-bedroom dating I come from. I want to build trust with you. I want to do right by you." He leaned back and spread his arms wide. "Believe it or not, there's more to me than this sexy body."

She laughed again, the rush of genuine gratitude unexpected. Maybe Glen was right? Maybe waiting till after the dust settled once they came clean with her family would enhance what they had brewing between them. And she was ready for something deeper. Ready for someone who valued her. It was obvious he was doing this for the right reasons. And it made her heart pitter-patter.

"Can you still kiss me?" she asked.

"Oh, yes. We're gonna get really good at kissing."

"Hug me?"

"Mmmhmmm."

"Rub my shoulders again when I'm stressed out?"

"Of course."

Becky rested her elbow on the table and parked her chin in her hand. "Okay. You win. For now."

The kettle on the stove started to whistle, and Becky pushed back from the table to get up.

"Stay put. I've got this," Glen said.

Easing herself back onto the seat, she watched him, in awe of his kindness. He asked where the teabags and cups were and if she wanted honey or lemon. Finding everything she pointed out, Glen finally presented her with a mug and sat in the chair right next to her. She could get used to a man waiting on her like this.

"This is... nice," she admitted.

"Yes, it is."

The dogs were sound asleep, and the fire was nothing but glowing embers in the hearth. Every time Glen shifted his weight in the kitchen chair, an occasional creak sounded. They were silent, their communication unspoken, with little smiles and nods of appreciation. She realized her recent burning desire was replaced with a new feeling—contentment.

Becky wanted to remember this moment for the nights when she'd feel a little bit tense and a little bit lonely. How he drew a line in the sand, adamant they not cross it until after they had an honest conversation with her family. The way he catered to her, wanting to please her. How he pushed his flannel sleeves up, revealing his thick forearms dusted with freckles and wiry hair. The way his large hands dwarfed the mug he sipped from, and how his eyes shown blue like the ocean when he peered at her over the edge through the hot vapors.

"Since your family won't be home tomorrow, do you want to go to church with me?"

Becky sputtered on a sip of tea, the word "church" coming from Glen's mouth shocking her, especially after their sexy rendezvous in the family room.

"What?" He grinned and set his mug down. "My sponsor suggested I find a local community church. I've been going for a few months. It's something I look forward to every week. Do you think it's weird?"

"No... I, uh, wasn't expecting you to ask me to go to church with you after I practically begged you to—"

"It's fine," he interrupted. "Just because I occasionally

go to church doesn't make me any less of a hot-blooded man, especially when I'm around you."

Becky swallowed hard.

"I can pick you up around ten. Afterward, we can grab some lunch somewhere."

"Or we could come back here, and I can make something?" The idea of spending more quality time with Glen was appealing.

"I don't want you to go to any trouble."

"It's no trouble at all. I do it all the time."

"That's why you need a break. Let me take you out for lunch." He picked up her hand and kissed her knuckles, pinning her with his stare. "Please?"

Her cheeks heated, not used to a man doting on her. She swooned. "Okay."

By the time Glen put on his boots, coat, and hat, it was nearing midnight. The light snow outside had stopped, the front lawn dusted in powder-sugar white.

At the front door on her tiptoes, Becky adjusted his coat collar. "You be careful going home. Text me when you arrive so I know you made it safe."

"Yes, ma'am." He smiled down at her. "I'll see you in the morning."

"Okay."

Glen leaned low and pressed his lips to hers, the rush of sweet desire immediate. How would she ever get through the holidays while craving this man's generous kisses?

"Hold that thought."

"What?" Becky blinked and stood there as Glen ducked outside and shut the door. Was that it? Was that goodbye?

Flustered, she cocked her head and listened to the sound of a truck door slamming shut, and then she remembered. The ribs…

Glen came back inside gleefully holding up the baggie filled with meat. "I almost forgot." He handed them off to her, the big dogs immediately interested in the scent and circling their legs.

"Get back, D. Go on, Jaxson," she scolded. Quickly, she trotted to the kitchen and tossed the baggie into the fridge. Shuffling across the wood floors, her heart beat wildly as she stared at the big lug of a man patiently waiting for her.

"Goodnight, Glen."

"Goodnight, Becky."

They kissed again, the tip of Glen's nose cold from being outside in the elements. She held onto his bicep as he opened the door, her hand sliding down the faded leather of his coat until their fingers clasped together in a final tug.

"Sweet dreams, Daisy Girl."

Becky let go with fingers outstretched until the last second and watched him walk out into the cold night, shivering in his absence. With the front door closed and locked, she peeked through the curtains and waited until the taillights of his truck disappeared over the hill in a cloud of exhaust. Leaning her head against the window, her hot breath made a foggy circle of condensation. Eyeing the mist, she used her index finger and drew a tiny heart on the glass.

She felt like she was floating through space. Untethered. Filled with awareness.

Becky hadn't realized falling in love could be so simple. Yet, so dangerous.

Chapter Twenty

GLEN

Glen enjoyed having Becky Bennett pressed warmly beside him in the back pew during the church service. It was nice having someone to sit with, the two of them listening intently to the pastor speaking about the power of gratitude. The seasonal message was appropriate, with Thanksgiving right around the corner.

The elderly, white-haired man spoke passionately from the pulpit and held a worn and tattered open Bible. His message hit home with Glen, the pastor suggesting how one should focus their thoughts upon the goodness of God and offer thanks for all He had done.

Glen was overflowing with gratefulness, especially having Becky in his life. How many days, weeks, even years had he spent traversing life alone, with no one and nothing to look forward to? Having a second chance allowed him to see clearly for the first time in ages how meaningful a sober life could be.

The uplifting message and music were the perfect start to their Sunday. And after a classic Southern brunch of chicken and waffles at the local diner, Glen suggested they do a little window shopping and peruse Main Street. The chilly temperature made it ideal for him to loop his arm with hers and snuggle closer. Usually, he'd keep his head down, face hidden beneath the brim of his hat. Over the last few years, he remained somewhat incognito out in public for fear of being recognized by the locals who knew his personal business. But so much time had passed since his dark days, and knowing the rest of the Bennett family was in another state made him feel freer with his public displays of affection.

Standing before the local bookshop, they eyed the display window already decorated with boughs of evergreen and twinkle lights. Stacks of books teetered precariously in an open Santa bag with a little sign on a chalkboard easel. An employee with excellent cursive penmanship had written a quote by Neil Gaiman, which read, "Books make great gifts because they have whole worlds inside them."

"I guess I need to start thinking about Christmas presents for my family," Becky said. "Walt enjoys books."

"Really?" Glen questioned. "I don't think I've ever seen Walt with a book in his hands in my entire life."

Giggling, she pulled him toward the door. "It's true. He loves presidential biographies and science fiction. Come on, let's see if they've got anything in here that catches my eye. This is a chance for me to get a head start on my Christmas list."

Glen loved how her smile beamed when she was happy, and he was eager to oblige. And besides, he didn't have anywhere else to be.

The bookstore's interior held rows and rows of books in every size, shape, color, and genre. The sweet musky aroma reminded him of a chocolaty latte, the redolent smell of paper and ink pleasing his senses. There were only a few customers in the store, and a woman with thin glasses perched on her nose kept watch, seemingly happy while reading her choice of books at the checkout counter. This left Glen and Becky on their own to discover hidden treasure.

Glen followed Becky from behind like a lost puppy, not knowing where or what to look at. He accidentally bumped right into her back when she stopped in the middle of an aisle.

"Oh!" she squealed.

"Sorry, Becky. I wasn't watching where I was going."

Turning around, she was nose to nose with him and smoothed the lapels of his coat, an action he was growing fond of. "Why don't you look around yourself and meet me at the checkout counter in about ten minutes? Who knows? You might find something special in here too."

Glen nodded. "Okay. See you in ten."

He ambled up and down the store's aisles, squinting at the rows of titles, unsure what to look for. But when he found himself in the Young Adult Fiction section, there was a blip of a memory tucked deep inside the confines of his mind.

He remembered sitting on the carpet in his brother Joe's room listening to him read a book, his brother's post-pubescent voice deep and warm. The book was about some kid neglected by his parents, used to taking care of things on his own. The story resonated in Glen's young mind because of his father's abandonment. He also loved the story because he was fascinated with cars. The boy in the book wasn't old enough to drive, yet he took off in a car, searching for an uncle, his journey turning into an adventure. Glen closed his eyes, overcome with the memory, and struggled to recall the book's title.

"Was it called, *The Car*?" he mumbled under his breath. It couldn't be this easy.

Running his thick fingers along the colorful spines of the books, his breath hitched when he landed on it. *The Car*, by Gary Paulsen.

"*Ha!*" he exclaimed, pulling it from the shelf. Flipping through the pages, he wasn't entranced by the teenager's story as much as the memory of Joe reading the book to him. His mind was flooded with recollections of his young life with just his mom and Joe, before his father ditched them. Before Joe was tragically killed.

"What did you find?"

Glen was startled by Becky's voice and slapped the book shut as if he were holding something illegal.

"What is it?" she asked, eyeing the book in his hands.

"It's... nothing. Just an old book I found."

Becky held her hand out. "Can I see it?"

Glen swallowed and relinquished the hardback into her hands. Becky immediately thumbed through the pages with curiosity. "This looks like something you might've read as a boy. Was this a favorite growing up? I mean, it's about a teenager and a car, so why wouldn't it be?" She giggled.

Glen felt his skin grow hot, his blood pressure rising like he was about to have a full-blown panic attack. She must have sensed his unease when he didn't respond. Locking eyes with him, she grabbed his forearm, her smile fading into a frown.

"What's wrong?"

"Nothing."

"No. It's something, Glen. Talk to me."

Glen licked his lips and motioned his head toward the

front of the shop. She shoved the book back on the shelf and barely kept up as he barreled out of the store, thankful for the rush of sweet cold air filling his lungs. Stressed, he paced a few feet before he turned around and walked the other way.

"Glen?"

He shook his head and continued down the street, unsure where he was headed.

"*Glen!*" Becky shouted.

He waved her off, but she persevered and caught up to where she trotted alongside him.

"Glen, please stop. Please tell me what's going on. I need to know what's wrong."

He growled and pointed at the coffee shop nearby. "Fine."

Several minutes later, they were seated inside the booth where he'd once made her laugh after intentionally dousing his whiskers in whipped cream. His hands shook, bringing a mug of black coffee to his mouth. The temptation to drink something stronger was at the forefront of his mind.

"The memories… they often hit me out of the blue," he explained.

"The book brought back a memory?" she asked.

"Yes." His eyes were downcast, staring at the dark liquid in his cup. "Joe used to read me the book I found in the store."

Becky reached for his hand from across the table. With their fingers clasped together, he held on for dear life.

"I know we don't talk about it—"

"Joe?" she interrupted.

His eyes flicked to hers, and he nodded, unsure if he should broach the awful, heartbreaking subject. But maybe it was time? He was falling in love with the woman sitting across from him, and the sooner they got this conversation over with, the better, right? And he wanted to tell her the truth so badly. He wanted to confess his deepest, darkest secret, which he'd never told anyone, including his mother and therapist. But he always chickened out, going into default mode, and sticking to the story where he blamed Becky's brother, Ted.

"I have a confession to make. I blamed Teddy for Joe's death. Even though he didn't pull the trigger, I still held your brother responsible," he said simply.

"I know."

"I hated him. I hated all of you." He swallowed hard, trying to keep his emotions in check. "I know hate is a strong word. But… after Joe was killed, I spiraled out of control. I went into a dark place, and my hatred consumed me." Little did Becky know, he hated himself most of all, but he wasn't ready to go there yet.

"I wanted revenge. I wanted… justice. And I guess in my state of mind, there was no justice because Joe was never coming back."

Becky's face had gone white, and she sat rigid in her seat, her hand turning ice-cold in his. But she didn't pull away from him.

"I know this probably brings up bad memories for you too, huh? The whole trial? And Teddy going to prison for all those years?"

"Of course it does." Her voice was but a whisper, her dark eyes holding deep sadness. "It was hard on all of us. But I can't even compare what I went through with how hard it was for you."

Glen inhaled sharply, struck by her empathy. Maybe… maybe he *could* open up to her and tell her everything. Tell her how sorry he was for taking out his rage on Ted.

Blinking back hot tears, he soldiered on. "Did you... did you hate *me* back then?"

Slipping her hand from his grasp, she seemed to shrink before his eyes. Her shoulders slumped, and she avoided his gaze. "Yes," she admitted. "I felt sorry for you first. My hatred didn't start until the night of the Harvest Hoedown last year."

Glen fisted his right hand and stared at his knuckles, remembering how his flesh collided with Ted's innocent face. How he couldn't stop himself, his pent-up wrath spewing out of him in the form of assault. He pummeled Ted over and over until Walt intervened and put a stop to the barnyard brawl. But his anger and vengeful heart wouldn't let up, and later in the night, Glen took it a step further when he and Ted were placed in the same holding cell at the county jail.

He nearly killed the man, brutally beating him and sending him to the hospital, where he was put into an induced coma for almost a week. Thank God Teddy didn't die. His miraculous recovery opened the door to Glen's freedom and healing. He owed Ted and Walt Bennett big time for saving his life and getting him back on track—and yet, he knew he was still deeply rooted in the same dark place of bitterness and couldn't fully move on from what had happened to Joe. He knew he could never fully be free if he withheld the truth about what *he* had done the night Joe died. He was the only one who knew his secret, which sickened him.

A nauseating feeling hit him in the gut, and he was sure it was pure guilt compelling him to spew his angry thoughts in front of Becky. It was a defense mechanism he used when he felt like he was losing control. And there was no turning back.

"Admit it, Becky. In hindsight, all of this was absolutely Ted's fault."

"*What?*" She stared at him like a deer caught in the headlights of an oncoming car. "Glen, I don't think we need to revisit any of this—"

"I beg to differ." He cut her off, unintentionally raising his voice. Inhaling a quick breath through his nostrils, he continued more calmly. "I'm sorry. But if you and I continue seeing each other, I think it's healthy to put everything on the table and talk about it."

Yeah, right, you stupid chicken shit. You're a liar, and you know it.

"I can't believe you still blame Teddy. You haven't forgiven him at all." Becky's lower lip trembled.

Glen ran a hand through his hair and harrumphed, his award-winning performance out of control. He couldn't stop. "Jesus, Becky. Come on. None of this would've happened if he hadn't driven his two dipshit friends to the convenience store where Joe was working. In fact, if he hadn't listened to his whiney girlfriend insist they needed more *beer* for the party, Joe would still be alive today, working on the farm with me."

"Now you're blaming *Robyn?*" Her voice arose in a high pitch as her eyes welled with tears.

Glen gritted his teeth, knowing he was intentionally lying to her. And he knew why: Because he'd rather live with the long-term consequences of lying than face the temporary pain of his truth. Everything he said came out in an accusatory tone. What in the hell was wrong with him? He was trying to cover up his culpability in Joe's death and prove a ridiculous point but realized every word falling from his lips was snappish, harmful, and nothing but bald-faced lies.

With his palms held up in surrender more for himself

than anything, he said, "All I'm saying is, look at the scenario from my point of view, okay? I'm not the bad guy here."

Yes, you are absolutely the bad guy in all of this!

"No one is the bad guy, Glen. What happened that night was a horrible, tragic accident."

"You're wrong." He vehemently shook his head.

"Well, I'm afraid we'll have to agree to disagree on this one." Swiping a napkin out of the dispenser on the table, Becky dabbed it under her eyes.

"I'm only trying to be honest with you. Isn't that what you want from me? Total honesty?"

Why couldn't he stop??

"I don't want anything from you."

He watched her stand and shove her arms into her coat. "Wait a minute. Don't get mad at *me*. I'm trying to… to open up and explain why I feel the way I do."

"I'm never going to understand how you can still feel this way after everything our families have been through. Aren't you tired, Glen? Don't you want to truly forgive and move on with your life?"

"I've forgiven Ted."

"You sure?"

"It doesn't mean I have to forget," he growled.

And I'll never forget what I did that night. I'll never forgive myself. My secret will go with me to the grave.

Becky buttoned her coat, noticeable tears streaming down her cheeks. "Then you really don't understand forgiveness at its core." She stood tall and thrust her chin into the air. "You're holding a grudge against an innocent man, Glen, hoping it will somehow punish him so you can feel righteous. Hoping you'll be protected from ever getting hurt again."

"Oh, I'll never be hurt again." He folded his arms against his chest and stayed seated, her comment raising his blood pressure. He was already devastated. He couldn't sink much lower than this and lobbed one last doozy at her.

"Let's just get one thing straight, Becky. Joe would still be alive today if it hadn't been for Ted and Robyn. End of story." His body trembled, knowing he'd gone too far. Knowing he'd dug his own grave with self-sabotage and self-hate, knowing he wasn't good enough for her.

Becky pursed her lips together and slowly shook her head. "What you're saying changes everything, Glen. If I had known this is how you really feel about everything that happened, I would've *never* started hanging out with you."

His eyes bore into hers, his words croaking in his throat. "What are you saying?"

She angrily swiped tears from her face, her last words a poisonous arrow shooting through his heart, mortally wounding him.

"Goodbye, Glen." She rushed toward the exit, nearly colliding with a waitress carrying a tray of decadent coffee drinks.

"*Becky?*" He stood and hollered after her, several patrons glancing his way. Slinking back into the booth, he hung his head, desperate to disappear.

What the fuck had he done?

Chapter Twenty-One

BECKY

Thanksgiving came and went in its usual hoopla of the family gathering and overeating around the big dining room table at Bennett Farms. Becky poured herself into the feast, making all her family's seasonal favorites. Her father, brothers, and their significant others helped her in the kitchen, and admitted she'd outdone herself, as usual.

The annual Christmas Tree Festival was next, her list of things to do a mile long. Hank and his fiancé, Ella Mae Miller, were home for the duration of the holidays leading up to Walt and Elyse's New Year's Eve wedding in Atlanta. Having her brothers and their partners around helped ease the pain in Becky's heart, not knowing how Glen was coping during the season, sure he was all alone.

Before his unfortunate angry coffeehouse confession, she'd had every intention of asking him to join her family for their Thanksgiving feast. But she shoved the invitation off the table after he blatantly blamed Teddy for everything. And even though his cruel words were a bitter pill to swallow, Glen's absence still left a gaping hole in her heart.

He'd sent several text messages apologizing profusely, blaming his harsh thoughts on seasonal depression. He told her he had added a second AA meeting to his weekly schedule and begged her repeatedly to forgive him. He even approached her near the big red barn one afternoon when he was on-sight working with Walt. But she waved him off, not mentally prepared to talk with him yet. The pained look on his face indicated how sorry he was, and she almost caved. But her loyalty to Teddy and her family trumped everything regarding reconciliation.

If Glen couldn't forget, then neither could she.

The cold December air chapped Becky's cheeks as she wandered through the pine forest, deep in thought. Her boots made a crunching sound against the pine needles littering the pathway. She could hear chainsaws in the distance, her brothers out in the back fields gathering the first pre-cut trees they'd have for sale just in time for the festival.

The annual celebration was a huge hit with Langston Falls locals. Folks came out in droves to pick out their farm-fresh Christmas trees, sample mulled wine, and other treats Becky's team prepared beforehand. There was also a new item on the menu—hot apple cider, thanks to Glen Kirby and his farm. Walt thought it'd be a good idea and insisted they have some signage marketing their upcoming apple-infused wine set to release in the spring. Walt had called it a "win-win."

Just thinking about the hot drink made her depressed, knowing she'd inevitably run into Glen at some point over the festival weekend. And why wouldn't she? Glen was now a staple on the farm—he and Walt very close to securing the new wine flavor for distribution.

"Hey, Becky! Wait up!"

She turned at the sound of her name and smiled. Ella Mae trotted toward her, the fluffy ball on top of her knitted beanie hat happily bouncing with each step.

Out of breath, Ella smiled. "What are you doing out here all by yourself? Can I help with anything?"

Becky swallowed hard, wishing she could be candid with her brother Hank's fiancé. Could Ella Mae help her navigate her dejected feelings? Would she have any advice on how to temper the anger she had toward Glen? Could she even find the words to explain her emptiness after saying goodbye to him?

"I'm just taking a break. You know, clearing my head before all the chaos tomorrow." She offered Ella a meek smile. "I was just about to start on the next project on my to-do list."

Ella Mae put her hands on her hips. "Well, put me to work. Hank's in the fields chopping down trees, and I have nothing to do. Let me help."

"Okay." The two of them started toward the barn. "Ella, can I ask you a personal question?"

"Sure. Fire away."

"How are you holding up during the holidays? Are you doing okay?" Their feet crunched along the path, Becky's question hanging in the pine-scented air.

Ella Mae's famous brother, country music star Travis Miller, died of an overdose, leaving Ella alone in the world. Thank God Hank was there for her, and now she had the entire Bennett family to call her own. Maybe Ella might have a few words of wisdom she could share regarding Glen as he navigated his sobriety and the holidays by himself?

"I'm doing alright. Travis and I were usually on tour during the holidays, spending Christmas and New Year's ordering room service in some fancy hotel, so it's not like

I'm missing any family tradition." She stopped on the path and looked up into the winter-gray sky in deep thought. "But I do miss him. Very much." She switched her focus toward Becky, her eyes misting with melancholy. "I don't think I'll ever stop missing him."

Becky nodded and offered her a timid smile. She felt the same way about her mama, the ache of missing her strongest during the holidays. Ella Mae had more in common with her than she thought. As they started walking again, Ella looped her arm through Becky's.

"The music has helped tremendously. Performing is when I feel closest to him."

"When you're singing his songs?"

"Yes. Our songs." She nodded. "And Hank I will be keeping Travis's legacy alive when we go back out on tour. We have more songs in the works with our upcoming album. Life does go on."

Becky thought about Glen and his legacy, the Kirby apple farm. A farm he was running all by himself with no complaints. If Joe were still alive, Glen would have help and wouldn't have to toil and labor alone. The thought made her sad.

"How many times did Travis relapse, Ella?"

She was quiet for a moment. "Too many to count. Travis was never fully committed to the process and failed to benefit from treatment time and time again. Breaking away from alcohol and drugs requires a huge effort."

She stopped on the path and shrugged, the sadness in her voice noticeable. "I think the only reason he ever went to rehab was to please me. I wish it would've been enough. He just didn't have a strong motivation to stay sober long-term. I wish he'd found a reason to get excited. You know, a reason to do the necessary work."

Becky wondered what Glen's motivation might be. But she knew he was doing the necessary work.

"Thanks for the explanation, Ella. I want you to know I'm glad you're here with us. You're part of our family now. I hope you're having fun."

She perked up. "I love it here. This place feels like home."

Becky smiled. The gorgeous and talented woman was a welcome addition to the Bennett family—another sister, much like Robyn, Elyse, and Samantha. Although Sam hadn't been around much over the holidays, which was something she needed to ask her brother James about.

"So, what else needs to be done today? I'm all yours, Becky."

"I've got poinsettias to put on all the tables and around the barn. And we've got a few more twinkle lights to tack up around the interior bar."

"Great! Let's knock it out."

Becky enjoyed working with Ella Mae. She was easy-going and fun to be around. They finished everything on her to-do list within a few hours, the farm slowly morphing into a festive Christmas atmosphere. By noon tomorrow, the place would be hopping with food trucks on the property, fire pits blazing with S'more stations, and holiday music blaring from outdoor speakers. She even had a cardboard cut-out of Santa himself positioned on an antique sleigh welcoming guests at the entrance to the farm. With her brothers running the hayride into the fields for those families who wanted to choose and cut their tree away from the pre-cut stash at the barn, it was sure to be a happy day.

Leaning low, Becky placed the last of the white poinsettias against the sliding barn doors and heard a distinct honk as a vehicle approached from a distance.

"Cool!" Ella Mae shouted.

Standing upright, Becky turned toward the honk, her mouth gaping instantly.

Coming around the bend was none other than Glen Kirby himself, seated behind the powder-blue 1960s Chevy pickup truck he'd fully restored. Anchored in the truck bed was a tall Fraser fir, the pine branches covered in lit-up twinkle bulbs.

Astounded, Becky approached the truck and marveled at the spectacle. Glen parked and proudly leaned his arm on the rolled-down window.

"Well, what do you think?" He grinned from ear to ear, the look of delight on his face evident. Gone was the despondent version of the man she'd left at the coffee shop, and she was intrigued.

Becky was aware of Ella Mae standing right next to her, thankful she was the one who replied.

"I think it's fantastic! The blue truck with the lit-up tree in the truck bed next to the red barn looks like a Christmas card." Ella went right up to Glen and stuck her hand out. "Hi. I'm Ella Mae Miller. I'm Hank's fiancé."

"Hey, Ella Mae. I'm Glen Kirby. I'm the one working with Walt on the apple-infused wine. It's so nice to finally meet you."

Ella turned toward Becky. "You've got to get some pictures. Isn't this a fantastic Christmas aesthetic?"

Becky nodded, her voice turned monotone. "Looks great." She stood there, not sure what to say or how to act. Ella seemed to sense her awkwardness.

"You okay?" She pressed her hand to Becky's arm and squeezed, her voice lowered so Glen couldn't hear.

"Sure. I'm fine."

"Alright. If you'll excuse me, I need to untangle another set of lights inside the barn."

Ella Mae disappeared, giving Becky and Glen some privacy.

"Hop in."

Becky furrowed her brow. "Excuse me?"

"You heard me. Hop in."

"Glen, I don't think it's a good idea."

Glen was undeterred. "Well, you specifically asked to be the first person to go for a ride when I finished with her."

Becky inhaled sharply and looked right at him, the walls she'd carefully constructed around her heart crumbling instantly. He remembered.

"Fine."

Before she could make her way to the truck's passenger side, Glen hopped out and gallantly opened the door in a grand flourish.

"Thank you," she said simply.

"You're welcome." The man hadn't stopped smiling.

With hands clutched in her lap, Becky made an effort to remain unruffled and aloof. But deep down, she was a mess. Part of her wanted to slide across the bench seat and press her lips to Glen's bearded cheek. The other wanted to scream obscenities at him.

Glen drove on the back roads passing barbed wire fences and dormant country meadows. Her bottom bounced on the seat with every divot they hit, the creaking and rumbling of the ancient truck making her wonder if the vehicle might fall apart any minute.

She glanced over at him and then back to the road. She wanted to remember the smiling version of Glen with pasture grasses flashing by the windows beyond the fence lines, the North Georgia Mountains towering in the distance. With his eyes hooded but bright with pride at his accomplishment, his red and green flannel underneath his coat buttoned up over a thermal undershirt.

Peering through the back window, she marveled at the Christmas tree still standing erect in the truck bed with lights ablaze as they hit another pothole.

"Are those battery-powered lights?" she asked.

"Yup."

"Are you worried the tree might fall over?"

"Nope. I've got it tied down real good with some bungee cords. Don't worry; it's not going anywhere."

She nodded. "What did you end up naming her?"

"The truck?"

"Yes."

"Well, here's the thing. I have a name in mind, but I wanted to run it by you first."

"Me? Why?" She eyed his hands gripping the steering wheel. Strong. Rough. Deadly.

Pulling the truck to the side of the road, he stopped and put it in park. When he turned to look at her, she noticed his face appeared thinner than the last time they were together a little over a week ago. Had he lost more weight? The thought immediately filled her with guilt, knowing she could have easily invited him to their Thanksgiving feast and fattened him up, her family welcoming him with open arms.

"Glen, I'm—"

"—Becky, please forgive me."

They both spoke simultaneously and smiled in unison at the realization.

"Becky, I was wrong to say all those things at the coffee shop. I've been wrong with many things in my life, and I'm trying to do better. I swear. I think it's just gonna take some time to learn new habits. Can you please find it in your heart to forgive me again?"

She wanted to forgive him. She *needed* to forgive him. But she was frozen in place, unsure which fork to take in the road.

"This is where we bend or where we break. And I sure as hell don't want to break off what I have with you, Becky. I want another chance. Can you please, *please* think about it?"

"Where were you on Thanksgiving?" she asked.

"What?"

"Thanksgiving. Did you go to Macon and spend it with your mom?" She prayed that was the case, sweet Mrs. Kirby doting on her only son with love and food.

Glen looked at the floorboard and leaned against the door of the truck. "I was, uh… I was at home."

"At home by yourself?"

"No."

"No?"

"Garth was with me." When their eyes locked, his smile was intact, his little joke not lost on her.

"Oh, Glen." She frowned. "I'm so sorry. I should've invited you to the farm. You could've spent Thanksgiving with us and wouldn't have been all alone." She was frustrated, her words coming out choppy and full of guilt.

Glen slid across the seat and gingerly put his arm across her shoulders. "Hey. Hey, it's okay. I was real busy fixing up Daisy. I've been working on her day and night. I wanted her all shined up to surprise you in time for the Christmas Tree Festival."

"What did you say?" Becky was wide-eyed. She watched him lick his bottom lip, blue eyes mapping her face.

"I wanted to surprise you for the Christmas Tree Festival."

"No, not that part. You said the name, 'Daisy.'"

Glen chuckled and scrunched his nose, realizing he'd let the cat out of the bag. "Yes. I named my truck Daisy. But only if it's okay with you."

"Of course, it's okay with me."

Gazing at him, he appeared a little softer around the edges, the scenic background beyond the truck looking like the portrait mode on her phone camera. Beneath those azure pools, she glimpsed a spark of something that sent heat swirling through her stomach.

"What do you want from me, Glen?" Her voice cracked with pent-up emotion.

"I want to be with you," he confessed, pressing his forehead to hers. "It's as simple and as complicated as that."

Chapter Twenty-Two

GLEN

Daisy was a massive hit at the Christmas Tree Festival. Families lined up for photos against the powder-blue vehicle, happy and cheerful in the holiday setting. Ella Mae was right—the backdrop of the poppy-red barn with the truck parked next to it looked like an old-fashioned Christmas greeting card.

"We may have to commission you to use your truck occasionally for marketing purposes," Roy Bennett said. The look of pride on his face wasn't lost on Glen.

Puffing his chest out with pleasure, he felt heat pepper his cheeks, unaccustomed to the feeling of pure satisfaction when it came to accolades of any kind, especially coming from a father figure like Roy Bennett. It was a hell of a lot better than all the criticism and shame Glen was used to.

"Anytime, Mr. Bennett."

"I agree," Elyse added. "I'm thinking we could do some marketing shots for your new wine label." She and Walt sat on the open lift gate and sipped hot apple cider. "You just say the word. I've got a great photographer in mind. The same one who's done some photos for Becky's brand."

The mere mention of Becky's name made his heart skip a beat. He tipped his cowboy hat before he shoved his hands into his front jeans pockets and nodded. "I'm up for anything. Happy to help."

"Good call, Elyse. You're always thinking ahead, aren't you, darlin'?" Walt palmed Elyse's denim-clad thigh and squeezed. The move wasn't lost on Glen as he scrolled the area for Becky, pining to be in her presence.

"So, when are we gonna get a taste of this new wine flavor y'all have been working on?" Roy asked.

"Soon, Dad. Very soon. In fact, I was thinking about unveiling it on Christmas Day before dinner." Walt's gaze shot to Glen. "But only if you're in town and can join us. Whatdyasay, Glen? You want to reveal our secret project on Christmas?"

All eyes were on Glen, and he shifted uncomfortably in his stance. "Well, I, uh… I'd love to. But don't you think we need to run it by Becky first?"

Walt furrowed his brow. "Why would I need to run it by Becks?"

"Run what by me?"

Becky came around the corner of the barn, her cheeks flushed, and her hands dug deep into her coat pockets. The sight of her knocked all the breath out of Glen's lungs, the yearning he felt for her hard to contain. But none of the Bennetts knew anything about their budding relationship, and he intended to keep it that way until she gave the green light.

"The boys were thinking about unveiling their new wine flavor at Christmas dinner," Roy explained.

"Oh." She flicked her eyes toward Glen. "You gonna be around on Christmas Day?"

Glen chuckled. "Well, I don't want to intrude on a private family gathering or anything."

"Intrude? Nonsense. I insist you join us. Especially if you and Walt want to reveal your new wine flavor." Becky's eyes shone bright with possibility, leaving Glen trembling in his boots. "I think it's a great idea."

"Then it's a done deal, Glen." Walt hopped off the truck and slapped him on the shoulder. "Christmas dinner at our house. Don't forget to bring your appetite." He leaned low and whispered in Glen's ear, "And the name you want to put on the wine label. Have you come up with anything yet?"

"Maybe?"

Walt winked at him. "Atta-boy." He stuck his hand out for Elyse to take, the couple ambling toward the S'mores area.

Roy tipped his hat and smiled. "I'm glad you're joining us, son. I look forward to the wine tasting too."

"Thank you, sir. I'm very much obliged."

Roy left Becky and Glen standing by the powder-blue pickup truck alone. She skipped toward him and squealed.

"How easy was that?"

"What do you mean?"

"I was going to ask everyone if I could invite you to Christmas dinner, but they invited you for me. Now you won't be alone, and we can be together."

"But we won't be *together* yet, right?"

Karen Carpenter's smooth vocals to the song, "I'll Be Home for Christmas" swirled around them, the music coming from the outdoor speakers. Touching the tips of her boots to his, the love light in Becky's gaze wasn't lost on him. "Soon, Glen. You can count on me." She leaned in and pressed her lips to his bearded cheek.

Glen gasped and took an intentional step backward, anxiously looking around the crowd. Had one of her brothers seen them? Was he about to get sucker-punched?

"Lighten up, Glen. No one saw anything."

"You sure?"

She nodded and motioned with her index finger for him to follow. He gave her a head start and slowly moseyed after her when she grinned over her shoulder, egging him on. He was like a hound dog following a whiff of a fox. A lovesick teen going after his secret crush. A horse out in the fields following the scent home to the stable after a long, hard day. Becky's perfumed trail filled his being with hunger and longing.

When he'd taken her for a spin in his truck named Daisy, they agreed to never bring up the subject of Joe's death again. And rightfully so. It was too painful for both of them. He needed to move on. It was all in the past, and he was more interested in his future—with Becky. If that meant compartmentalizing his grief and blame when it reared its ugly head, so be it. He'd do just about anything to be with his daisy girl.

Glen watched Becky duck inside the main house through the back door into the kitchen. Standing on the stairs leading up to the porch, he turned one last time and eyed the crowd milling around the barn area, ensuring the coast was clear. The scene was festive, the twinkle lights, food trucks, fire pits, poinsettias, and music creating the perfect vibe for the Christmas celebration. He was proud of Becky's efforts, her talent in everything she touched amazing him.

The screen door groaned on rusty hinges before he

opened the solid door into the kitchen. Remnants of festival food packaging and stacks of homemade Christmas cookies made him pause. Becky was nowhere in sight.

"Becky?"

He was met with silence and continued through the hallway off the great room. Eyeing the staircase, he knew it was the pathway to her bedroom on the second floor. Looking over his shoulder one last time, he wondered if she was playing hide-and-seek, just like in the old days. Well, two could play this game.

Placing his boot on the first stair, he moved with quiet steps until he was on the second floor. Looking both ways up and down the hallway, he edged his large body against the wall and slowly ambled to Becky's bedroom. The door was wide open, her unmistakable scent causing warmth to spill into his chest, pooling and spreading with pining. Palming the door wider, he gasped when she jumped out from behind it and squealed with glee.

"*Boo!*"

"Jesus, Becky. You scared the shit out of me!"

She grabbed him by the hand, pulled him inside, closed the door, and locked it.

"What are you doing? We can't stay in here. What if they find us together?"

"Hush, Glen." She pushed him against the locked door and tossed his hat toward a nearby chair. Grabbing his face, she locked her lips with his.

Glen was tentative at first and held her by the waist. But his desire took over, and he moved his hands to her head, pulling her taught against him. Their mouths and tongues came alive with passion, her sweet breath filling him with life.

"I'm sorry about what I said at the coffeehouse, Glen. I

didn't mean it," she managed to say between nips and kisses.

"I'm sorry too."

Glen lifted her into his arms, her booted legs wrapping around his torso as he moved them toward the bed. Within moments, her back hit the soft mattress, his weight pressing into hers as they continued to kiss in between panting breaths. Everything about Becky exuded femininity, from her soft cheeks, to her pale-pink nail polish, to her golden hair spread across the forest green pillows. The rainbow unicorn he'd won for her on Halloween was wedged between the bed and the wall and made him grin.

"Glen." His name fell from her lips before she kissed him long, hard, and deep.

He threaded his fingers through her hair, aware of the smoldering heat trapped inside the bulky fabric of his winter coat. She hummed against his mouth, and he let it reverberate throughout his body before he groaned and forced himself off her.

"Don't leave yet." She was leaning back on her elbows, her hair disheveled, and her eyes piercing him with a look he knew full well—one part longing, the other part lust.

Glen wanted to protect her. She was sacred to him, and he didn't want to share her with anyone, their secret safe from the world. But he had another secret roiling in his belly, one he knew he needed to share with her. He was convicted by this skeleton in his closet, the very thought of saying it out loud leaving him paralyzed with fear. Sitting next to her, he offered Becky his hand. Lacing her fingers through his, she gently squeezed.

"I want you to accompany me to the beach after Walt and Elyse's wedding."

"What?" he whispered, struggling to hear her over his thundering heart.

"I booked a trip to the beach, and I don't want to go alone. I want you to come with me."

He let go of her hand and shifted to face her. Pushing her hair back from her face, he tucked a thick strand over her ear. The way she gazed at him with those dark eyes full of longing and trust left him shattered to come clean. But now wasn't the time.

"Before or after we tell them about us?" he asked.

"I don't know. We'll have to see how things play out at Christmas and then at the wedding."

She dragged the tips of her fingers across his hairy cheek, sending ripples of pleasure to his core. The thought of having Becky alone on a Florida vacation sounded mighty fine to him. But his grin fractured with uncertainty. There was so much they needed to discuss between themselves and then with her family before he dared to dream of traveling out of town with her.

"Are you scared to tell them?" he asked.

"Not anymore."

Glen puckered her mouth with his fingers and stared into her dark eyes. They were deliciously and dangerously tangled up in each other's world, and he was desperate to kiss and touch her a little bit more. Desperate to tell her his secret. But he held back and shoved the urge away.

He pressed a lingering kiss to her swollen lips before he stood and lovingly gazed down at her. "Then I won't be afraid either."

Nope. He wasn't afraid. He was *terrified*.

Chapter Twenty-Three

BECKY

Becky piddled nervously while arranging appetizers on the big island in the kitchen. Christmas morning had flown by with a dizzying array of unwrapped presents, and family gathered around the tree in matching seasonal pajamas. After a hearty brunch, including a few mimosas, everyone dispersed and changed clothes. The relaxed atmosphere was everything she ever wanted during the holiday, but one person was missing—Glen. Thank goodness he was coming over for their annual feast and to unveil the new wine he and Walt had finally created.

She'd changed into one of her new sweaters, a sexy white cashmere number that hung romantically off one shoulder. After coming downstairs, her brothers reactions were perplexed by the sultry way she was dressed. As if an entire morning lounging in holiday-themed pajamas wasn't provocative enough. Even Robyn and Elyse were wide-eyed but thrilled by her dramatic transformation.

"You look beautiful," Robyn commented.

"Thanks, Robyn. I went shopping a few weeks ago and treated myself."

"As you should," Elyse concurred, coming up alongside her. "Girl, I may have to borrow this for my honeymoon."

The three females giggled. For Elyse to want to borrow anything of Becky's was comical. The dark-haired, blue-eyed beauty was a regular fashionista when it came to clothing. Although she had toned it down a bit since meeting Walt and moving to the country. It wasn't unusual to find Elyse wearing blue jeans and boots more regularly, her high heels and red lips only coming out for work occasions. Becky loved that Elyse was more relaxed around them, happy she would be her sister-in-law in the next week.

"I think I'll freshen up before the big wine reveal." Elyse smiled and wiggled her perfect eyebrows.

Teddy approached and wrapped his arm around Robyn's waist, his wedding band glinting in the Christmas tree lights on display in the family room. "You look pretty, Becks. What's the occasion?"

"Teddy!" Robyn admonished, elbowing him in the ribs.

"Ouch! What?" he laughed.

"It's Christmas Day. It's just a sweater, Teddy. I wanted to look nice, especially with the wine reveal."

Ted nodded. "Well, you look real nice."

"Thanks."

The kitchen island was covered in various appetizers and charcuterie boards, the entire family enjoying the afternoon of nibbles, football, and fellowship. A giant turkey roasted in the oven, and everyone pitched in with the side dishes.

Robyn and Teddy brought a mixed green salad topped with cranberries, pecans, and homemade dressing. Walt and Elyse prepared a spicy squash casserole and a traditional green bean casserole with crunchy onion topping. Hank and Ella Mae insisted on trying a new sweet potato soufflé with a marshmallow cream topping. Poor James was all alone in his cooking endeavors, his contribution a prepackaged tray of macaroni and cheese. Samantha had decided at the last minute to join her family on a rare holiday ski vacation, leaving James sulking and alone.

"Your mac 'n' cheese looks delicious," Becky kidded, leaning against his shoulder.

"Shut up," he chuckled. "You know I'm not any good in the kitchen."

"I know. It's the thought that counts."

James lifted a glass of Bennett Farms wine to his lips and took a sip. "It's gonna be a spread, like always. Did you make Mama's famous mashed potatoes?"

"Of course I did. With giblet gravy too. And I made the cranberry gelatin salad and Memaw's cornbread stuffing. Oh, and a few loaves of homemade bread. I also saved a couple of jars of homemade strawberry jam you love so much just for you."

James slung his arm across Becky's shoulders and squeezed. "I hope you know how much we appreciate all the trouble you go to. Seriously, Becks. You're the best. You always make the holidays extra special."

"Aww. You know how much I love catering to all you frat boys."

The big dogs barked, nails clicking on the hard-wood floors as they scrambled to the door. Becky inhaled a deep breath knowing Glen had finally arrived.

"Merry Christmas, Glen," Roy heartily announced. He welcomed him inside with a bear hug.

"Merry Christmas." Glen set a large bag on the floor.

He took off his coat and cowboy hat, handing it to Roy as the family offered greetings.

Becky stayed in the kitchen and watched the heartfelt scene unfold. Glen was dressed in black denim and a crisp, white collared shirt. His beard was neat, and his hair recently trimmed. He panned the room, blue eyes landing on hers. A slow smile unfurled from his whiskered lips as he picked up the bag and approached her.

"Merry Christmas, Becky. You look… damn." His eyes held hers with pleasure.

She felt her cheeks heat, aware of her entire family watching them.

"Thank you. Merry Christmas, Glen. What have you got in the bag?"

Glen pulled out a vintage white casserole dish with blue cornflowers decorating the side with one hand, and a large bag of tortilla chips in the other. He presented his wares to her with a wide grin.

"What is it?"

"Cheese dip."

"Cheese dip?" She giggled.

"Yes. You told me to bring a traditional appetizer my family served on Christmas Day. Well, this is about as traditional as we got. Cheese dip was our favorite while we watched the big games. It's also something I can't mess up." His chuckle was deep and warm, and Becky had to curl her lips together to thwart off a gigantic smile.

"I might need to pop it into the microwave and warm it up." He walked by her carrying the dish in a whoosh of manliness. "The great thing about cheese dip is you can reheat it as often as you want, and it won't go bad."

"I like the sound of that. Easy-peasy."

Walt slapped Glen on the back while the appetizer

heated in the microwave. "I've got glasses already set up for the wine tasting whenever you're ready."

"Walter, he just got here. Let the man relax first," Elyse chided alongside Walt. She'd refreshed her lipstick, the fiery red matching her holiday nails.

The microwave dinged, and Glen pulled out his contribution, setting it on the island with all the other appetizers. "It's okay. I'm ready whenever y'all are." He dipped a chip into the melted cheese and popped it into his mouth, grinning while he chewed. "It's perfect. Try it, Becky."

She took a chip from the bag and dipped it into the gooey, melted mess. "Mmmm," she concluded. His blue eyes sparkled as he winked at her.

It was nice having the entire family gathered in the family room, the scene festive with an undercurrent of excitement. The giant Christmas tree was loaded with collected ornaments from over the years, twinkle lights shining like tiny stars in the cozy space. The big dogs lounged across their beds, and Glen's coat hung by the door, reminding her he was staying for a while. It was nice seeing him all dressed up, his eyes lighting up every time he looked at her. She felt a magnetic pull toward him and couldn't contain her enthusiasm, knowing he was proud of what he and her brother created.

With the large family scattered across every available seat in the family room, Glen and Walt stood in front of the hearth, each holding a bottle of wine. The clear glass revealed the faint color of the honey liquid inside, condensation peppering the unlabeled chilled bottles. Becky handed out stem-less glasses to everyone before sitting on the arm of the sofa next to her father. He patted her knee, his eyes darting to hers with pleasure.

As Walt and Glen came around the room and filled

everyone's glass, Walt spoke with evident pride in his tone. "This is a Bennett Farms first, y'all. Two families blending organic grapes and apples into something extra-unique."

Becky locked eyes with Glen as he leaned low and poured wine into her glass, her genuine smile intentional. She continued to watch him go around the room and serve her family, his care and loving manner filling her with hope.

Finally, Walt poured his own glass and held it into the air. "I believe Glen and I have come up with something special here." He clamped his free hand on Glen's shoulder. "It's been my pleasure working with you, bro. You've been a regular face here at Bennett Farms, and I feel like we've come full circle."

Becky blinked back tears, the poignant moment one she wanted to stamp on her memory for those times when she might feel a little uneasy when considering their past.

"This wine will please every palate at the table," Walt continued. "It's a perfect semi-sweet, semi-sparkling combination with a rich red apple taste. And I know it will be a huge hit with our customers and a real lucrative brand to boot. Cheers, y'all."

Becky brought the glass up to her nose and inhaled a deep breath. The wine held definite fruit and floral notes with hints of oak and vanilla. Her taste buds collided with the sweet flavor, the crisp texture and fruit reminding her of baked apples in wrinkled tin foil on an autumn day, prepared by a handsome farmer wearing flannel. Glen's contribution was all over this glass of wine, and she was pleased.

"Mmmm, I like this," Roy exclaimed.

"It's good," James added.

Glen stood stoic, holding the empty bottle in his hands. He hadn't participated in the tasting, fixated on everyone's reaction to the taste. Taking in all the comments, he seemed genuinely pleased.

"Have you come up with a name for this wine?" Hank asked. Ella Mae was seated on his lap, the two cozy and snuggling between sips.

"Well, the name is up to Glen," Walt replied. "He hasn't even told me what he's come up with yet, so this will be a real surprise for all of us."

All eyes, including Becky's, landed on the big man.

"Well, what is it?" James asked. "What did you name this new wine?"

Glen cleared his throat. "First off, before I reveal the name, I'd like to thank all of you for welcoming me back to Bennett Farms after all these years. I'd especially like to thank Walt for coming up with the idea for a new wine blend and helping me out so I can repurchase my farm free and clear. It's been a real pleasure working with you, bro." He thrust his hand out, and they shook before Glen smothered Walt in a bear hug, slapping him aggressively on the back. Watching the two of them was like observing a film reel of their past when they were best friends growing up together without a care in the world.

"I, uh... I know things haven't always been easy between us."

Becky noticed Robyn lay her head against Teddy's shoulder. Ted kept his gaze fixed on Glen, unruffled by the comment.

"To be a part of something from the ground up has been... amazing. And I never realized how much went into creating a new wine flavor. Y'all are insanely talented."

The family chuckled.

"But here's the thing. I didn't have to think twice when Walt asked me to come up with a name for this particular flavor. Because you see, this wine is sweet. It's light and crisp, like the perfect fall day. There are hints of my ma's baked apples and your Mama's delicious apple pie recipe." He focused on Becky and smiled. "And y'all know how much I love a good pie."

Becky giggled, enthralled by Glen's heartfelt speech.

"And even though I don't drink alcohol anymore—"

"Getting close to one year sober," Walt interrupted, slapping Glen on the back again. Hank whistled, causing the big dogs to hoist themselves off their beds, big tails wagging and James wrangling. There was laughter and congratulations, Becky's heart about to burst through her soft sweater with love and anticipation.

"Like I was saying," Glen chuckled. "Even though I don't drink anymore, I knew I wanted this particular wine to embody the sweetness and the amazing grace I've felt since coming to work here."

He scanned the room taking in each family member present. This moment was special, and flashbacks of all the good times they'd shared instantly filled Becky with contentment. White cream on whiskers. A cloudless sky riding in an antique truck named Daisy. Apple orchards and barbecue smoke. Shoulders pressed together in a church pew. A sunset with the scent of pine in the air. A silly unicorn in rainbow colors pressed against her pillow. Becky felt herself settle, pure gratitude filling her with emotion.

And when Glen's eyes landed on hers again, she held her breath.

"With your permission, Mr. Bennett, I'd like to name this wine after your beautiful daughter."

The room hushed, her name off his lips sounding like a love song.

"*Rebecca Rose.*"

Chapter Twenty-Four

GLEN

Glen was overwhelmed by the applause, the Bennett brothers and their father rising from their seats and surrounding him with heartfelt congratulations. Even Teddy commented on how the name of the new wine was the perfect choice.

Glen had hit the proverbial grand slam.

Scanning the room for Becky, her dark eyes pinned him with her stare, something sweet and sincere passing between them. Between the solid handshakes and hugs, back slaps, and approval from her family, he was feeling it all.

"Well? What do you think? Do I have your permission to name this new wine after you?" He stood right before her and nervously waited for her official response.

She didn't say anything. Instead, she wrapped her arms around him and pressed her nose into the crevice of his neck. Glen turned rigid, aware of several pairs of eyes taking in the exchange. Patting her awkwardly on the back, he cleared his throat.

"I take that as a yes?"

When she pulled back from him, her eyes were muddled with tears. "Yes." She was breathless. "That's the nicest thing anyone's ever done for me."

His emotions bubbled up, and he thought he might lose it. Thankfully, Walt interrupted them with his loud enthusiasm.

"*Dude*! How'd you get so poetic, huh? I thought you'd name our wine something boring like 'Red Apple' or 'Apple Blend.' Naming it after my beautiful sister? Bravo, man." The two men high-fived.

"I've got a calligraphy artist working on ideas for the label already," Glen said. "And don't worry, it'll still blend with Bennett Farms branding, only a little more feminine in the lettering."

"Sounds amazing. I can't wait to sign off on it."

Becky sniffled, her eyes bright with happiness. "I need to check on the turkey. Do you boys mind gathering the wine glasses when everyone is finished?"

"We can," Walt reassured.

Glen watched her move through the crowded family room, the perpetual smile on her face a reminder he was the one who'd put it there.

"Are you sure nothing happened between you two when we were in Nashville? I mean, naming our wine after my pretty little sister…." Walt gave Glen the side-eye. Was he on to him?

Glen chuckled and started gathering wayward wine glasses. "Rebecca Rose Bennett has class, Walt. And she puts up with a lot of shit taking care of everybody around here. She's also sweet, just like the wine. She deserves a label with her name on it. It's as simple as that."

"Simple, huh? If you say so." There was a teasing tone to Walt's words, and Glen knew he'd dodged a bullet. But moving forward, he needed to be careful. Becky's tender hug in front of everyone was a sure-fire giveaway something was going on between them. He'd have to keep his distance for the rest of the day.

But as the big group gathered around the table for the holiday feast, Glen found himself sitting right next to Becky. He was sure this was intentional. The festive meal was everything he ever imagined it could be—and then some. The food was delicious, and the company was even better.

For the first time in years, Glen felt like he belonged somewhere. It was as if he'd gone back in time to those innocent days of youth when laughter reigned, and heartache wasn't even a blip on his radar. When the Bennett boys were his brothers from another mother and included him in their daily lives.

But the icing on his cake was having a beautiful woman sitting beside him, her soft hand resting on his thigh. Stroking her skin underneath the shroud of tablecloth, he realized this was what had been missing from his life all along. He didn't know falling in love could be so simple. His daisy girl and her lovely family gathered around the table. A turkey leg and fresh vegetables on a pretty plate. Candlelight flickering among crystal wine glasses filled with the bounty of his harvest. The cavernous void in his heart overflowing with love and forgiveness.

Glen exhaled a long, slow breath. Rolling his shoulders back, he allowed himself to linger in his happiness.

"Did you get enough to eat?" Becky asked.

"Plenty." He nodded and noticed her peony pink nails against the crystal wine glass she held. The color reminded him of the sky the night they watched the sunset over the mountains. He sure would like to spend the rest of his sunsets with her.

"You really are beautiful tonight." He kept his voice low, the urge to stroke the exposed skin of her bare shoulder where her white sweater dipped, tempting him.

Her cheeks flushed, the color matching her delicate nails. "Thank you," she whispered.

"You're welcome."

Glen reached for his water glass and noticed Robyn staring at him across the table. He offered her a timid smile and looked away. It wasn't until after dinner he realized she was on to him.

"May I speak to you in private, Glen?" Robyn asked.

He held a stack of dirty plates and set them near the sink. Becky was busy packing leftovers, the kitchen crowded and lively with the entire family helping.

Robyn motioned for him to follow her down the hallway and into Mr. Bennett's office.

"Close the door," she commanded.

Glen did as he was told and shut the door with a click. "What's going on, Robyn?"

She leaned on the edge of the mammoth desk and gripped the overlap. Her blonde hair spilled over her shoulders in waves against her red sweater, and Glen had a flashback of when they all attended the same local high school. Robyn had been homecoming queen her senior year, her red sequined gown stamped in his memory as she stood with a golden crown on her head on the football field with Teddy by her side.

"Tell me what's going on between you and Becky."

Glen frowned. "What do you mean?"

"Come on, Glen. We all see the way you act when you're around her. It's obvious you have feelings for her."

His pulse ticked with worry. How was he going to get out of this?

"Nothing is going on between us, Robyn. She's my friend. I'm… I'm blown away I'm even here tonight."

"You should be."

"What does that mean?" Glen did his best to remain calm and stoic, his heart thundering with each lengthy second.

"Stay away from Rebecca Bennett, Glen." Robyn exhaled a long breath. "You can't be with her—*ever*."

"What are you talking about?"

Robyn stood and folded her arms against her chest. "You almost *killed* my husband." She emphasized the word "killed" and waited for a beat before she continued.

"Now, I know everyone in this family has moved on and forgiven you. And… and that's great. And I know you've gotten help, and you're sober, which is incredible. But you and I know it's easier to forgive than to forget." She took a step toward him. "We will *never* forget what happened, do you hear me? And besides, things between you and Becky wouldn't work out anyway. She's precious to this family, do you understand?" Robyn pointed at the door. "And if you ever laid a hand on her, those men out there would rip you to shreds, and I, for one, would help them hide your body."

There was fire in Robyn's eyes, and her lips quivered as she attempted to keep her anger in check. Glen kept his mouth shut.

"Now, I won't cause a scene out there, Glen. I want you to enjoy Christmas and the fruits of your labor. And I want you to know I liked the wine and the name you chose. It's brilliant."

Glen held his breath, sensing she had more to say.

"But you need to let Becky down easy. I see the way she looks at you too, and it scares me."

"Scares you? How?"

"You have deep-seated rage in you, Glen. I don't care that you've been to rehab and you're not abusing alcohol and drugs anymore. But you have to know you have a predisposition to violence, probably going back to the environment you were raised in without a father. Biological factors are going on here, Glen."

Bristling in his stance, he clenched his teeth. He knew Robyn was knowledgeable in the law world, but to compare him to some kind of serial killer?

"You've got it all wrong, Robyn."

"Do I?" Her eyes squinted in defense. "I've known you for a very long time, Glen. You've always been anti-social. You lack common empathy and compassion. My God, when you attacked Teddy in the jail cell and almost beat him to death—"

"Robyn, please stop," he begged. "I wasn't in my right mind that night. It's not a personality trait or a tendency. I was fucked up, but I've gotten help. I'm *not* the same person I used to be."

Tears shimmered in Robyn's eyes, and she swiped at her face. The diamond in her wedding band glinted in the light. "After all the trauma Becky's been through at such a young age losing her mother, and then everything with Teddy... I worry she'll steel her heart against others if she gets hurt again. Do this for Becky, okay? Do this for Teddy. Do it as a sacrifice for all the pain and suffering you've put me and this family through."

Glen swallowed hard, his throat closing around his words. "What exactly is it you want me to do, Robyn?"

Robyn got right up into his face, and he braced himself for her reply.

"Continue living your life sober and working hard to get your farm back. But stay away from Becky and find someone else."

Chapter Twenty-Five

BECKY

Becky wiped a tea towel across the blue cornflowers on Glen's vintage casserole dish and set it on the kitchen counter, a hint of a smile dancing in her eyes. The entire afternoon had been magical, and she still couldn't fathom having a wine on the market named after her.

Scanning the great room, she noticed Robyn enter from the back hallway with Glen trailing behind, the look on his face none too pleased. Scowling, she flicked the dish towel over the edge of the farmhouse sink and walked toward him. When their eyes met, something strange and foreboding passed between them.

"I hand-washed your casserole dish so you wouldn't have to take it home dirty. It's sitting on the counter."

"Thank you," he mumbled.

Furrowing her brow, she reached out and touched his arm. "You okay?"

His sigh was audible. "I'm fine."

"What's wrong?"

"Nothing." He shook his head and plastered a fake smile

on his face, his eyes the color of an impending storm. Dark and unsettled.

"I had a real good time today, Becky. Thank you for your hospitality."

"Wait. You're leaving?" She followed him toward the front door.

"Yes. I forgot to tell you, I'm, uh, heading to Macon tomorrow first thing. You know, to spend some time with my ma during the holidays."

Becky watched him shrug on his coat. "Oh. Well, tell her I said hello and Merry Christmas."

"I will."

Becky remained by the door and watched him make the rounds saying goodbye to everyone. She was confused by his abrupt departure and had an inkling Robyn had something to do with it. With the casserole dish in one hand, he grabbed his cowboy hat off the coat rack with the other and shoved it on his head. He was really leaving.

"I'll walk you out," she announced.

"No, Becky. You don't have to. It's freezing outside."

"I want to." She grabbed the nearest coat off the rack and stuffed her arms through the sleeves.

The two of them exited onto the front porch, the crisp air a stark contrast to the warm and cozy family room. Becky breathed in the scent of burning wood and evergreen, their boots crunching along the pebbled pathway filling the silence. Glen's truck was parked farthest away from the home among her brothers' trucks and Teddy's Jeep, out of sight from the house's front windows. The hinges on the truck door squealed open, and Glen bent low to set the casserole dish on the seat and reach for something inside.

"Merry Christmas."

Becky gasped as he presented her with a small red box adorned with a self-adhesive bow stuck to the lid. "What's this?"

"Open it and find out."

She lifted the lid revealing a small silver bracelet tucked inside. Taking it out of the box, she admired it from side to side.

"Those are little daisy charms. It reminded me of you."

Her eyes flicked to his, the warmth from his gaze lighting up her cheeks. "It's perfect." She handed him the empty box and quickly put the jewelry on, overcome with gratitude. "I have something for you too. Wait right here."

She sprinted toward the front porch and pulled a flat, wrapped package from behind a large planter. The gift was left hidden on purpose, a present she meant to give him earlier but was sidetracked by the wine reveal and Christmas feast. Rushing back to him, he stood tall, dumb-struck as she presented him with the package.

"Becky, you didn't have to."

"But I wanted to." She planted her hands on her hips and nodded. "Go on. Open it."

Glen ripped the paper off in one sweep, revealing a customized steel sign the size of an album cover. The top part featured a vintage pickup truck design, and the bottom was personalized with his last name, "Kirby," etched into the metal.

"I hope I got the truck model right."

"You did." He stared at the gift in his hands with awe etched across his features.

"I figured you could put it up in your workshop or something."

Glen nodded. "This will look real good in my workshop, Becky. It's the nicest gift I've ever received."

Becky beamed, excited he was so happy. "And I love my gift too." She held up her wrist, displaying the delicate daisy charms.

Glen slid the metal sign across the front seat of the truck. "Come here."

She walked into his embrace and clung to his large frame.

"You make me very happy, Daisy Girl. Do you believe me?" His low voice rumbled in her ear, his hot breath grazing the shell of her ear.

"You make me happy too."

"Merry Christmas."

"Merry Christmas, Glen."

Becky felt him kiss the top of her head, the gesture sweet and gentle. She stepped back, and he got into his truck. The engine roared with life as he rolled down the window and rested his coated forearm on the edge.

Coming right up to the window, she pressed her hands into the thick fabric. "So, I guess I'll see you in Atlanta for the wedding?" she asked.

"I'll see you in Atlanta."

"Don't forget to pack for our beach getaway. It might be cold this time of year, so bring layers."

"Layers. Got it."

Becky grinned and leaned in through the window, kissing him on the cheek. Watching him back out of the parking space, she lifted her hand in a little wave, the charm bracelet happily tinkling against her wrist. When he gave her one last look full of longing and desire, she pressed her lips to the tips of her fingers and blew him a final kiss.

And she didn't care if anyone inside the house saw it.

"How's my girl? You must be tuckered out after today." Roy patted the empty seat on the couch beside him, and Becky sat down.

Snuggling next to her father, she stared at the hypnotizing flames in the fireplace and yawned. "It's been a long day. But a good day."

"I agree. Did you get everything you wanted for Christmas?"

Becky eyed the daisy charm bracelet on her wrist and nodded. "And then some."

"How about the new wine name? You sure you're okay with it?"

"Yes, Daddy. I'm sure."

"Well, Glen Kirby certainly surprised us all, what with the flavor and then the name. That boy sure has come a long way. I'm proud of him."

Becky couldn't help the half-grin donning her face. "I'm proud of him too." Shifting, she slowly stood and stretched. "Goodnight, Daddy."

"Goodnight, darlin'."

"Goodnight, everyone."

"Goodnight," her brothers echoed, eyes glued to the football game on the big screen. Ella Mae looked like she was asleep, snuggled beside Hank, and Elyse and Walt had already gone home for the night.

Becky flicked off the kitchen lights on her way to the stairwell, ready to crawl into her comfy bed and sleep. As she rounded the corner, she almost collided with Robyn coming out of the half-bath.

"Oh! Sorry, Robyn. I'm half asleep," Becky giggled.

"No worries. Teddy and I are about to head home. Thanks for everything you did today to make Christmas so special. You always go above and beyond, just like your sweet mama used to."

"She taught me well." Becky was flattered by the comparison. "I'm sure I'll see you this week before we head to Atlanta for the wedding. Goodnight." She started for the stairs and stopped when Robyn called after her.

"Wait a minute, Becky."

Turning around, she squinted in the dim hall lighting, suddenly feeling the weight of the long day on her shoulders. "What is it?"

Robyn reached for one of her hands and squeezed it gently, her voice but a whisper. "What's going on between you and Glen Kirby?"

A shot of adrenaline coursed through Becky's veins, instantly waking her. Her voice scratched with unease. "What do you mean? We're... friends."

"You know what I mean. We all see it. The way you look at each other. The way your face lights up when you're talking to him. I'll bet you intentionally had him sit right next to you at the dinner table so y'all could hold hands under the tablecloth. Am I right?"

Heat scorched Becky's neck and cheeks, and she huffed, letting go of Robyn's hand. "You don't know what you're talking about."

"I think I do, Becks. And I'm worried about you."

"You're worried? Why?"

"Because you're playing with fire, and you know it."

Becky gritted her teeth. "You spoke to Glen about this tonight too, didn't you? It's why he left early. That's why his happy mood turned sour. What did you say to him, Robyn? What are you trying to prove?" The two women were in a standoff, and Becky's breathing turned heavy.

Her secret relationship with Glen suddenly wasn't much of a secret anymore.

"How could you even think of starting up something with Glen, of all people, Becky? For heaven's sake, he almost killed my husband—your *brother*." The tone of her voice held desperation.

Robyn had always advocated for Teddy, her love for him since they were high school sweethearts like something from a classic romance novel. Their love was strong and had weathered many torrential storms. Becky felt sick to her stomach, knowing she'd caused her sister-in-law pain and angst. Sitting on the wooden stairs, she hung her head.

"Robyn, you know how much I love Teddy and how I would never do anything to cause him more pain."

Robyn sat next to her and wrung her hands in her lap. "But that's exactly what you're doing. It's one thing being friendly with Glen on the farm while he's working with Walt. It's quite another to see him flirting and baiting you at a family dinner."

Becky jerked her head to look right at Robyn. "Baiting me? What does that mean?"

"Come on. You know as well as I do the man has a vengeful heart. He can't be trusted. He'd do just about anything to get his farm back. And to get his claws into Bennett Farms—"

"Stop it, Robyn. You've got it all wrong," she interrupted in defense. "Glen does not have a vengeful heart. He's worked really hard to get to where he is today. He's changed."

"Maybe he has changed… for a little while. But what will you do the next time he's enraged and starts swinging, maybe even at you? Or when he loses control and falls off the wagon? Are you strong enough to withstand his anger?

His… his *fury*? The man has had a vendetta against this family for years. What makes you think he's not using you to get back at everyone? Have you ever stopped to think about it? What if there's a strong possibility he's been stringing you along to get exactly what he wants?"

"Enough," Becky barked. She stood and scowled at Robyn, her fury bubbling beneath the surface.

"Y'all can have your own opinion about the man. But I'm here to tell you, he's *changed*. He's been sober for almost a year. He's restored an entire antique car. He goes to church on Sundays. And tomorrow, he's driving to Macon to visit his mama for the holidays." She shivered and steeled herself with resolution. "That doesn't sound like the kind of man who has any kind of *vendetta* against me or my family." She turned and trotted up the stairs.

"*Becky!*"

She stopped and kept her back toward Robyn, listening to her last words.

"I love you, Becky, and I don't want you to get hurt. Glen is a recovering addict, plain and simple. I just want you to think about how there are no guarantees with where his life is headed."

Becky turned around, her voice trembling in response. "You're right. There are no guarantees in any of our lives. But I have faith in Glen. I have faith in love and forgiveness. And isn't that the ultimate lesson we're supposed to learn anyway?"

Robyn sighed and arose from her seat on the stairs. "You've forgotten the most important part of all of this."

"What?"

"Your family will never allow this relationship to happen, and you know it."

Becky thrust her chin into the air. "Well then... you really don't know my family, then."

Turning, she rushed through the hallway and into her bedroom, slamming the door shut. She paced back and forth before she sat on the edge of her bed. Swiping the stuffed unicorn Glen had won her off the pillow, she gripped it hard against her chest and rocked back and forth, Robyn's words messing with her confidence.

What if she was right? What if this was all some sick joke, and Glen was stringing her along?

Running her hands across the rainbow-colored mane of the stuffed animal, her new charm bracelet caught her eye. She brought her wrist up to her mouth and pressed a lingering kiss on the jewelry, hot tears coming to the surface.

There was only one way to get to the bottom of this. She needed to have a heart-to-heart with Glen Kirby. But it would have to wait until she could talk to him in person at Walt's wedding in Atlanta.

Chapter Twenty-Six

The week between Christmas and New Year's Eve went agonizingly slow, especially with Glen being out of town. Thank goodness Walt and Elyse's wedding was on the horizon, keeping the entire family busy with preparations.

Becky and her brothers were attendants in the ceremony, along with Elyse's sister, Ava, and her brother-in-law, Rick. And her four-year-old nephew, Jagger, was the ring bearer. It was turning out to be a real family affair, the wedding held at Live Oak Studios in Atlanta, the same studio where Elyse and Walt met when Becky almost auditioned to be on a cooking competition show on the Cook USA Network.

Almost.

Thinking back to the uncomfortable time a year ago, Becky wondered what her life would've been like if she'd gone through with the audition and made it. Would she have won and been the host of her own network cooking show by now? Would she have relocated to Atlanta and found a quaint townhome with a little patch of earth to start a garden? Or would she have turned into a cosmopolitan girl like Elyse, challenging herself to live in a high-rise in the concrete jungle wearing expensive sweaters and shoes?

She knew the answer. No way.

Becky was a small town country girl at heart. She wasn't cut out to be a big city girl, let alone the host of her own freakin' television show. It wasn't meant to be. The glitz and glam and the widespread sexual misconduct in the industry were something she wanted no part of, thank you very much.

Elyse found sponsors for Becky's YouTube show which leveled her up to monetization. And a bonus for all her hard work was being able to film everything from the safety of her family kitchen at Bennett Farms. She couldn't have done it without Elyse. And now, because of her brand's success, she was working with a legit publishing company that wanted to publish *The Farmer's Daughter Cookbook* featuring family recipes she shared on her channel.

Celebrating Elyse was something Becky looked forward to after everything the woman had done for her. And seeing her brother Walt over the moon happy was all she ever wanted for him.

"Which one?" Elyse asked.

Becky was lying on top of Elyse's bed watching her pack for the wedding weekend, clothes and shoes strewn about the room. Her future sister-in-law held up two dresses, one in black with a plunging neckline and one in bright pink with mid-drift cut-outs. Leave it to Elyse to dress to the nines; the rehearsal dinner party tomorrow night at the Sun Dial restaurant on top of the Westin Peachtree Plaza building in downtown Atlanta sure to be an unforgettable kick-off to the wedding weekend.

Becky sat up and tilted her head, eyeing the two dresses.

"Well, the black dress is certainly sexy, and Walt will go bonkers when he sees you in it. But I like the bright color of the pink one, and I think it's a happier choice for the happy occasion."

Elyse nodded. "Let me try it on." She hightailed it to the bathroom and shut the door, leaving Becky alone.

Teddy and Robyn were already in Atlanta, staying with her lawyer father in his downtown high-rise overlooking Centennial Olympic Park. Thank goodness too, because Becky hadn't spoken to Robyn since their confrontation in the stairwell on Christmas Day. She knew she needed to make amends so they could enjoy the wedding without ill feelings toward each other, but she wasn't sure how.

Robyn had rocked her world with her insinuations and judgmental comments regarding Glen. And how would she react when he showed up for the ceremony and saw them hanging out together?

Leaning back against a pillow, she eyed Glen's last text message sent earlier in the day.

See you soon, Daisy Girl.

The text made her smile. She looked forward to seeing him too. But she was more excited about their trip to Sandersville Beach together *after* the wedding. Becky still hadn't told her family Glen was joining her. The timing was all wrong. And what they didn't know wouldn't hurt them. Right?

She wanted to be alone with Glen. She *needed* to be alone with him. There would be plenty of opportunities to tell everyone about her and Glen's relationship afterward. Until then, keeping things on the down low would be challenging, especially at a beautiful wedding celebrating true love.

Elyse stepped out of the bathroom wearing the bright

pink dress, hands palming the fabric. "Well? What do you think?"

Becky sat up and nodded. Elyse looked like a cover model for *Glamour Magazine*.

"It's perfect."

"Hmmm. I think you're right."

Becky watched Elyse pilfer through several boxes of shoes, looking for something to match her dress. "Elyse, can I ask you something?"

"Sure."

"Has Walt truly forgiven Glen Kirby, or is he placating him until he can buy back his farm?"

Elyse jerked her head to look right at her. "That's a pretty loaded question, Becky."

"I know. I'm sorry. I just... I want to know what everyone is thinking."

Elyse sat on the edge of the bed and patted Becky's leg. "You want to know if your family would support you and Glen dating, don't you?"

Becky's eyes widened, her confession slipping out of her mouth quietly, "Mmmhmm."

Elyse offered a sad smile. "What happened between your two families was heartbreaking. But as an outsider looking at things now, it's refreshing to see how much love and forgiveness have transpired. For Walt and Glen to make amends and work side by side is a miracle in and of itself."

"I agree."

"When I first met Glen last year during the snowstorm, he wasn't in his right mind. He was sick, Becky. Thank God Walt and I were there to help him. Seeing him clean and sober now, I admit, I like the guy. He's kind. He's a hard worker. And he's certainly smitten with you."

Becky gripped Elyse's hand. "And I'm smitten with him.

But I know my brothers and dad will freak out if I tell them I want to date Glen. They might've forgiven him, but they'll never trust him again."

"Do you trust him?"

Becky bowed her head and frowned. Now it was Elyse's turn to ask a loaded question. But she and Glen still had so much to talk about. She had a hunch he was keeping something from her and wanted to get to the bottom of it. Still, she trusted her gut, and her gut was telling her everything would be okay.

"I think so."

Elyse's smile lit up her gorgeous face as she squeezed Becky's hand. "If you can trust Glen, you'll be more forgiving, and he will see that you believe in him. When a man knows you have his back, he'll give you the whole world— and then some."

Tears welled in Becky's eyes as she nodded, thankful for Elyse's words of encouragement.

"Becky, I knew the minute he boldly announced 'Rebecca Rose' as the new wine name, Glen was all in. That man would walk through fire for you."

"Oh Lord, is it obvious?" She laughed, causing tears to sluice down her cheeks.

"Aww… come here, sweet girl." Elyse opened her arms wide, and they hugged. "Trust your heart. Be true to yourself, and I promise the rest will fall into place."

The caravan of Bennett trucks and cars converged on Atlanta on a mild winter afternoon. The entire wedding party and out-of-town guests stayed in a nice hotel near Live Oak Studios and the downtown area. Becky had a room all to herself, and she hung her bridesmaid dress in the closet with cheer, the lavender color feminine and the style flattering on her curvy figure. She had plenty of time to take a luxurious bath in the decadent marble tub, and she enjoyed playing dress up for the rehearsal, opting for a light pink pantsuit and matching jacket, the color scheme intentional so she'd match Elyse's bright dress for the occasion.

The hungry wedding party headed into the city after the ceremony rehearsal, which took less than thirty minutes in a convenient hotel ballroom. The rehearsal dinner was a loud, boisterous affair at the fancy Sun Dial restaurant atop the tallest hotel in the Southeast. The establishment was known for the breathtaking 360-degree panorama view of the magnificent Atlanta skyline, and it was the perfect space for a romantic meal celebrating Walt and Elyse.

Roy bought out the entire dining room for the festivities, and the family and guests enjoyed a plated dinner of signature entrées and high-dollar wine. The city glowed at sunset, the colors of the sky reminding Becky of the night when she and Glen watched the sun go down together at Bennett Farms.

Just thinking about her burly apple farmer had her stomach doing flips. She was anxious to see him again, ready to have a heart-to-heart before they spent an entire week alone at the beach.

Samantha sat right next to Becky at dinner. She hadn't seen much of her over the holidays and was surprised by her bold comment. "Rumor has it you and Glen Kirby are becoming good friends. James told me about the new wine he named after you."

Becky blew out a long breath and spoke with a soft tone. "I had no idea he would name the wine what he did."

"You sure? Y'all were awfully chummy on Halloween when you danced with him."

Becky shook her head and pressed a linen napkin to her lips. "That was months ago, Sam. I hardly think one Halloween dance is why he named the wine after me."

"Well then, why do you think he did it? Robyn told me she thinks Glen is doing this on purpose. God knows he's had a vendetta against your family for years."

Becky tossed her napkin next to her salad plate and glared at Sam. "What is wrong with y'all? Huh?" She didn't mean for her response to be so loud. Her expression twisted with frustration as a few heads turned in their direction.

"Becky, darlin', you okay?" Roy asked from across the table.

"I'm fine, Daddy," she said. Her smile was sweet and accommodating. She did her best to tamp down her anger during Walt and Elyse's special dinner.

Lifting her wine glass to her lips, she took a hefty swig. Her brother, James, put his arm across Sam's shoulders and leaned in. His voice was hushed so the others couldn't hear.

"Do you ladies need some more wine?"

Becky set her empty glass back on the table. "Sure."

"I don't think wine will solve this," Sam said.

"Solve what?" James asked.

"Your sister is playing with fire. She needs to be careful."

"Sam...," he warned. "You said you wouldn't discuss this during the wedding weekend."

"Well, I've changed my mind. Glen will be here tomorrow, and we'll all have to watch these two flirt and carry on like there's nothing wrong with it."

Becky spoke through clenched teeth. "There *is* nothing wrong with it, okay? Stop badgering me, Sam."

Sam turned and stared at Becky, her facial features morphing with concern. "I'm sorry, Becky. But your brothers and your father aren't going to say any of this to you because they don't know how. But you need to hear it from someone."

"Sam," James warned again.

"Please, James. Let me finish, and then I won't say another word about it all weekend. I promise."

"And do I get a say in this?" Becky sat rigid in her seat, aware of Robyn and Teddy trying not to make it obvious they were watching the scene unfold.

"Just hear me out for a few seconds, okay? A relationship with someone with an alcohol or drug addiction is dangerous. It can lead to unhealthy stress and abuse."

"Glen is *sober*, Sam. He doesn't do that anymore."

"But like I've told you before, statistics are not in his favor."

"*Enough*, Samantha," James scolded.

"Fine." Sam calmly set her napkin beside her plate and rose from her seat. "You can't say I didn't warn you. Now if you'll please excuse me, I must run to the ladies' room."

Becky watched her leave and then turned toward her brother with a scowl.

"I'm sorry, Becks. She has the best intentions, just not the greatest execution. It won't come up again, I promise."

"And what do you think about all of this, James? The ladies in this family have had their say. What about you and Daddy and our brothers? Have y'all been talking about me behind my back? Concerned about your poor little sister who doesn't know any better?"

James ran a hand through his dark hair and shook his head. "Now isn't the time or the place to get into this, okay? I'm sorry Sam went there, and I promise it won't happen again. Please, enjoy your dinner and the rest of the weekend. We can circle back to this later."

Becky looked around the table at her family among the other guests, her eyes landing on Walt and Elyse. Their foreheads were romantically pressed together, and he said something to make her blush. God, to have a love like theirs, out in the open, the two of them ready to soar into their life together as a married couple. Flicking her eyes back to James, she quickly nodded and held her empty wine glass toward him like a petulant child, the delicate daisy charms around her wrist pinging the crystal. He smiled, ready to accommodate her.

Filling her glass, their eyes met, something honest and trustworthy passing between them. James knew exactly what was going on between her and Glen Kirby. And she was thankful he was giving her space to figure it out on her own.

Chapter Twenty-Seven

GLEN

Glen shifted uncomfortably on a white wooden folding chair, the tie around his neck a little too tight for his liking. He was intentional with his aisle seat on the last row in the studio venue, hiding in the shadows, away from the bright lights aimed at the wedding party on the sound stage. He knew a few folks weren't too keen on his presence as of late, and he wanted to stay out of their way.

God, Becky was beautiful. He couldn't take his eyes off her. The way her lavender dress hugged all her curves in the right places. Her cheeks flushed with brotherly love as she lovingly gazed at Walt and Elyse standing before the female wedding officiant. The smell of fresh flowers permeated the air, the simple bouquet in her hands the color of a mountain sunset. Her golden hair hung around her shoulders in soft waves, and the perpetual smile on her gorgeous face indicated she was happy.

Glen swallowed hard, his primal need to touch her intense. He hadn't seen her in over a week, their communication relegated to sweet texts and an occasional phone call when she could get away from her family.

His suitcase was loaded and sitting in the cab of his truck in the parking lot, the anticipation of spending an entire week with Becky at the forefront of his mind. Their plan was to discreetly leave directly after the wedding reception. She'd told him she didn't want her family to know he was coming along. Not yet. He couldn't blame her. The backlash would've caused a rift during the wedding celebration, and that's the last thing he wanted. Her little secret was safe with him.

"I now pronounce you husband and wife," the officiant announced.

Glen watched Walt lean in and reverently cup Elyse's face, pressing his lips to hers. Jealousy shot straight to his heart, not toward Walt and Elyse per se, but toward the possibility of having his own happily ever after like them. To witness such a milestone in his friend's life was a gift, and he was thrilled for Walt. Still, the longing for a genuine love connection like his friend's was a natural response. Glen said a little prayer in the shadows, hoping he might achieve the same dream one day.

Violin music played, and the giddy bride and groom pranced down the center aisle. Walt spotted Glen and grinned from ear to ear, holding out his hand for a high-five. Chuckling, he slapped the groom's hand and watched the wedding party exit the studio in a parade of black tuxes and lavender dresses, Becky bringing up the rear.

When their eyes met, she offered him a dazzling smile and winked. Something sweet and secretive passed between them. Glen was feeling extra happy between the joyous mood in the room, his beautiful daisy girl rocking his world, and the anticipation of having her all to himself in a secluded cottage on the beach.

Following the crowd of beautiful people into a larger studio across the hall, he was taken aback by the transformation inside. The popular Rupert's Orchestra was already playing familiar swing music as staff handed out champagne flutes to all the guests. Glen shook his head and politely declined.

The round tables for the formal dinner were decked out in stunning linens of violet and elegant floral centerpieces in shades of sherbet. Large swags of fabric draped across the dark ceiling, tying into a massive chandelier in the center of the room. Twinkle lights had been added, giving the space a softer, quixotic touch. Glen felt like he'd stepped onto a set for a romantic movie, sure there were large cameras filming everything. He stood slightly taller when he realized Becky was heading straight toward him.

"There you are," she exclaimed, holding her arms out for a hug.

He was stiff in her embrace, aware of her entire family in the room. Still, to have her in his arms was what he'd patiently waited for all week. Patting her on the back, he broke their connection and took in her beauty from top to bottom.

"Good lord, Daisy Girl. You're a sight for sore eyes."

Her face shone with adoration as she straightened his tie. "You clean up real nice, Glen. You're so handsome."

"Thank you." His face was on fire beneath his neatly trimmed beard, sure he was turning the red color of the Bennett Farms barn.

"I'll be right back after the wedding party introductions," she said. "Go grab a sparkling water from the bar. There's one on both sides of the room."

"Okay," his voice scratched.

She nodded, and he watched her disappear into the crowd. The chandelier lights dimmed, and the band leader's voice boomed over the sound system.

"Ladies and gentlemen. Let's give it up for the Bennett/Farrell wedding party!"

The Bennett siblings walked out onto the dance floor along with Elyse's sister, Ava, and her brother-in-law, Rick, who held their four-year-old son's hand. Everyone smiled and waved at the crowd, who politely applauded. Before the wedding weekend, Becky had filled Glen in on Elyse's Kansas City family. He learned the four-year-old was named Jagger, after rock legend Mick Jagger. Apparently, the couple had met on a blind date at a Rolling Stones concert. The cute little boy was decked out in a miniature tuxedo, his ring-bearer duties completed for the night.

"And now, please welcome your bride and groom, Mr. and Mrs. Walter Bennett!"

The crowd erupted in a frenzy of cheers and applause as Walt and Elyse walked out onto the dance floor, hand in hand, waving at their guests. Elyse wrapped her arms around Walt's neck as the orchestra played the Frank Sinatra classic, "The Way You Look Tonight."

Glen noticed Becky's expression from afar as she stood by her father, the two of them watching Walt. A look of sisterly love glowed on her gorgeous face. The happy bride and groom giggled and whispered into each other's ears while they danced, Walt's hands slowly moving down Elyse's exposed back and eventually settling at the top of her bottom covered in white lace. At the song's end, the two hugged and kissed while the wedding guests looked on with joy.

The music segued into the Lee Anne Womack country

song; "I Hope You Dance." Walt held Elyse's hand and approached her father, the two men hugging briefly before Mr. Farrell and his daughter took to the floor. Walt ambled over to Becky, took his sister into his arms, and started dancing with her.

The moment wasn't lost on Glen, knowing their mother, Lillian Bennett, was undoubtedly missed. Losing her to cancer was a tragic loss. Watching from afar, his eyes pooled with tears as Becky filled in for her late mother. She kept dabbing at the corners of her eyes while Walt glided her across the space. As the song came to a close, he whispered something into her ear, and Becky threw her head back and laughed, the poignant moment filled with nothing but love.

The band leader encouraged guests to come out onto the dance floor. While some did, others made their way to the beautiful tables, looking for their assigned seats in anticipation of the delicious meal. Glen stood slightly taller when he realized Becky was headed toward him again.

"I think my bridal party duties are over for the evening." Her face was flushed, her eyes bright with unshed tears. "Let's find our place settings and catch up."

Glen nodded and followed Becky through the crowd toward a big table near the front of the room. He immediately noticed a place card with his name calligraphed next to hers.

He leaned close to her and whispered, "Are you sure I should be sitting next to you?"

"It's fine, Glen. Elyse is the one who came up with the seating arrangements, not me. And don't worry. We're all spread out. Elyse wanted each of us in the wedding party to be at a table with the other guests."

"Oh."

Glen ended up sitting next to Becky and one of Elyse's

male cousins, the other Bennett family members dispersed throughout the room. The dinner music was festive, and the food was delicious. The menu wasn't particularly fancy but flavorful. They dined on beef tenderloin and herb-roasted chicken served with mashed potatoes, asparagus, and Brussels sprouts. Of course, endless bottles of Bennett Farms red and white wines were served, along with several rousing champagne toasts offered during the meal from Walt's brothers. Glen felt like he was in a dream among the candlelight and the food with his hand firmly planted on Becky's thigh, hidden in the folds of the tablecloth throughout most of the meal. In a couple of hours, he wouldn't have to hide once he had her all to himself.

"Excuse me," Roy Bennett announced from the microphone center stage. The patriarch of the Bennett family looked regal in his black tux and Stetson cowboy hat. Folks dinged crystal glasses with silverware, trying to get everyone's attention. As the room hushed, he cleared his throat.

"As I stand here today, watching my son marry the love of his life, I can't help but reflect on my own marriage and the lessons I've learned along the way. If I may, I'd like to offer you a few words of wisdom as you begin this next chapter in your lives."

"Sure thing, Dad. Fire away," Walt encouraged.

Roy nodded and pulled reading glasses and a wrinkled piece of paper from his tux jacket. "First, always remember to communicate openly and honestly with each other. Communication is key and the foundation of any strong relationship. It's always important to listen and understand each other's perspectives."

Glen felt Becky lean into his shoulder, her big brown eyes fixated on her father. A subtle waft of her perfume tickled his nose, and he breathed it in, the warmth of her feminine body permeating his.

"Second, always make time for each other," Roy continued. "Life can get pretty busy, but it's important to make sure your relationship is a priority. Set aside time for date nights, weekend getaways, and spending quality time together."

"Spoken like a true romantic," Becky whispered wistfully.

Glen nodded, thankful to be in the room filled with so much love and wisdom.

"Third, always be willing to be forgiving. Son, I know you've had firsthand experience with this one, and I'd just like to say I'm proud of you for being willing to forgive and move forward."

Glen stiffened in his seat, aware of the hidden meaning behind Mr. Bennett's words. Becky patted his thigh as if sensing his unease.

"And finally, always remember why you fell in love and decided to get married. Keep your love and passion alive, and never take each other for granted. Marriage is a journey, and it's important to enjoy the ride..." Roy suddenly choked up and swiped the glasses from his face. "You've got to make the most of every single moment you have together... until the very end." He nodded and stuffed the paper and glasses into his jacket. "That's it. Y'all don't need some old man blubbering away like an idiot. Congratulations, you two. I love you both dearly."

Walt stood and clapped his hands together, the crowd joining with a standing ovation. Glen watched as the two men bear hugged, Roy Bennett obviously overcome with emotion.

The band started to play a familiar tune, and Glen sniffled. "You, uh, wanna dance?"

She looked up at him and smiled. "I thought you'd never ask."

He licked his lips and nodded. Taking her by the hand, he whisked her onto the dance floor among the other guests as the band played, "At Last." He knew he wasn't the best dancer, but he was blissfully happy moving to the sensual rhythm of the love song.

"Are you having a good time?" Becky asked.

"It's always a great time when I'm with you." He smiled down at her, not giving too much away, aware of Teddy and Robyn, James and Samantha dancing mere feet from them. When someone tapped his shoulder, he turned rigid. Looking behind him, his gaze landed on Hank and Ella Mae. The couple didn't seem fazed by Glen dancing with Becky at all.

"Great night, huh? Dad hit it out of the park with his speech." Hank grinned from ear to ear, dancing with Ella in his arms.

"He sure did," Becky shouted over the loud orchestra.

Hank shifted his focus to Glen. "Hey, man. Thanks for dancing with my sister. Do you mind if I cut in for a minute?"

Glen stopped and purposefully let go of Becky. "Be my guest."

He watched Hank take his place as Ella Mae filled the void where Becky stood. It was awkward dancing with a stranger, although the times he had been around Ella had always been pleasant.

"I think you should go for it," Ella said, leaning into his ear so he could hear.

"Pardon?"

"I think you should ask Becky Bennett out… on a date." The woman was smiling at him as if she had it all figured out. Little did she know he and Becky were about to embark on an entire week sequestered in a tiny beach cottage on the coast with only one thing on their minds.

"You think so?"

Ella nodded. "I know so. Becky likes you, Glen."

Fire erupted on the back of his neck, and he blinked several times, unsure how to respond. Had Becky been confiding with Ella Mae about the two of them? Did Ella know about his sordid past regarding the Bennett family? Did she know he was a recovering addict like her famous country music brother, who died of an overdose?

"You know the Bennett boys are mighty protective of their little sister."

"I had a protective brother too, Glen. They'll always be that way. Stop treading so lightly. Be upfront and honest about how you feel. I think you might be surprised by everyone's reaction. You and Becky deserve to be happy."

The song ended, and Glen stood there, unsure of what to say.

"I think they're about to cut the cake in a minute," Hank said. "Come on, Ella. Great seeing you, Glen."

"You too." He watched the happy couple disappear into the crowd.

"Was it awkward for you, dancing with Ella Mae?" Becky asked.

"No. It was fine. She uh… she said you liked me." He couldn't help the lopsided grin donning his face.

Becky smirked and looped her arm through his, leading him toward the cake station. "If she only knew the half of it."

Chapter Twenty-Eight

BECKY

Becky stared at her reflection in the bathroom mirror. These were the last moments before her vacation of a lifetime began with Glen Kirby.

Smiling, she fluffed her hair and reapplied her lipstick. Her mouth held the sweet taste of wine made from grapes grown on the hillside outside her childhood home. The taste reminded her of all the beauty of her past and the promise of her unfolding future.

The clock had struck midnight, and Walt and Elyse's New Year's Eve wedding reception was winding down. It was almost time for the newly married couple to say their goodbyes—and for her and Glen to depart. They planned to drive through the night to Florida; the eight-hour trek made a little easier split between two drivers. She still hadn't told anyone she included Glen in her beach getaway plans, and she wanted to keep it that way. They believed she was renting a car for her adventure and leaving first thing in the morning. Until she could have a sit-down conversation with her family, she wanted to protect what she and Glen had. It was sacred, and she wasn't ready to share it with anyone.

Touching a tissue to her lips, she remembered Glen's midnight kiss stolen in the shadows away from everyone else. The swoony feeling came over her again, knowing they would have an entire week of make-out sessions and then some. She pictured him, and heat began to pool at her center. His blue eyes. His mouth. His broad shoulders. His barrel chest and bulging arms. Those hands that earlier, tenderly caressed her thigh under the table so no one could see.

Inhaling deeply through her nose, she shook off her random pining and put her swoony feelings on the back burner. She needed to focus on the present. Stick to her goal and get them out of town without anyone knowing. Remain calm. Cool. Like she wasn't lying to her family. But she was. And it left her unsettled. They were so close to the finish line. She could do this. She had to. She *wanted* to.

Exiting the bathroom to the sounds of the wedding band playing a rowdy rendition of "Shout," she was taken aback when she almost collided with her brother, Walt.

"Hey. Why aren't you out there dancing? Isn't this one of your favorite party songs?" She grinned back at him and noticed his undone bow tie hanging around his neck.

"I was looking for you, Becks."

"Me? Why? Do you need help with something? Where's your bride?"

Walt ran a hand through his dark hair, his expression hard to read. His nose and cheeks were red, indicating he'd had his fair share of celebratory wine.

"I'll get right to the point. Is something going on between you and Glen Kirby?"

Her mouth suddenly went dry, and she assumed he'd

witnessed her midnight lip-lock with Glen. "Who told you that?"

"Doesn't matter. Just answer the question, Becks."

"Glen is my friend, Walt. I like him. So what? Like everyone else, we danced at your wedding, and he kissed me at midnight. What's the big deal?"

"The big deal?" His voice held incredulousness. "Word has it you and Glen are sneaking around and doing more than just a wedding dance or experiencing a New Year's Eve kiss together."

Becky harrumphed. "Tell me who gave you this information, Walt. Clearly, they're blowing this way out of proportion."

"Like I said, it doesn't matter. Is it true? Are you sleeping with the enemy?"

Becky felt her cheeks explode with heat and took a step back. "Walt, this is not the time or the place to discuss my love life—"

"Then it is true. You're sleeping with him," he interrupted, his tone exploding.

Becky started to walk past her broody brother, her mouth clenched with fury. But he grabbed her by the elbow and pulled her to a stop. Their eyes met, something confusing and cautionary passing between them. Had Elyse spilled the beans? No. Knowing how Walt might react, she wouldn't have done that, especially on their wedding day. Then who did?

How dare someone in the ballroom say something to her brother, knowing he'd get riled up. This was why she didn't want anyone to know about her and Glen until after the family celebration. This was the reason she needed to keep their relationship a secret. And wasn't Walt the one who invited Glen in the first place?

"My God, Becky. You know what went down with Glen and Teddy and me. You were there for all of it. Have you already forgotten? All the fucking tragic history our families share? Trust me. You don't want to get involved with Glen. He's not the right man for you."

"And how do you know, huh, Walt?" She planted her hands on her hips in defiance. "How come you can work with him and act like y'all are buddies like old times? And furthermore, how come you invited him to your wedding if you hate him so much?"

"I don't hate him."

"You want to know what I think? I think you haven't truly forgiven him. You say you have, but by how you're reacting to something bogus someone told you, I can tell you haven't. And for the record, I can do whatever the hell I want when it comes to Glen."

"There it is. I knew it. You're sleeping with him."

Becky gruffly crossed her arms in front of her chest. "Sorry to disappoint you, dear brother. But I'm not sleeping with him. I'm afraid you've been misinformed." She tilted her head into the air with confidence. "And besides, it's none of your business who I date or sleep with. I'm a grown-ass woman, and I don't need you or anyone else in this family telling me what I can and can't do."

Walt's expression turned crestfallen, and he tried to back-peddle. "Becks, I only have your best interests at heart. You know that. But believe me, Glen Kirby is not one of them."

The sound of a male voice clearing his throat interrupted their standoff.

"Is everything alright?" Glen came from around the corner, his stormy eyes wide with apprehension. But there was something else in his cautious approach. It was the way he stood beside her in a protective stance, the heat from his body instant.

"Speak of the devil." Walt glared at Glen, his hands fisting at his sides. "Are you sleeping with my sister?" he spat.

"*Walter!*" Becky admonished.

Glen remained calm and aloof, his focus on Walt never wavering. "No. Although, she is right. It's none of your business."

"Fuck you, Glen. How dare you go after Becky after everything you've put my family through?"

"Walt, you don't know what you're saying. Glen has been nothing but respectful toward me. I promise." She boldly stood in between the two men. "Why are you doing this? You should be on the dance floor celebrating with your new wife!" She trembled, fearing her tipsy brother might throw a punch in his agitated state.

"I'm doing this because I love you, Becks, and I don't want to see anyone else in our family get hurt by this guy." His eyes narrowed as he stared Glen down.

"I'm sorry you feel this way," Glen said. "I consider you my best friend, Walt. You saved my life. You're like a brother to me. Always have been. And I'm honored you allowed me back into your life and for inviting me to your beautiful wedding tonight." His chest rose in a deep intake of air. "You were the one who once told me if I 'take the bull by the horns' and do all the hard work to overcome my addiction and anger, I'd become a man of humility and my life would take on new meaning. I did it, Walt, and it worked. And along the way, I admit, I've developed feelings for your sister."

Becky tensed, and Walt growled.

"Dude, it can't happen," Walt seethed between gritted

teeth. "It will never work, and you know it. I'm sorry, but I can't have you dating my little sister. Period. Not after everything that's happened between us." Walt held his hand out toward Becky. "Come on, Becks. Let's get back to the reception."

Becky shifted her gaze between the two men, torn at what she should do next. She was astounded when Glen offered his hand too.

"Are you ready to go, Becky?"

The tension in the small hallway was thick, the thumping rhythm of the music matching the pace of her quickening heart rate. She had two choices: go with her brother and keep the peace within the family, or follow her heart and experience a passionate week with Glen, away from the painful memories of their past.

Without hesitation, she slid her hand into Glen's and squeezed.

"I'm sorry, Walt. I love you. I do." Tears welled in her eyes. "But I have to follow my heart on this one, just like you did with Elyse." She pulled Glen by the hand, anxious for a quick getaway before all hell broke loose.

"*You're being reckless, Becky. You'll see!*" Walt hollered after them.

Chapter Twenty-Nine

GLEN

The view from the little cottage Becky rented for the week was breathtaking, the stunning sights of the water and shoreline rendering Glen speechless. He'd never been to the beach before; the ocean was something he'd only seen in pictures or in the movies.

He stood on the weathered top stair of the back deck and stared beyond the natural bulging sand dunes in awe of the vast ocean stretched out to eternity. He felt small in comparison, his sense of wonder close to overwhelming.

The salty, January wind whipped at his hair as the loud roar of the Atlantic Ocean coming ashore in crashing waves seemed to applaud his arrival. He shifted in his jacket against the noon-day chill and watched the seagulls walk along the frothy shoreline, leaving tiny trails of y-shaped footprints in the sand. Growing up, he never understood why everyone made such a fuss about vacationing at the beach. But now, he understood. Between the salty air and sand and the sky kissing the dark, pulsating water of the ocean, the seashore was a magical place.

But his mood was overcast, much like the sky, and the steady sounds of water and wind lulled him into a sleep-deprived state. He was exhausted from the emotional climax of Walt's wedding and the eight-hour drive from Atlanta, the lack of sleep blurring the edges of everything into a hazy vignette of colors. His fingers twitched, and he had an overwhelming urge to scoop up large handfuls of sand and watch the grains slip through his fingers. His life was in free fall since his brother's passing, everything he touched tainted with his guilt. There was a hole in his heart as deep as the ocean water reflecting in his sad eyes.

But he held hope there was a remedy to his heartache. Today was a new day in the new year, and it was finally time to turn the page. It was time for him to come clean and tell Becky the truth.

The walkway boards leading to the beach were gray and weathered from the elements. Glen stepped onto the sand and lingered momentarily on the grainy path. The wind blew his hair, and he squinted, looking up into the sky dotted with storm clouds. His chest rose as he inhaled the seaweed scent of water, the sound of the waves thunderous in his ears.

Slowly walking along the shoreline, he marveled at the ocean and stood at the surf's edge, careful to stay back from the frigid froth potentially soaking his boots. With his hands on his hips, he lifted his head toward the sky and shut his eyes.

"I'm sorry," he whispered into the sea breeze, his voice cracking with pent-up emotion, hoping his brother could hear him wherever he might be. His jaw clenched, and more tears leaked from the corners of his tightly shut eyes into his beard. "I'm sorry for what I did. But I'm going to make it right somehow. I promise."

Glen opened his eyes and squatted near the water's edge, palming the sand with trembling hands. It was gritty, wet, and cold to his touch. Scanning the horizon, he could make out a boat in the distance headed north past the pier. There was no one else on the beach, the open stretch of sand in front of the cottage deserted except for Glen. But he wasn't alone. He could feel Joe's presence as if he were standing right next to him on the shore.

A tiny ember of hope ignited in his core, knowing deep down his brother had always been for him and not against him. He knew if Joe were alive today, he'd tell him to get over himself and move on.

Glen sighed and gripped the back of his neck in exhaustion before he trudged back toward the beach cottage along the wooden walkway. The saw grass swayed back and forth in the breeze as the residence came into view. He paused and took in the sight of the humble abode, knowing Becky was inside sound asleep.

They'd arrived in the morning, sleep-deprived and woozy from the wedding and traveling and fell into the king-sized bed with nothing but sleep on their minds. But sleep evaded Glen, and he ended up staring at Becky up close as she lay beside him in a deep slumber with shadows and light highlighting her face.

For her to choose him was a gift he wasn't taking for granted. He had no ulterior motive when it came to Becky. She was his crush in his youth, the chances of ever being this close to her as an adult, like finding a pirate's treasure chest hidden in the deep blue waters of the ocean. From the first moment they kissed, his lips burned, and surges of pleasure so intense ripped through him. They were like two stars exploding in the heavens, bright bursts of light and heat burning through the atmosphere.

And now he had her all to himself. He was more than ready to explore every curve of her delectable body and claim his forbidden love once and for all. But he wouldn't, he *couldn't* move forward with his romantic intentions until he came clean and purged the deep, dark secret he'd kept guarded in his heart since the night of his brother's tragic death.

Glen could've told her the truth during the eight-hour drive through the middle of the night, but he needed to concentrate while he drove on the dark interstate alongside all the big rigs. He decided he'd have a sit-down heart-to-heart with her after they rested and tell her everything— even if it meant he might lose her altogether.

He owed her that much. He owed it to her family. He owed it to Joe.

Sliding the back door shut, Glen shrugged off his jacket and hung it over a chair in the small kitchen. He was surprised when Becky shuffled out of the bedroom, hair mussed, and a crease embedded along her supple cheek from where her head had been pressed against the pillow.

"Good morning," she uttered. "Or should I say, good afternoon?"

Glen moved toward her instantly, wrapping his arms around her and hugging her close. He breathed in her scent and pressed his lips against her ear, whispering, "Good afternoon, Daisy Girl."

"Mmmm," she moaned lazily. "You smell like the ocean."

Cupping her face with his hands, he kissed her long and hard, his heart racing with lust, desire, gratitude, and awareness. Between the sounds of the ocean filtering in through the window seams and the pleasant hum of her mouth molded against his, he wanted to bottle up this moment and savor it forever.

Glen knew what he wanted. He wanted Becky Bennett. But the only way to have her completely was to come clean with his wicked past.

Tracing the swell of her cheek with his thumb, their eyes locked. Blood roared in his ears as he mustered the strength to finally tell her.

"I need to talk to you—" his voice faltered, his throat closing around the words.

"Okay. You want me to make some coffee first?" Beneath the warmth of her brown eyes, he glimpsed a spark of something that sent a tiny curl of trust through his stomach.

"No." He took her by the hand and guided her to the sofa. The view of the beach and the expansive ocean beckoned him to chicken out, jump in, and drown in his sorrows.

Becky sat next to him, the grip of her fingers in his intensifying. "What's wrong?"

This was it—this was the moment he'd always feared finally coming to fruition. There was no turning back.

Glen cleared his throat and turned to face her. "There's something I need to tell you. Something I've never told anyone before, not even my own mother. It happened on the night Joe died."

Becky's brow furrowed. "Go on."

Glen nodded. "I knew Teddy and Robyn were going to be at the college bonfire party. Joe mentioned it to me at home the day before because he'd sold a bunch of beer and wine coolers to some of the college kids." He let go of her hand and stood, pacing in front of Becky with rattled nerves.

"Being a stupid underage high school kid, I thought it'd be fun to crash the party—"

"You were there?" Becky interrupted, her eyes holding confusion.

"Briefly."

"How come Teddy and Robyn never told me this?"

Glen inhaled a deep breath and licked his lips. His voice was barely a whisper. "Because Teddy and Robyn didn't know I was there."

"I don't understand. You were at the party, and they didn't see you?"

Glen couldn't look at her anymore, her beauty and innocence slicing through him like a hot knife. The pain consumed him as he finally let go and purged his secret, his words coming out quickly.

"I snuck into the party, Becky. I parked my truck down the road and climbed over the fence. No one saw me. No one knew I was there. I wanted to swipe a few free beers and call it a night. But I got greedy when I saw the stash of booze in someone's pickup truck with the liftgate open. The music was thumping, and college grads danced around the huge fire. No one noticed me when I grabbed two cases of beer off the truck's back end. I was quick and ran through the field to escape in my vehicle unseen."

Glen paused and pressed the heel of his hand against his forehead. With his eyes closed a strangled cry erupted from his mouth.

"It's my fault they ran out of beer that night. If I hadn't taken those two cases, Teddy, Robyn, Max, and Ethan wouldn't have gone to the quickie mart where Joe was working to get more. Max and Ethan wouldn't have put on those ski masks to prank my brother, and Max wouldn't have pulled the trigger on the gun he didn't know was loaded."

Visions of Joe being shot moved through his mind on autopilot, the horrific, relentless reel torturing him with unfathomable regret. One bullet to the face killed his brother instantly.

"I thought I was cool and clever scoring those two cases of beer. I sat in the storage shed and got shit-faced, passing out and scaring my ma when she couldn't find me the next morning—when she had to tell me my brother was *dead*."

Glen sobbed, the memories hitting him like a ricochet of machine gun bullets, the pain breaking him in two.

"Oh, God. I can't tell you how many times I've wanted to tell you, Teddy, and Walt. I even thought about coming clean with the judge who sentenced Ted. But I was a fucking coward. I had to find a way to change the narrative in my mind, so I... I wouldn't go crazy and kill myself. That's why I blamed your brother and everyone else. I tried to convince myself it *wasn't* my fault. But deep down, I knew it was all along. I'm the one who should've been sentenced. *I'm* the one to blame. I'm the one who killed my brother."

His shoulders shook with grief and guilt, his tears fueled by shame and a broken heart.

"Give me a minute, Glen," Becky whispered. She stood on wobbly legs and disappeared into the hall bathroom. A moment later, he could hear her crying from behind the closed door.

Collapsing on the sofa, Glen's head swam with his admission. He leaned his head back and listened to the pounding of the surf outside compete with the roar of his heart in his ears. His fists clenched, and he pummeled a nearby throw pillow with his hand and sobbed. He cried just as hard when he was told his brother was dead. Unlike the tears he shed then, these were fueled by the possibility he might have blown whatever chance he had with Becky. His heart was utterly broken, and he had no more anger or regrets to tamper with what he'd done.

He heard Becky's footfalls cross the wooden floors and felt her hands press against his cheeks, holding his head steady. He steeled himself to face her, blurry eyes flicking to hers. Up close, her beautiful image was warped in a stain of watery colors from behind a veil of tears.

"I'm so sorry," he wept uncontrollably.

"Oh, Glen," she cried. The sadness in her voice wrecked him. "I'm sorry you've been carrying this secret and punishing yourself all these years. It's not your fault."

"But it is," he choked.

"You are not to blame."

"Yes, I am."

"It was a tragic accident. It's *not* your fault."

Glen didn't reply and sucked in shaky breaths of air, her words pricking his mind with the faintest hope. He desperately wanted to believe what she was saying and move on from his misery. If she didn't blame him, perhaps the entire Bennett family wouldn't either. Could he dare to believe he'd finally turned the page? Could he finally move on and live his life free from this unbearable burden?

She sat next to him and hugged him close. He buried his face in the crevice of her neck as they both sobbed together.

"It's not your fault."

Chapter Thirty

BECKY

The clouds were dense and dark over the ocean. Undaunted, Becky wanted to squeeze in a walk along the shoreline before the nasty weather hit. She wanted to give Glen time to calm down after his confession, his feelings raw and tender. The wind whipped at her hair, and she squeezed his hand, heartbroken and ruminating about what he'd told her. Her sadness felt heavy, knowing how much Glen had suffered all these years. And he'd gone through it entirely alone. Everything made sense now—his anger, the drugs, and his thoughts of suicide.

Glen had been lost, like a ship at sea, and moving forward, Becky wanted to remind him everything would be okay. She wanted to reassure him his life mattered and that he meant something to her.

As the pregnant clouds loomed low, ready to burst at any moment with a cold drenching rain renewing the shoreline, she found herself prompted to silently pray. She asked for God's presence to hang low in Glen's life like those clouds, to burst open so the floodgate of heaven could dispense every blessing and promise and wipe away every guilt-stained tear.

Suddenly, the immediate gush of a full downpour descended from the sky.

No tentative sprinkles were preparing for the thunderstorm. Just, all at once, the sky opened up. Instinctively, she grasped Glen's hand, and they tore across the beach toward the cottage, dashing for the warmth of dry shelter. Her heart raced, and Glen slowed to a stop on the weathered boards of the deck, even though the rain continued pelting them with its noisy hammering.

He let go, stood tall beneath the pouring heavens, and opened his arms wide. Becky watched in awe as he turned his face upward into the falling raindrops. A beaming smile spread across his bearded features. It was as if he completely surrendered himself, allowing the cleansing water to wash away his pain right before her.

Blinking against the deluge of frigid water, she panted, aware of a delicious curl of warmth spreading low through her stomach. Glen's stormy eyes held hers, his hot breath making a cloud in front of his face. He lowered his hands to his sides and blinked back at her, the two of them very much aware of the rumble of thunder and desire surrounding them.

Becky had been so close to making love to Glen when they'd first arrived in Sandersville Beach. It was nice seeing him relax after the long travel night, his face lighting up at the sight of her when she came out of the bathroom dressed in her nightgown. They lay comfortably in the king-size bed, his large body giving off heat next to hers. Eyelids heavy with sleepiness and lust. It was nice being pressed against him, his breath a gentle rush of air against her ear, whispering goodnight. The way his palm covered the entire expanse of her thigh, thick fingers squeezing and causing goose bumps to erupt across her flesh.

She'd felt a magnetic pull toward Glen since the day she dropped off a homemade apple pie as a peace offering. But it was intense now. Deeper. More vulnerable. Honest. She loved being with him and seeing bits of his true self unfolding right in front of her. But they'd fallen asleep, their night of pleasure paused. And now? Now she was more than ready to take things to the next level.

Reaching for him through the pounding rain, his wet fingers surrounded hers, and he pulled her flush against his soaked chest. Gazing into his eyes, she saw history. He gave her a knowing look, a half-smile curled across his lips. There were no more secrets hidden there beneath his beard. The brawny man stood raw and exposed, beckoning her to let go of the past and fall into his strong arms. He licked his bottom lip, eyes mapping her face and messy wet hair hanging over her shoulders. She shivered with want, the cold rain seeping through her clothes.

"I'm a drowned rat," she giggled.

His smile tipped up into something beautiful, and he used his index finger to gently move a wayward strand of wet hair behind her ear. She inhaled deeply and held onto the moment, her heart beating faster and faster. A low rumble of thunder rattled the windows, and she knew with the truth out in the open, cleansed by the rain, she would never look at him in the same way again. Something had shifted between them, and she waited, listening for a moment longer before he melded his lips with hers. His hands combed through the sides of her hair with tenderness, holding her head steady as she blossomed like a daisy in the hot mountain sun of Georgia, the manifestation complete.

"I need to get you out of these wet clothes before you catch a cold." His voice was deep with arousal.

"Yes," she whispered against his fevered lips, aching for more.

He opened the sliding glass door of the cottage and guided her over the threshold, holding her hand. Once inside, they shrugged off their dripping coats. Hugging herself with arms crossed against her chest, she watched him. Glen's back was to her, his flannel shirt stretched across his broad shoulders as he hung their coats over the kitchen chairs to dry.

"I want you, Glen," Becky said in a rush of words.

He jerked his head to look at her, his eyes dark and wild.

Some secret part of her opened up, unraveling and unspooling in the tiny kitchen by the sea. She'd been thinking about Glen this way since their first kiss on the wrap-around porch of her childhood home. And now, she didn't know whether it was because they were alone and away from her overprotective family or if it was the freedom she had by completely ignoring her social media channels for the last few weeks. Maybe it was being secluded in the romantic beachside cottage with the burly man or his complete honesty in telling her the truth. Whatever it was, she was eager to take their relationship to the next level.

Glen Kirby pushed at her seams—his sexy-as-sin stare, the smell of rain on his hot skin, his sweet lips in a passionate kiss, and the anticipation of feeling him deep inside her. She was coming undone and thought her heart might burst.

Offering her his hand, he didn't say anything and led her to the primary bedroom in the back of the house. The sound of rain drummed on the metal roof. Soothing. Sexy. The sound was punctuated by the occasional rumble of thunder. With the door closed, he cupped her cheeks and kissed her again, long and hard and deep, his tongue sweeping between her lips. Glen backed her up against the door and caged her in with his muscular arms, devouring her mouth and lighting up every nerve ending in her body. Becky reached between them and slid her hand over his bulging jeans, desperate for skin on skin.

"God, I want you, Glen," she whispered urgently. "I want you so bad."

They abruptly stopped kissing, and he stepped back, silently studying her for a moment.

"What?" she asked.

Her lips tingled with pleasure, and her insides burned. She was sure her panties were soaked with more than rainwater. Tilting her head, she demurely batted her lashes at him, feeling self-conscience from beneath his bold, stealthy stare.

"You don't want to make love to me?" she asked.

Glen ran his tongue across his lower lip and nodded. "Of course, I want to make love to you, Becky. I've wanted to for a long time."

"Then what are you waiting for?" She lifted her thick sweater over her head, tossing it onto a nearby chair. Standing in front of him with her ample chest rising and falling in deep breaths beneath her lacy bra, she reached around her back and unhooked the garment. She caught his expression as he watched it fall into her hands.

"Do you like what you see?" she whispered.

Glen's eyes were dark, his usual blue irises eclipsed by his dilated pupils fixated on her chest.

"Of course, I like what I see. You're a dream."

"Then touch me, Glen."

The strong column of his throat moved in a heavy

swallow as he took a tentative step toward her. His hands covered her fleshy mounds, and he squeezed while exhaling a long, slow breath.

"You're so beautiful."

"Take off your shirt. I want to feel your skin pressed against mine." Part of her wanted to draw things out, but the other part felt like if she didn't hurry things along, he might disappear before her eyes, their forbidden desire kept shrouded in darkness.

Glen didn't bother to unbutton his shirt in his haste. Instead, he ripped the flannel open, buttons flying and scattering across the hardwood floors. He was quick with his undershirt, peeling the fabric over his head, revealing his solid chest smattered with hair. He moved forward and pressed his bare skin to hers, dragging the tips of his fingers across her cheek.

"Better?" he uttered.

"Maybe."

She was flirting with him, giving him the go-ahead to strip down to nothing. Heat flared in his eyes when he understood. She watched with bated breath as he shucked off his boots and unbuckled his belt, letting his jeans drop to the floor around his ankles. Glancing at the bulge in his boxers, heat flooded her core. She crossed her arms against her chest and tapped her foot. This induced a low chuckle from Glen. He smirked and lifted the edges of his waistband, peeling his underwear off slowly, intentionally. He stood naked before her.

Becky gaped at his size, aroused by the sight of this magnificent, naked man. He was a beast, his muscles evident from his strong biceps to his thick thighs and substantial cock.

He mocked her, mimicking her stance and crossing his

arms against his chest. She braced herself against the door and pulled off her shoes, aware of him watching her every move. Her breasts hung heavy, and as she unzipped her jeans and lowered them down her legs, she heard him exhale a slow and steady breath.

"Damn, Daisy Girl. You're the most beautiful woman I've ever laid eyes on."

She stood before him with nothing but a thin veil of lace between them. He palmed the tiny pink bow at the center of her panties, making her gasp.

Leaning low, he whispered in her ear, "Lay on the bed."

Becky nodded and edged herself onto the mattress. Glen lay beside her, his fingers dangerously close to her soaked nub as he rubbed her bare thigh. Peeling her last layer off, the scent of desire permeated the air.

Their mouths hovered inches apart, breath hot, and hearts pounding like the rain against the windows. Straddling her waist, he leaned lower and pressed his hands on either side of her head, his face hovering over hers. The heat emanating off his skin was soothing.

"What do you want?" he asked.

"I want you, Glen. All of you."

Delicious heat unfurled between her legs as she opened up for him. With deft fingers, he stroked her center, and she shuddered with desire. She yelped at the first sweep of his tongue, her body writhing euphorically beneath him. He was priming her pump and wouldn't let up, her first orgasm quick and ripping through her in a flash.

Glen was pleased and reached over her to open the nightstand drawer where he'd placed more than just his wallet. A few seconds later, he knelt between her legs and rolled a condom on. She'd seen other guys awkwardly handle this move before, but that was right after high school when she dated a string of geeky, skinny guys. They were nothing like the man hovering over her now.

Glen was rugged and robust, mature and protective. Everything about him exuded masculinity and testosterone, from his bearded face and a smattering of hair on his broad chest to his solid body and rock-hard dick.

She took in a deep breath, filling her lungs with his scent. Forever, the smell of this man would live in her memory, packed away with the sweet aroma of apples and the verdant perfume of pine.

He teased her with his sheathed penis in his hand, and she whimpered. "Please, Glen."

He slid into her tight opening, his voice deep and coated with arousal. "Damn, you feel so good." He found a rhythm, pulling out slowly and thrusting back into her with easy strokes, his skin pressed against hers. A low, husky moan escaped his mouth, the sound sexy and forbidden.

She inhaled deeply, drunk on the heat of his skin and how he filled her. His masculine weight between her thighs. His hands gripping her ass like he owned her, vocal about how much he enjoyed touching her. Tasting her.

He would slow down, and she would beg him to speed up, needing him harder and deeper. He wasn't aggressive, but took it upon himself to understand her needs. She raked her nails across his back, gasping at how deep he plunged into her, wishing this moment would last. Wishing she could stop time altogether and stay wrapped up in his arms. Wishing they could stay holed up in the charming beach cottage forever.

Becky let go, unashamed and reckless in the way she wanted him. And he seemed to want her just as much, the growl of her nickname on his lips sending her higher and higher. She arched her back and begged him not to stop, rocking her hips until she spiraled out of control and careened off the ledge in a hot burst of light and colorful ecstasy. The surges of pleasure in the aftermath of their lovemaking were so intense, she felt like she was floating through space, every nerve ending filled with sensation.

Afterward, they lay beside each other, their arms and legs tangled atop the twisted sheets. They were hot and sweaty, heavy breaths inhaling and exhaling among the rumbles of thunder and pouring rain.

"I once told you that after we kissed, I wouldn't pursue anybody else for the rest of my life. And now that we've made love, I'm doubling down on my promise. I've completely fallen for you, Becky," Glen panted.

He shifted in the bed to face her. "I don't care about anything anymore except you and your happiness. Today was the most important day of my entire life. Thank you for listening to me and not judging me. Thank you for inviting me to come here with you." He ran his index finger across her swollen lips. "This feels like the right time to say it... I love you."

Becky's eyebrows shot up in surprise. "You love me?"

"Yes. I love you. I've wanted to tell you for a while. I've never said those words to anybody before... words that are rare and incredible, and saying them feels ecstatic, like a release." He threw his head back onto the pillow and laughed out loud. "Like a verbal orgasm."

She giggled in response and leaned her arm against his chest, resting her chin in her hand. "Say it again."

Their eyes locked, something honest and extraordinary passing between them. "I love you, Daisy Girl. Do you hear me? I love you. Only you."

"I'm glad," she replied. "Because... I love you too."

Chapter Thirty-One

BECKY

"Am I awake? Or am I dreaming?" Becky yawned.

Snuggled naked against Glen's hip, her eyelids felt heavy. The sound of the falling rain lulled her into a state of twilight sleep.

"You're awake," Glen chuckled. "Do you want me to turn on a light? It's kind of dark outside."

"No. Don't turn on the light. It's cozy here in bed with you. Mmmm," she hummed, blissfully happy and satiated from their afternoon delight. "I'm sorry about the forecast. I heard the beach was lovely this time of the year. Not too hot and not too cold. I didn't realize it was the rainy season."

"The rain makes it romantic being secluded indoors with you," he replied.

Smiling, she sighed in agreement. "Talk to me. Tell me something more about you."

"Something more? You know pretty much everything there is to know about me. The good, the bad, and the ugly."

"Tell me about…," she thought for a moment. "Tell me

about your nighttime routine at home. Do you watch television in bed? Does Garth sleep with you? Do you sleep with a nightlight or a sound machine on?"

Glen was quiet as if mulling over his response to her barrage of random questions. "I don't have a TV in my bedroom. And I don't have any kind of sound machine. And I hate to admit it, but Garth does sleep with me at night. He curls up by my head or at the end of the bed near my feet."

"Aw, that's so sweet."

"And most nights, I fall asleep with the lights on."

"Do you eventually get up and turn them off?"

"No, I don't."

"Why not?"

"Well, at first, I thought it was because I'm naturally lazy, especially when I'm dog-tired. It's hard getting up from my bed after a long day of manual labor."

"Makes sense you'd be too tired to get up after you're already comfortable."

Glen nodded. "But the more it happened, I began to realize it was something else. I leave the lights on because… Since Joe died, I get into my head when I'm alone in the dark. My room changes shape and fills with shadows, and I literally trip over the mess of my life."

Becky turned rigid next to him, his confession heartfelt and sad. "I'm sorry."

"Don't be sorry. Things have changed since you entered the picture."

"So, moving forward, do you think you can sleep with the lights off?"

"I think so. Can I tell you why?"

"Tell me."

"Because *you* are the light in my darkness."

She hummed against him. "Your words are beautiful. You're a poet."

"And I didn't even know it," he rhymed.

She smiled against his skin, drunk on love and lack of sleep. She was thankful they were talking about their lives, grateful she'd found someone. With Glen by her side, she knew she'd never be lonely again.

"Glen?"

"Hmmm?" he mumbled, drawing lazy circles up and down her arm.

"I'm at a point in my life where I'm not searching for crazy love anymore." She made air quotes with her fingers. "I want… quiet love. Patient love. Happy love. I want to be understood in love."

"But you have love, Becky. You have it with me, and your entire family adores you."

"I know. But it's not the same. What I have with them is… lonely love."

"I don't understand."

"Let me explain. My mom was my best friend in the entire world, and when we lost her, it was a hard adjustment being the only female in the family. I didn't have a mother figure I could depend on. I mean, sure, I have a few female friends whom I adore. But the bottom line is, I've been incredibly lonely, Glen."

"I'm sorry, Daisy Girl. When do you feel lonely?"

"I think I'm lonely the most at night, like you. Especially at dusk, when the world looks a little too soft around the edges. When I'm not sure if I'm still awake or I'm dreaming. And then I wake up hugging a pillow that feels like a human, so I start my days a bit sadder than I would've hoped."

"I can totally relate."

"I knew you would. The other day, I was in town at the coffee shop scrolling through recipes for my upcoming cookbook when a couple walked in, arm in arm. I observed them, and do you know what the guy did?"

"What?"

"He ordered coffee for her. He had her order *memorized*. I know it sounds silly, but I was floored. It was weird because, at that moment, my loneliness consumed me. I wanted what they had. I want a man who's memorized my coffee order." She sighed, thankful for his undivided attention while listening to her story. "And by the way, I prefer chai tea, not coffee."

"I'm taking notes," Glen whispered with reassurance.

"I find myself lonely at dinner time back at the farm, even though I'm cooking for an army of men in my family. Most of the conversations are about farming or upcoming wedding showers and plans for my brothers, which is fine. Honestly, I've been lonely for such a long time it's become part of my normal everyday routine. Before I met you, I was devastated at the idea of not having someone who adores me. Someone special, like my brothers all have, to call my own. I have so much of myself to pour into someone. I've waited for love a long time."

"Patient love," Glen reminded her.

"Yes. Patient love."

She sat up and tugged on the sheet to cover her breasts. "I know you shouldn't depend on one person to be your only source of happiness. But the absence of someone special in my life has been the entire reason for my *unhappiness*. Am I making any sense?"

"Perfect sense, Daisy Girl."

The look of love emanating from his handsome gaze

was everything she'd ever hoped for. Smiling, she lay back down against his side and closed her eyes.

"And then you came along, Glen. And just like that, I'm not lonely anymore."

———

Sandersville Beach was a hidden gem nestled on the east coast and nicknamed Florida's "Little Village by the Sea." After a few precious hours of sleep, Becky and Glen ventured out into the tiny beach town in search of a hearty meal. A place called The Shack was right around the corner and offered the best and cheapest breakfast and lunch in the area. Unfortunately, the place closed at two o'clock sharp, leaving them hungry and disappointed in the pouring rain.

Driving through the arts district known as Pineapple Grove with windshield wipers thumping against the front windshield, Becky sat in the passenger seat and eyed several art and photo galleries along Main Street. She mentally took notes on which ones she might want to visit after they'd found a place to eat. She also spotted a small town bakery aptly named Daisy Cakes. She took it as a sign from the heavens she was meant to be here in the sleepy little beach town and couldn't help the immediate smile unfurling from her lips. They'd have to visit the bakery for sure.

The Brew Dog Pub was their best option during the rainy weekday afternoon. Glen hoisted the large door open, and Becky was thrilled by the interior. While researching rental places for her much-needed vacation, she learned Sandersville Beach was a town known as an artist's Mecca, with many businesses decorated with local creatives' wares. Looping her arm through Glen's, they moseyed to an empty corner booth in the back of the restaurant and sat at a sturdy table. The seats reminded her of old church pews, the hard bench made more comfortable with well-worn cushions in deep shades of red. Sliding opposite each other, she shrugged off her coat and eagerly peered at the menu.

"I'm starving," she proclaimed.

"Me too."

After a waitress with colorful tattoos running up and down both arms took their order, Becky interlocked her fingers on the varnished tabletop and took in Glen's rugged good looks across from her. She was more than ready to continue their deep dive into each other's lives, especially after spending the afternoon vulnerably lying naked next to each other.

"You look beautiful tonight."

"Tonight?" She giggled. "It's only four o'clock, Glen."

"Well, it feels like night." He reached across the table and held her hand. "There's another night I remember you looked beautiful too. You were wearing a purple shirt, tight jeans, and cowboy boots. I was a senior in high school, and you were an incoming freshman. I was a freak, and you were going to be the prom queen."

"Stop. You were a baseball star right alongside my brother Walt."

"True. But I was still a rebel back then. I remember this particular night pretty vividly. A million stars were scattered across the night sky, and you smiled at me from across the flames of a bonfire. Your smile rivaled those stars. Do you remember?"

Becky furrowed her brow, wracking her brain to remember what night he was talking about. "I'm sorry, I don't."

"No worries. When you smiled at me, my hands immediately turned clammy, my heart raced, and I had butterflies in my stomach."

"Oh, no," she giggled. "Did I say anything to you?"

"No. You just smiled, and that's all it took. I swear that's the moment I fell in love with you."

"When I was a geeky freshman? And from one smile?" She was awestruck by his memory, his recollection sweet and romantic.

"Yup. One cute grin from my daisy girl, and I was a goner." He touched the dainty charm bracelet circling her wrist. "And here I am today with you as a twenty-eight-year-old man, and my heart's still racing, butterflies are assaulting my stomach, and I have clammy hands again. I guess what I'm trying to say is that some things never change. My heart's always had a special place for you, Becky Bennett. Having a front-row seat in your life, and growing up with you and your brothers has been a privilege. I'm very fortunate."

"I am too."

The waitress dropped off their sodas and a big basket of calamari. Becky's eyes lit up at the sight of the food, her last meal a measly granola bar before their walk on the beach when the rains came through.

Chewing, Glen dipped a second deep-fried tentacle into the ramekin of spicy mayonnaise. "What do you want?"

"I haven't decided yet. I think I'm going to go with a classic cheeseburger."

He chuckled and popped the calamari in his mouth. Wiping his lips with a paper napkin, he swallowed. "That's not what I meant."

"Oh?" She slurped a gulp of soda from her straw. "Then what did you mean?"

"What do you want out of life?"

Becky tilted her head and took in the colorful artwork for sale hanging from the paneled walls of the pub. Most of the scenes were beach-related, the swirling shades of greens and blues vibrant in the dark space. But one painting spoke to her; a watercolor rendition of a charming southern cottage surrounded by colorful flowers in all shapes and sizes.

She gave Glen her full attention and grinned. "I want a comfortable home to call my own someday."

"Describe it to me. Help me picture it."

"It's white with yellow shutters. And the kitchen overlooks a huge garden where I can wear floppy hats and overalls and grow all the pretty flowers and vegetables." Her face flushed with heat, the excitement in her voice unmistakable.

"Anything else?"

She sat up perfectly straight and nodded. "Yes. I want a back porch with two rocking chairs where we can sip iced tea in the summer and hot apple cider in the winter. A place where we can watch all the sunsets."

Glen studied her from across the table, the blue in his eyes matching some of the vibrant ocean paintings on the walls. He was relaxed and, dare she say, completely happy for the first time in a long time. And she knew it was all because of their time spent together.

"Okay." His voice rumbled with pleasure.

"You promise?" She gave him the side-eye, her tone teasing. She liked making plans with Glen. She liked knowing she'd found her person.

"Mhmm. I promise. I'd like to spend the rest of my sunsets with you, Daisy Girl."

Chapter Thirty-Two

GLEN

The week-long downpour carved out rivers in the sand, the beach littered with random bits of nature washing ashore in the churning waves. The sky remained gray without a trace of sunlight, but Becky's face shone bright like a lighthouse through the storm.

Glen's mind played back the entire week repeatedly on the long drive home. He could taste the salty sea on her lips and still hear the residual roar of the tide in his ears. Their last morning snuck in through the window, and they laid there for hours, listening to the surf come and go, holding each other tight. He lived those seven days a million times in his mind. They were the best seven days of his life.

"Are you nervous seeing your family again?" He glanced at Becky, who sat in the passenger seat, her face unreadable as she stared out the window.

"I'm not nervous. I'm annoyed."

"Annoyed? Why?" He was curious.

She shifted uncomfortably, her pretty brow furrowed as she leaned her head back against the seat rest.

"My daddy's texted and left several voicemail messages over the week checking in on me. And each one of my brothers has texted too."

"Let me guess. They're worried about you being alone with me, am I right?"

Becky huffed. "I replied and told them to mind their own business. But you know they're not gonna let it go. At least Walt is still on his honeymoon, and I won't have to face him yet."

Glen swiped a hand down his whiskered chin. "Do you want me to talk to them?"

"No. I can handle it. But thank you." She smiled sweetly before turning her attention back to the dismal weather outside.

Becky dozed the last hour of the drive while Glen navigated the home stretch, and by the time the truck sped under the large Bennett Farms sign, and up the steep hill toward the farmhouse, the late Sunday was starting to fade beyond the mountainside. Taking in the substantial home, he noticed Mr. Bennett exit the front door with the big dogs flanking his sides. The man stood alone on the top step, hands planted on his hips, looking like a father waiting for the prodigal son, or in this case, the prodigal daughter. Glen felt like a teenager again, about to be scolded for having Becky out past curfew.

"Let me do all the talking," she said.

"Okay." He got out of the truck and hurriedly opened the door for her.

"Hey, Daddy," she greeted.

"Hey, darlin'. Welcome home."

Glen stayed busy gathering Becky's luggage from the truck. With his arms loaded, he watched her kiss her father on the cheek before they hugged. He kept his distance and waited dutifully for instructions.

"Come on in, Glen. You can set those bags in the foyer."

"Yes, sir." His heart blipped with hope. Maybe this wasn't so hard after all?

He followed Becky and her father inside and set the bags down. The dogs acted happy to see him, and he bided some time patting their heads.

"Can you give us a minute, son?" Mr. Bennett asked.

"Of course."

"Sit down and make yourself comfortable."

Glen watched the pair disappear down the hall, Becky flashing him a smile and mouthing the words, "Don't leave." Gripping the back of his neck, he paced in front of the fireplace hearth and could make out their voices in the background. He crept to the beginning of the hallway and listened, thankful the door was cracked open just enough to hear their conversation.

"We were all worried sick about you, sweetheart. I don't understand why you left the wedding the way you did. Why you left without saying goodbye? And why didn't you tell us the truth about what was happening between you and Glen? Walt's the one who told me. And when you didn't respond to my phone calls—"

"Daddy, I texted you back," Becky interrupted.

"I would have preferred to hear your voice."

"I would've preferred to have been left alone on my vacation. My God, you had every one of my brothers trying to get through to me. I worked hard for this vacation. I wanted to be left alone."

"Alone with Glen Kirby."

There was silence, and Glen strained to listen.

"I've known Glen and his family since he was born. But he's not the one for you, darlin'. Your brothers will all tell you the same thing. He's a nice boy, Becky. But he's—"

"He's what?"

"He's a sinkhole. I don't know how else to explain it. He's gonna pull you under, and you're gonna end up heart-broken or pregnant."

"*Daddy!*" she admonished, her voice rising.

Glen took a step back, his heart plummeting to his feet. This is how Roy Bennett really felt about him?

"We all think it's best if you don't see him romantically anymore," Roy stated with finality.

"Oh, so I'm supposed to follow orders from you and the boys? Is that what you're saying? I'm not eighteen anymore. I'm a grown-ass woman."

"Becky, darlin', you're a young, vibrant woman with her whole life ahead. Stringing along Glen Kirby is only going to weigh you down."

"You are not in charge of telling me who I can and cannot love."

Glen froze, the word "love" out in the open. Pressing his lips together, he held his breath.

"Love?" Roy questioned.

"Yes, Daddy. I love him."

Roy exhaled an exasperated sign. "Darlin', you don't know the first thing about love."

"Oh? And you're the expert? Mama left you behind on the farm to go to art school. She was following her dreams. And then y'all had to get married because you pulled her into your sinkhole and knocked her up with Teddy, and she never got to live out those dreams." A sob escaped her mouth as if realizing her hurtful, angry words.

"I'm sorry, Daddy. I didn't mean it. I know you and Mama loved each other until the very end. I do. But now, I'm following my heart and doing what makes me happy for a change. Isn't that what any parent wants for their daughter?"

"Of course. But his violent history? He will destroy you—"

"Stop it," she interrupted.

Glen leaned in, straining to hear.

"Daddy, listen to me. I met somebody, okay? He's got gorgeous blue eyes. He opens doors for me. He goes to church on Sundays. He likes vintage cars and trucks. He loves his mama, and it's true he went through a hard time. But he's not bitter; he's *better*. And you know what? I'm the one who pursued him in the first place. But he held back, wanting y'all's blessing before we took things any further. He's respectful, and he's got a kind heart, and he would never, *ever* lay a hand on me. Because if he did, he knows every one of you would rip him to shreds. He's not after my money, the farm, or anything else. The only thing he's after is my heart. And Daddy... I've already given it to him."

Glen shook his head, tears pricking the corners of his eyes, bewildered by her heartfelt speech. He'd eavesdropped enough and decided to give Becky and Roy some space before things got even more heated or they roped him into the conversation. This was between Becky and her father.

Quickly, he scurried to the front door and slipped outside. He was halfway to his truck when he heard Becky call after him.

"*Glen*! Wait!"

Turning around, he watched her run toward him with her arms open wide. Tears streamed down her beautiful face, and on instinct, he opened his arms, and they collided in a hug.

"My family isn't too happy with us."

He closed his eyes in defeat and squeezed her body tight, his voice a rough whisper against her ear. "What are you going to do, Daisy Girl?"

"I don't know."

Glen held her at arm's length searching her face for answers. "What about this past week at the beach. You told me you love me."

"I know. And I do. And it was wonderful sharing my vacation with you." She paused, averting his intense stare. "But maybe you were right. Maybe... maybe we should've waited, especially with our family history. Maybe we need to let more time go by so everyone can calm down."

Glen fumed. "It's about the money, isn't it? They're worried I'm after your money. Am I right? So I can buy back my farm? Spend it all? Have my claws in the only Bennett female as revenge for what happened to my brother?"

"No, Glen. You've got it all wrong," she cried.

The front door opened, and Roy Bennett came onto the front porch and eyed them with unease. Glen lowered his voice and pinned Becky with his stare.

"Will you just love me for who I am right now? It was real easy when we were alone at the beach, away from the entire Bennett jury."

Becky pursed her lips, her dark eyes muddled with confused emotion.

"It's not gonna be easy to get all of them on our side. In fact, it's gonna be tough. But I'm willing to work at this every day because I love you. Only you. I've loved you for a lifetime, before all the pain and suffering. And here's the best part. Now that we've gotten through all that, I know we can get through anything."

Becky lowered her face and stared at the ground, tears sluicing down her cheeks. With tenderness, Glen tipped her face upward with his fingers to where she had to look right at him.

"Will you do something for me right now? Please?"

"What?"

"Put the past on a shelf and imagine your life a month from now. Hell, *fifty years* from now. Do you see me in it? Are we sitting on the back porch of our white house with the yellow shutters watching the sunset? Because if you can't picture it, you shouldn't fall in love with someone like me. You know why?"

"Why?" she sobbed.

"Because I'm the guy who will give you your heart's desire. I'll work my fingers to the bone to make it happen. I'll kiss you when you're wearing your floppy hats out in the sunshine in your flower garden. I'll drive you into town and place your order for chai tea. I'll win you every single goddamn unicorn at the Halloween festival until the day you die. I will *patiently* love on you, and I will make sure you are never *ever* lonely another day in your life again." He pulled her flush against his chest and palmed the back of her silky hair as she wept in his arms.

Roy disappeared inside the house, giving them space.

Glen pressed his hands against Becky's cheeks and held her face.

"Your dad's right—I *will* destroy you in the most beautiful way possible. And if you decide you want me to leave, then *you* will have to tell me, not them. But be warned, I won't make it easy for you because I'm a crazy man in love," he chuckled. This induced a meek smile from Becky's lips.

"I love you, Becky. I do." He placed a chaste kiss on her forehead, his last words to her a warning.

"But if you do ask me to leave, I won't go quietly. And you'll finally understand why most storms are named after people."

Chapter Thirty-Three

BECKY

Becky filled a pot of water at the sink and stared out the kitchen window at the big red barn among the grayness of the winter day. Vivid memories of her and Glen's beach getaway were at the forefront of her mind; every touch, every smile, every moment, a kaleidoscope of color and warmth and love.

She hadn't seen him in almost a week, both agreeing to keep things on the down low until they could have an adult conversation with her entire family after Walt and Elyse returned from their honeymoon. That was three days ago.

Time was like the tide back at the romantic beach cottage, coming and going like clockwork, her mind rewinding each day spent together away from her concerned family—away from the reality of her judgmental brother, Walt.

Speak of the devil.

While surveying the farm property out the window, she watched Walt and Teddy amble out of the barn. They wore thick winter coats and smiled from underneath their cowboy hats. Immediately, she was annoyed, knowing they had their wives waiting for them at home. They didn't have to convince anyone in the family who they wanted to spend their lives with, so why did she?

The water in the pot overflowed, soaking her hands. Startled, Becky turned off the faucet and wiped her hands on a nearby tea towel.

"Becky?"

Inhaling a sharp breath, she turned to see Glen standing near the kitchen island. He held his hat in his hands, his manly presence invading the room like a thick perfume.

"Glen? What are you doing here?"

The strong column of his throat moved in a swallow. "Walt texted. Said we had some wine business to take care of before the spring launch."

"Oh." She moved slowly opposite him on the other side of the island, hands gripping the cool marble ledge.

"I've missed you, Daisy Girl."

Becky's heart ached, and she blinked back at him, memorizing every angle of his face. The way his hair was slightly matted from wearing his hat. His intense eyes the color of a rhinestone sky, full of hope and longing.

"I've missed you too."

"Walt's gonna have questions. Maybe it'd be a good idea if you came with me to get this conversation over with." He moved around the corner of the island and stood next to her, the wish in his low voice noticeable. "I want to be with you, Becky. Only you."

Heat flooded her core being in such close proximity to the man she claimed she loved. But did she really love him? Or was what they had nothing more than a romantic tryst. A dangerous liaison. A reckless affair. If she truly loved him, why hadn't she fought for him?

"I'm strong enough to be your man…," he admitted softly. "… if you'll let me."

His words ripped her apart. He was ready, willing, and able to be with her, and she'd made him wait. And for what? An impending conversation with her family convincing them this was her choice and not theirs? Respect was a two-way street, and she'd been driving down a one-lane road for too long.

Glen reached for her face and dragged his fingers down her cheek. Becky closed her eyes and pressed her hand against his, leaning into him. Her mind reeled, her body instantly coming back to life from his touch.

He wasn't some one-off dude she'd shared her vacation with. No. She was head-over-heels for this man. He rolled into her life like a storm, without warning. He *was* the storm, and she was wrecked, in a good way. Hurricane Glen ruined her.

"You're right, Glen. It's time to set the record straight and stop tiptoeing around my family's feelings. You're my man, and it's time I stuck up for you."

His smile was immediate, and he raked his fingers into her hair, holding her face with tenderness. When their lips melded together, every last day she'd spent without him vanished in a heartbeat. She was right where she was meant to be—in his arms. Glen felt like home.

With her mind made up, she grabbed him by the hand and pulled him into the mud room. Quickly, she shrugged on her coat. A rush of cold air hit her face instantly as they walked outside and down the walkway toward the barn. Teddy and Walt stood still and watched them approach, Becky intentionally holding Glen's hand firmly in hers. She wasn't about to let go.

Walt's face morphed from awe to disgust in an instant. "What the hell are you doing?"

"Well, Walt, as you like to say, 'I'm taking the bull by the horns.'" She confidently tilted her chin into the air with gumption and looked back and forth between her brothers, assessing their reactions. Teddy remained passive, the look on his face filled with sadness. Walt grew increasingly bothered, his eyes shooting daggers at Glen.

"This is fucked up, and you know it, Glen," Walt said with a cocky grin.

"Good to see you too, Walt. How was the honeymoon?" Glen asked.

"Don't change the subject."

Glen waited for a beat, his nostrils flaring with resolution. "I love her, Walt. And she loves me. You might as well accept us this way because I'm not going anywhere."

He squeezed Becky's hand, and she had to blink at the pressure building from behind her eyes. He was standing up for her, and she wasn't about to crumble into an emotional heap because this was an uncomfortable conversation. She continued to stand tall, to stand for what she believed in. And she believed in Glen.

Walt spat on the ground and clenched his fists with unease. "You've always done this. You have a track record for wanting the things you know you can't have."

"*Walter!*" Becky admonished.

He smashed his index finger into Glen's chest and got in his face. "You saw what my family had and set your sights on all of it. And this is how you weasel your way in, right? Convincing my little sister, you're the cat's meow. Well, we all know you're nothing. You're an angry, unsatisfied addict who will break Becky's heart, and you know it. And I, for one, will not stand by and let that happen."

"Walt, you need to calm down," Teddy gently advised. He pressed a hand on Walt's shoulder, which he hastily shrugged off.

"Fuck Glen, Teddy! Aren't you sick of him and all his twisted antics? Aren't you sick and tired of waking up every day with a lifelong limp because of what he did to you in that jail cell, not to mention the *years* you spent behind bars for a crime you didn't even commit!"

Teddy hung his head as Glen turned rigid next to Becky, the fury in his being noticeable. She wasn't about to let these two get into another barnyard brawl because of her. She gripped his bicep with her free hand and did her best to soothe him.

"Don't listen to Walt. It doesn't matter what he thinks," she reassured.

Walt's eyes turned to slits, the next few sentences out of his mouth an ultimatum.

"You still owe me for your farm, Glen. And you owe my family for all the bullshit heartache you've caused over the years, and you know it. It's your choice, and I'm gonna let you choose. Your farm—or my sister."

Glen released Becky's hand and pushed back against Walt's chest. "How dare you?"

"How dare me? How dare *you*, you son-of-a-bitch!" Walt pushed back.

Becky rushed to Teddy's side, pleading with him to make the two men stop. "Please, Teddy. Make them stop. Don't let them do this again. *Please!*"

Her voice pitched into a high wail and must've caught the attention of James and Roy from inside the barn. They rushed outside, the concerned expressions on their faces evident.

"What the hell is going on here?" James asked.

"Stay back!" Walt waved a hand into the air, his eyes fixated on Glen's face. "This is between me and him. Go ahead, Glen. I'll even let you throw the first punch." Walt pointed at his cheek, egging him on.

"Boys, please. Let's take this inside and hash it out peacefully," Roy implored.

"I don't want any trouble, Mr. Bennett," Glen admitted, his eyes never leaving Walt's. "But no one can tell me who I can and can't love. And I love your daughter."

Walt reared a fist back and struck Glen in the jaw, the sickening thump causing Becky to shriek. Roy and James immediately grabbed Walt by the arms and held him back.

Teddy gripped Glen by the arm, begging him to stay calm. "Don't do it, Glen. Don't start up with violence again. Please."

Glen ran a hand down his beard and shifted his jaw, ensuring he was still in one piece. He forced a chuckle from his lips, knowing he was throwing gasoline on Walt's anger. "Damn, Walt. You hit like a wimp."

Walt growled, lunging at Glen again. But Roy and James firmly held on to him, preventing another strike.

But what happened next was surreal, the slow-motion movements of Roy Bennett shutting the fight down in a millisecond.

"Daddy?" Becky watched in horror as her father let go of Walt and crumpled to the ground, one hand clutched to his chest. "*Daddy*?!" Rushing to his side, he remained unresponsive, lying on the dirt.

"Dad?" Teddy kneeled and leaned an ear next to Roy's mouth. "He's not breathing!"

"I'm calling 9-1-1," James panicked, pulling a cell phone from his pocket.

Distressed, Walt fell to his knees next to Becky and

gently patted Roy's face. "Dad? *Dad*! What happened? Did we hit you? What the hell happened?"

Becky frantically looked up at Glen, who stood nearby, his hands clenched and the shocked expression on his face heartbreaking. "Glen?" she pleaded, not knowing what to do.

Their eyes locked, and his chest rose in a deep air intake as if he understood the assignment.

"Move back," he instructed.

Becky gave up her spot next to her father and watched in awe as Glen unzipped Roy's coat and leaned his ear close to his mouth.

"Don't touch my father," Walt yelped. His initial anger had dissipated, his voice cracking with worry.

Glen was undeterred. "Either you give me space, or your father dies right here in front of you and your siblings. Is that what you want?"

"What? *No!*" Walt struggled to stand and got out of the way. "Do what you gotta do, Glen. Please."

Glen ripped open Roy's flannel shirt. "I'm trained in CPR. I think your father's gone into cardiac arrest."

Becky gasped and watched Glen tilt her father's head back with gentleness. He explained he was opening the airway and listening for breathing. When he realized Teddy was right, and Roy wasn't breathing, he placed his hands one on top of the other with interlocked fingers in the middle of his chest and started performing compressions while staying calm and composed. At one point, he quickly asked Becky to pull off his heavy coat, the act of CPR intense and tiring. His muscles bulged against his thermal shirt. And was he humming through gritted teeth to the rhythm of "Staying Alive?"

An ambulance siren could be heard in the distance, and

as James waved the big rig down the hill next to the barn, Roy regained consciousness.

"*Dad!*" Walt hollered with relief, quickly coming to his side.

"What... what happened? Did I pass out?" His face was ashen, and his speech warbled and slurred.

Glen politely stepped back, allowing Becky to take his place. She leaned low near her father's neck and sobbed. "Oh, *Daddy*."

The paramedics were quick, and Roy was strapped onto a gurney with an oxygen mask pressed over his face. As the ambulance drove away, leaving a plume of dust in the Bennett siblings' wake, Walt kicked at a rock with the pointy tip of his boot.

"He's gonna be okay," James reassured, slinging an arm across Walt's shoulders in brotherly comfort. "We need to meet the ambulance at the ER."

"Goddammit," Walt cursed, wildly looking around. "Where's Glen?"

Holding his coat, Becky scanned the area and realized Glen must have snuck away while the paramedics performed their job. "Maybe he went inside. He must be pretty freaked out after this."

"Ya think?" Walt chided. "Now I'm the one who owes Glen... everything. He just saved our father's fucking life."

Chapter Thirty-Four

GLEN

Glen's adrenaline rush resuscitating Mr. Bennett had vanished, leaving him depleted. Exhausted. Sucked dry. He almost felt like he was hung over after a hard night of drinking and drugs—almost.

It was hard to believe he was the only adult in the group who knew CPR, thankful he had the skills to help Roy at that moment; skills he learned at the local fire department's Friends and Family CPR class a few months prior. But he also knew the man had a long road to recovery ahead of him, the statistics dismal.

In his training, he'd learned most people who experienced cardiac arrest didn't survive. Those who did were at risk for brain injury, changes in quality of life, and physical and psychological well-being. He knew Roy was in good hands at the hospital now, but an even bigger question lingered in his mind:

Was this his fault?

After parking his truck in front of his house, he slammed the vehicle door shut and strode swiftly toward his shed.

He'd neglected to get his coat back from Becky, hightailing it out of there once the paramedics arrived. Scrubbing his hands up and down his cold arms, he cursed under his breath, the guilt in his gut consuming him. The sliding shed door groaned on rusty hinges, the light of day revealing his powder blue antique truck inside.

Daisy.

Glen climbed into the driver's seat, shutting himself inside. Gripping the steering wheel until his knuckles turned white, he kept it together, taking intentional deep breaths in and out, in and out. Closing his eyes, he felt the volcano in his gut rumbling, his emotions threatening to burst. He'd walked a long road at war with himself and his past addiction. He faced his shame regarding his actions, focusing on the person he wanted to be. He worked toward new goals. He fucking fell in love.

Knowing he'd escaped the prison of substance abuse, he knew he could accomplish anything he set his mind to and work hard for it. As he grew in his sobriety over the last year, he was acutely aware of his lifelong struggle when it came to relapse, especially during hard times. But he knew deep down to his core he was less likely to fall because he had someone in his life who had a close eye on him. Someone who could save him from himself.

Images of Becky's fear-stricken face left him shaken. She turned to him for help when her father collapsed, and he was right there. And he'd do it all over again in an instant.

But there were other faces in the mix too. Teddy, a gentle giant who didn't deserve Glen's wrath back in the day. He was a man who'd overcome so much in his young life, his forgiving heart and perseverance a testament to his character. And then there was James, the Bennett brother Glen always considered to be the true leader in the family.

He was a fair man who kept the peace between everyone. Of course, James went into protection mode, calling 9-1-1 when his father was in dire straits.

The youngest brother, Hank, reminded Glen of a human version of a Labrador Retriever. He was happy-go-lucky, everybody's best friend. The kind of guy who'd give you the shirt off his back. Glen wondered if Hank had been called, the Nashville country singer pursuing his dreams with the love of his life by his side. Would Hank come home at the drop of his cowboy hat? Absofuckinglutely.

And Walter. Glen's best friend from childhood and his nemesis in adulthood. The one Bennett in the family whose temper closely matched his own, going from zero to death row in a heartbeat. Walter's expression bothered him the most. He helplessly watched Glen bring his father back to life, the look of shock and profound awe a climax in their relationship. Was this the end for them? Or was it only the beginning? Was Glen a hero or a villain in Walt's eyes? Only time would tell.

And what about Mr. Bennett? Seeing his lifeless body lying on the dirt would haunt Glen for years. Roy was the only father figure he'd ever known. A man he looked up to. A man whose influence in his life served as an emotional substitute for the biological father he never knew. Holy shit, if Roy had died in Glen's arms, there's no way he would've ever recovered, his slip into relapse inevitable. And Lord knows, the Bennett siblings might've blamed him all over again. His life would've been over, kaput. His chances with Becky stripped away for good.

But that's not what happened. Roy lived, and he was hopefully recovering in a nice warm hospital bed with his beloved family gathered all around.

And where did that leave Glen? He was alone. Shivering. Sobbing in the front seat of his restored truck and contemplating the taste of alcohol on his lips. He was only one drink away from hell.

Swiping hot tears from his bearded cheeks, he glanced through the truck window at the customized sign Becky had given him for Christmas hanging on the wall. It was the size of an album cover, the top part featuring a vintage pickup truck design, and the bottom personalized with his last name, "Kirby," etched into the metal.

Glen was a simple, hard-working man. He came from a long line of Kirby apple farmers. Unbeknownst to Walt, he wasn't looking for a pot of gold, a sugar mama, or a get-rich-quick life. Those ideas were not what living meant to him. And with everything his family and the Bennetts had been through, Glen knew God had been good to him. Better than He had to be.

Glen let go of the steering wheel and leaned back against the seat. What did it all mean? He'd lost so much over the years: his brother Joe. His house and farm. His mental and physical health before he got help. Could he stand to lose even more when it came to Becky and her family?

And there it was.

His mouth dropped open with the epiphany when he realized this wasn't solely about Becky Bennett at all. Yes, he was madly in love and wanted to carve out a simple life with her by his side. But he had to admit, he also loved her brothers and her father. Glen was a man looking for a sense of belonging. For trust, comfort, care, and happiness. And the Bennetts had always been right there, a few miles down the road. He'd found his family with them, and they'd become his lifeline—to live.

An overwhelming feeling of peace swept over him, and

he knew what he had to do. Cranking the engine, he put the antique truck in drive and slowly pulled out of the shed. He was a man on a mission, ready to face the Bennett jury. Prepared to meet—his family.

———————

The Langston Falls emergency room was relatively quiet. Glen arrived coatless, thankful for the warm interior inside. Looking around, the Bennetts were nowhere in sight.

"Excuse me, ma'am?"

"Yes?" A friendly nurse looked up from her station.

"I'm looking for Roy Bennett. He was brought in earlier by ambulance."

The nurse typed a few clicks and nodded. "Are you part of the family?"

Glen waited for a beat before he confidently nodded. "Yes, ma'am."

She stood and motioned with her hand. "Follow me. I'll take you back to the private waiting room where they all are."

He nodded and gripped the edges of his cowboy hat with both hands. The nurse motioned to a closed door at the end of a long hallway.

"They're in there."

"Thank you."

Glen waited until the nurse was out of sight and prepared himself. He settled his hat back on his head and fisted his hand, gently knocking on the door. James's face appeared within seconds, his eyes going wide at the sight of him.

"Hey, James. I—"

James didn't let him finish. He lunged at Glen, hugging him with force.

"Boy, am I glad to see you."

Glen was stiff in his arms, and when James pulled back, he was smiling. "We've been waiting for you. Dad is doing okay, thanks to you. I can't even begin to tell you how grateful we all are."

"*Glen!*" Becky pushed between James and Glen, nuzzling her body against his. "I was worried about you."

"I'm sorry I made you worry. Are you okay, Daisy Girl?"

She nodded against his chest and looked up at him with happy tears glimmering in her eyes. "Come inside and wait with us."

Glen eyed James for permission and was thankful when he nodded.

With Becky's arms still around his waist, he took off his cowboy hat and nervously glanced at Teddy, Robyn, Walt, and Elyse. Samantha was noticeably absent, as were Hank and Ella Mae. But he knew it would take Hank and his fiancé time coming from Nashville.

Teddy boldly ambled toward him. "What you did back at the farm…," Teddy choked with emotion and took a beat to regain his composure.

Robyn immediately comforted him. "It's okay," she soothed.

Teddy stared right at him. "Thank you," he whispered.

Glen couldn't speak and offered Ted and Robyn a quick nod. Shifting his focus to Walt, he couldn't tell if the man was pissed or happy, ready to punch or hug him. Elyse stayed seated, the sweet expression on her face indicating Walt wasn't any of those things.

Walt slowly approached, and Glen held onto Becky a

little tighter. And when Walt thrust his hand out in a shake, Glen knew they could be friends again—*brothers* again.

They aggressively shook, Walt's grip competing with his, making him laugh with joy. Glen took it a step farther and pulled Walt in for a group hug with Becky in the middle. Teddy joined in with one arm slung across Robyn's shoulders, the other slapping Glen on the back. Elyse arose from her chair and snuck her way in next to Walt. And James spread his arms open wide, finishing their circle.

And that's what they were, a circle of love connected in hope and perseverance, forgiveness and unconditional love. They'd overcome adversity and unfathomable pain, the odds of reconciliation not in their favor. But somehow, by the grace of God, Glen had come full circle.

And he was never letting go.

Chapter Thirty-Five

BECKY

A nurse gathered the attention of everyone in the waiting room with a quick knock on the door. All heads turned to look at her.

"Excuse me. Mr. Bennett has a request. He'd like to speak privately to his daughter." She smiled, her focus squarely on Becky.

"Just me?" Becky pointed at herself, stunned her dad didn't want her brothers in the room.

"Yes, ma'am."

She palmed Glen's chest. "Will you be okay while I go talk to him?"

"Of course." He smiled. "Take your time. I'll be right here waiting for you. I'm not going anywhere."

Becky grinned, stood on her tiptoes, and gave Glen a quick peck on the lips while her brothers and the girls watched without a trace of disgust or disappointment in their expressions. It felt freeing to offer public displays of affection without criticism.

The nurse escorted Becky through the hospital hallways

to the intensive care unit, where her father received post-resuscitation care. Stopping outside the closed door, she asked, "Is my dad going to be okay?"

The nurse offered a reassuring smile and nodded. "I'll let the doctor explain everything to you and your brothers after he makes his rounds. Roy is a strong man. He's having difficulty concentrating and may seem lethargic to you, but his prognosis is good because he was resuscitated."

Becky blew out a relieved breath. "Thank you."

"You're welcome."

Becky followed the nurse inside the room, overwhelmed by all the tubes and machines beeping and buzzing around her father as he lay propped up in the hospital bed. His eyes were closed, his features calm and relaxed. He appeared to be napping.

"Should I come back later?" Becky whispered.

The nurse peered at a heart monitor, each sharp blip on the screen indicating her dad was very much alive. Pressing her hand against his shoulder, Roy blinked open his eyes in confusion.

"Hi, Roy. Your daughter is here to see you now."

He looked from the nurse to Becky, who stood at the foot of the bed.

"Hi, Daddy." Her voice cracked with emotion. She'd never seen her father look so frail.

"Hey, darlin'. I'm sure glad to see you."

The nurse edged her way to the door. "If you need me, just press the green button on the large remote on the side table. Roy knows where it is."

Becky nodded. With the nurse out of the room, she rushed to her father's side and sat in a chair conveniently beside the bed. Gently, she held his hand, her brow furrowing with concern.

"How do you feel?"

Roy squeezed her hand and sighed. "I feel like I've been hit by the old barn tractor. If I fall asleep on you, don't worry. I've been told dozing is part of the recovery program."

Becky grinned, knowing her dad was being cheeky. "Why did you only want to see me and not the boys?"

Roy motioned toward a tumbler of water with a built-in straw on the side table. Becky was quick and held it for him as he took a small sip.

"I owe you an apology," he said, licking his lips.

Becky set the water back on the table. She needed clarification. "Why do you owe me an apology?"

Her father was careful with his words, his concentration evident. Each word out of his mouth came out excruciatingly slow. Becky realized it would take some time for him to return to his former robust and larger-than-life self.

"When your mama died, you filled a void in the family. You took care of all of us."

"I love taking care of all of you. It's my job. And I will take extra care of you when you return home."

Roy chuckled. "I know you will, darlin'. You always do. But who's taking care of you?"

Becky scowled. "I don't understand."

He shifted against the pillow behind his head, his eyelids droopy with fatigue. "It's time for you to go after your dreams, darlin'. Just like your mama wanted to—"

"Daddy," she interrupted. "I didn't mean to say those awful things to you about Mama. I was angry and hurt. Please forgive me."

"There's nothing to forgive. You were absolutely right."

"I was?"

"Yes." His grip on her hand lessened as his body relaxed into the bed. Was he about to fall asleep?

"You want me to leave so you can rest?"

"No," he whispered, closing his eyes. "I want you to live your life in whatever way you choose. I've been selfish over the years, keeping you at the farm. It's just hard for me to let go. It's hard knowing my baby girl has grown up. And Glen Kirby…," his voice trailed off.

Becky was all ears, anxious to hear what her dad had to say about the man she was in love with. "Tell me, Daddy."

His brow furrowed above his closed eyes. "That boy isn't a sinkhole. I see how your face lights up when he's in the room. It was the same thing with me and your mama. Glen is solid. Hard-working. And he's loyal, to a fault."

Becky waited patiently for him to make his point and squeezed his hand.

His voice turned raspy. "Glen almost took a Bennett's life. But then he redeemed mine." The easy grin on his face was full of warmth and paternal love. "I'd say he's even, don't you think? You have my blessing, darlin'. Go… live your life. Love your life. You only get one. Make it count."

Becky swallowed a lump in her throat and laid her head against her father's arm. His chest rose and fell in even breaths in slumber, his blessing everything she ever wanted.

Glen wasn't a villain anymore. He was a hero. He was released from blame, free and clear. Becky and Glen were finally liberated, and it was time for her to claim what was rightfully hers on her own terms: a life to call her own.

Leaving her father slumbering peacefully in his hospital bed, Becky returned to the private waiting room where her brothers, the girls, and Glen awaited. Swinging open the door in a rush of happy energy, she nodded and eyed the handsome brood.

"Daddy's gonna be okay, y'all. His speech is slow, and he gets tired easily, but we had a nice chat. The doctor will be by after his rounds to give us the low down on his recovery." She sat beside Glen, and he put his arm across her shoulders, pulling her close.

"Thank God," Walt exclaimed.

"Good news, Becks. Hopefully, we can see him later too," James said.

"And when the doctor comes by, we want to ask him about CPR classes," Teddy added.

"CPR classes?" Becky asked.

"Yes. Glen was telling us how easy it is to get certified in training. He took a class at the local fire station," Teddy explained.

"And it would be good to know with all the tourists and field workers on our property," James said. "Maybe even purchase one of those AED machines to have on-site too. I think it'd give us all peace of mind in case of another emergency, don't you think?"

"Great idea," Becky agreed among the positive responses from everyone in the room.

She turned and looked at Glen, reminded of something he'd once said. Walt had told him if he stayed honest and paid it forward someday, he'd become a man of humility, and his life would take on new meaning. Glen more than paid it forward. He saved their father's life.

"What?" Glen grinned, snuggling closer to her.

"Nothing. I'm just—happy."

"I am too," he whispered in her ear.

It was nice being pressed against him, his body warm and his whiskers soft against her cheek. She'd felt a certain pull toward Glen, and now, their secret was out in the open. She loved being with him, seeing small traces of his humble self he did his best to hide. His loyalty and his patient love coming to the surface from a man no one else ever really got to know. Glen filled the empty, lonely places in her life slowly, carefully, with his easy smile and quiet, loving spirit.

There was no need to figure out her next steps because suddenly, she felt like she could breathe again. And she didn't want this feeling to ever go away. She wanted it to last for a lifetime.

Chapter Thirty-Six

GLEN

"Hank and Elyse will be here tomorrow," Becky said.

She flicked on the lights in the kitchen, the farmhouse eerily quiet in the evening hour. She was glad her brother was coming home from Nashville, knowing the family was in an all-hands-on-deck situation regarding their father. The doctor told them recovery from cardiac arrest would take time and would include physical therapy and ongoing heart care to prevent another episode. He'd have follow-up appointments and prescribed medication, and they even talked about hiring a nurse to help on the farm for the first month or two.

Her father's cardiac arrest changed Becky's attitude about life. Of course, she wanted to help her father get back to where he was physically and emotionally. But she also realized she needed to take time for herself too. She started looking outward again, excited to share her life with her special someone out in the open.

She grabbed the tea kettle from the stove and filled it at the sink. "We have the house to ourselves tonight. James took the dogs to the carriage house. Are you hungry? I could make us some scrambled eggs or maybe a sandwich?"

Glen came right up behind her and wrapped his arms around her waist, nuzzling his nose in her hair.

Becky giggled. "You're tickling me."

"I want to do more than tickle you."

She set the kettle in the sink and turned around so they were nose to nose. She hung her arms lazily over his broad shoulders and gave him her best come-hither stare.

"Kiss me," she whispered.

Glen nipped at her lips, his grip on her body intensifying as he tucked his nose into the space below her ear before dragging his face down and pressing tiny kisses against her throat.

"Mmmm," she hummed. She slipped her hand between his legs, and Glen immediately exhaled a low, husky moan, his lips melding with hers and his tongue sweeping between her teeth. Delicious heat unfurled from her center, spreading slow and sweet.

"The bedroom?" she asked.

"Yes," he hissed, hoisting her into his strong arms and carrying her easily.

Her back hit the soft mattress within moments, and his weight pressed into her. The tips of his fingers traced the outline of her breasts, moving lower to her sweet spot, sending ripples of pleasure to her core. He painted a picture with his hands, teasing and taunting, his lips on fire with heat and desire. She was desperate to feel him inside her again.

"God, I want you," she pleaded.

They scrambled to get undressed, throwing their clothes this way and that. He quickly grabbed a foil packet from his wallet and sheathed his engorged penis with a condom.

Becky inhaled sharply, the weight of his masculine hips between her thighs such a turn-on she thought she might burst before they started. She ran her hands over his shoulders and ass, begging him to go faster. Glen groaned and crushed his lips to hers in a passionate kiss, doing the opposite. He moved slower. Deeper.

"You're. Killing. Me," she exhaled in a staccato breath.

"But what an incredible way to die." He grinned and made a little circular motion with his hips that had her dangling over the edge.

Their mouths hovered inches apart, her teeth pressed into her lower lip to keep from moaning. Her passion for Glen was so immense she thought she might split in two. And now that they were officially together, she wasn't frantic or panicked someone might find them in this once forbidden situation. Now she was driven by love and desire, freedom and undeniable pleasure.

Becky clung to him, and he sped up, pumping her hard and fast. Grinding against him, she felt a familiar tingle in her tummy as if she were about to nosedive into a freefall.

"I'm gonna come," she panted, barely able to get the words out.

"I want you to," he growled. He thrust his tongue into her mouth and kissed her long and hard and deep, threading his fingers through her hair and tugging at the roots.

She writhed rapturously beneath him, the tunnel vision indicating she had reached the mountaintop and was ready to soar. "Oh... *God*!" Her vision blurred, and she struggled for her next breath. Only it wasn't a breath but a scream of pure ecstasy.

Glen's arms flexed, and she could make out every sinewy muscle as he braced himself for an orgasm. His nostrils flared, and he grunted, his release a beautiful vision of strength and power.

They lay there panting in the aftermath side by side, not saying a word. Becky snuggled into his arms, and Glen kissed her temple. She wanted to bottle up this moment, his body hard and warm beneath the sheets. The sounds of the house settling in the night. The hoot of an owl outside the windows and the bed creaking from their weighted blissful-ness among the twisted sheets. He held her so close she could feel his heartbeat.

"Glen?"

"Hmmm?"

"You're gonna own your farm outright by the end of summer, I promise."

"What are you talking about?"

"I'm going to help you."

Glen abruptly sat up, his brow furrowed with displea-sure. "I am *not* taking any of your money to buy back my farm from your brother. That's exactly what they've all been worried about."

Becky grabbed the stuffed rainbow unicorn he'd won for her on Halloween from behind her pillow and threw it at him. Startled, Glen caught it and frowned. He was not amused.

"That's not what I'm proposing," she said.

"Well, you must have something pretty spectacular up your sleeve if you think I'll own my property by the end of summer. It's going to take me years."

"No, it's not. Hear me out." Becky couldn't contain her excitement. "Didn't you and Walt come up with a new wine recently? A wine deliberately created to help you in the re-purchase of your property?"

"Yes?" Glen was hesitant in his reply.

Becky flicked her long hair over her shoulder with confidence. "And didn't you name the wine after a certain goddess you love?"

Glen chuckled. "Rebecca Rose. Yes."

"And isn't Rebecca Rose moi?" She palmed her bare chest, her enjoyment tenfold enticing him with her plan.

"Yes. I named the new wine after you. What's your point?"

"Well, I, Rebecca Rose, have a huge social media following and a hit YouTube show. I also have a new cookbook coming out this year." Her enthusiasm took over as she shifted to her knees, making the mattress bounce. "I've been talking with Elyse about this. I'm already doing influencer marketing with my channel for other branded content. Why not add the Rebecca Rose label to the mix?"

"Influencer marketing?" Glen pinned her with his stare, trying to track what she was saying.

"It's a collaboration where a brand gives me their product for promotion and selling purposes. It's a surefire way to expand the reach of your wine brand through social media."

Glen ran a hand down his bearded chin, the light bulb going off behind his blue eyes. "And you think it could work?"

Becky held his face in her hands. "I *know* it will work. I've sold thousands of other products through my accounts. Things like cookware and dishes. Why not promote a delicious wine named after me? My super fans will go nuts knowing the wine was made on the farm where I film episodes of my show. And all proceeds will go toward paying off your debt. It's a win-win for us both."

Glen locked eyes with hers. "You'd do that for me?"

"Of course. I love you, Glen."

His breathing hitched, and he nodded, sliding his fingers into her hair. "I love you too, Daisy Girl. So much."

He pulled her forward in a hug, his voice dropping to a whisper. "I want to do everything for you. I want to give you your dream house with yellow shutters and a porch. I want to plow the earth for your gardens and watch you walk among the daisy paths. I want to buy you overalls, win you stuffed animals, and order you chai tea." His arms squeezed her tighter, and she clung to him just as hard.

"And I want to watch the rest of my sunsets with you until the day I die." He dropped his forehead to hers, calloused fingertips dragging down her cheek. "I'll give you patient love, and you'll never be lonely again." Glen's smile made her heart beat double-time.

"Promise?"

"I promise."

They fell back among the wrinkled sheets, arms and legs entwined, feet playing footsie. Closing her eyes, Becky willed herself to remember this moment, knowing she wasn't dreaming. Happy she was wrapped around Glen and not a pillow.

Pressing her palm against his chest smattered with damp hair, she felt his heart thumping steadily and hoped he could somehow feel it: Everything she hadn't said yet. Everything she wanted to do for him in the future—their future.

"Glen, wherever you are in the world is where I want to be."

Entwining his fingers with hers, he pressed their hands against his heart. "You promise?"

"I promise."

Next in The Bennetts of Langston Falls Series

The Bennetts of Langston Falls Series

Fearless LOVE

KG Fletcher

vinci-books.com/fearlesslove

**On the run, searching for safety—but love could be the
ultimate risk.**

She's on the run. He's her safe haven. But falling for him could
cost her everything. When a single mom and a small-town hero
become unexpected roommates, love is the last thing they expect—
but exactly what they need. *Fearless Love* is a steamy, emotional
small-town romance.

Turn the page for a free preview…

Fearless Love: Chapter One

JAMES BENNETT

Sometimes, the universe makes it crystal clear when it's time to make a move. Like the kind you make in a good game of chess. But before you get started, you should consider all aspects of a move since the consequences cannot be undone. James Bennett believed the advantages of his decision outweighed the disadvantages, and his next move was not a mistake but an essential milestone in his and Samantha's relationship.

And he was ready for a checkmate.

Entering the five-star Speckled Trout Restaurant on the outskirts of Langston Falls, his heart blipped with hope. The interior was intentionally dim; the candlelight glows from each table giving off a quixotic vibe for those weekend couples looking for a little more romance. Although he didn't get the specific table he requested, he thought the romantic atmosphere might work in his favor. It couldn't hurt, right?

He stared longingly at the view beyond the large

windows across the expansive terrace, wishing for a spot where he and Samantha could dine al-fresco among the big porch heaters and crackling fire in the outdoor fireplace. Hues of pink and orange highlighted the stunning backdrop of the long-range mountain view, the winter sunset clocking out at half past six.

But the outdoor space was already filled; reservations for a prime table required weeks in advance before the Valentine's Day weekend surge. Still, the interior was nice, the vibe everything James wanted it to be for this important milestone in his life. Now, if he could only calm his nerves.

James waited for Samantha for almost forty-five minutes. She was usually irritatingly punctual, a pet peeve of hers in her law enforcement career monitoring her assigned parolees fresh out of jail. But since the holidays, his brother Walt's New Year's Eve wedding in Atlanta, and his father's cardiac arrest and hospital stay, it felt like they hadn't seen each other in weeks, hence the romantic dinner reservation and the decision to take things to the next level.

He was anxious to talk to her about moving in together once and for all. Having a few drawers in his dresser and closet space for some hanging clothes wasn't cutting it anymore. At least she'd texted, letting him know she was running late and would be there as soon as possible.

He wondered what delayed her. Was she at a halfway house getting someone signed in? Or maybe she had to collect another urine sample from one of her parolees for a drug test? Perhaps she was helping a colleague take a violator back to rehab or the county jail?

James had never been fond of Samantha's job, which often put her in dangerous situations. And don't get him started on how it seemed like she was on call twenty-four hours a day, including weekends. He'd never understood her willingness to help out the low-life thugs in her occupation. But hadn't she helped his oldest brother, Teddy, when he was released and out on parole? And he was *nothing* like most of the degenerates Sam worked with daily.

He remembered the moment they met, like it was yesterday. Samantha "Sam" McNeil was Ted's assigned parole officer and she visited Bennett Farms to check in on him. When his big dog, Jaxson, jumped up on her, she lost her footing and fell flat on her ass. From the moment he touched her hand to help her up from the ground, he knew she was someone special. Their connection was instant. It was magic.

Too bad they had to wait until her time as Teddy's parole officer was completed before they could officially date; relationships between officers and members of a parolee's family frowned upon. Still, they managed to keep things on the down low, meeting for coffee or lunch and biding their time with lengthy phone conversations when she was off the clock.

Samantha was instrumental in helping his family through the legal mumbo jumbo when Ted unintentionally violated his parole after an unfortunate incident at the Harvest Hoedown a year and a half ago. It was the same night family neighbor and nemesis, Glen Kirby, punched Sam in the face during a barnyard fight, resulting in a sinister black eye.

But all those painful memories were behind them now —or were they?

It seemed everyone in the Bennett family had moved on and found love. Teddy was free and married to his high school sweetheart, Robyn. Walt was also a newlywed, his recent New Year's Eve wedding in Atlanta to television producer Elyse Farrell, a huge family celebration. His youngest brother Hank was engaged to famous country music songwriter Ella Mae Miller, and his sister, Becky, was in a relationship with their former feuding farming neighbor, Glen Kirby. How the heck did that happen?

"Hey." Samantha whooshed in and sat across from him, the candles flickering and highlighting her flushed cheeks.

James was taken aback and arose from his seat to assist with her winter coat. "Here, let me help."

Samantha waved him off and scowled. "I've got it." She demonstrated her independence, never allowing him to fuss over her.

He reluctantly sat down and watched her fumble with the heavy fabric. Her dark hair was pulled back into a tight bun, and she was still dressed in her work clothes and sensible shoes. Picking up a thick menu, she peered at the specials from behind black-rimmed glasses— her *work* glasses.

"Have you ordered anything yet? I'm starving."

James frowned and eyed the empty table setting in front of him. He'd been sipping on nothing but water while he patiently waited for her.

"No, I haven't."

Samantha glanced over the top of the menu at him with wide eyes. "Then what have you been doing here for the last forty-five minutes? Staring into space?" She laughed at his expense.

James cleared his throat and tried hard not to come across as a grumpy boyfriend. "I've been waiting for you. I thought maybe you'd gone home to change, but I can tell you're still in work mode. What happened this time?"

Samantha sighed, took her glasses off, and set them on the white tablecloth. Before she could respond, a waitress appeared and took their drink order. Sam was cordial, smiling as she ordered a champagne cocktail and an expedited crab cake for starters. James decided on a recommended local craft beer.

"You don't want an appetizer?" she asked as the waitress flitted away.

James reached for her hand across from him and squeezed. "I want to know what's been happening between us, Sam."

She averted his gaze and pulled her hand from his grip, grabbing her linen napkin to clean her glasses. "I'm fine, James. I'm just... late."

"Are you going to tell me why?"

"Maybe."

"Maybe?" James chuckled. He decided to change the subject. "I miss you, darlin'. I feel like we haven't spent any quality time together since Walt's wedding and Daddy's hospitalization."

"By the way, how's your dad doing? How's Roy?" Her brow furrowed as if she was genuinely concerned.

But Sam hadn't made it to the hospital since his dad was admitted over two weeks ago. She'd told him she was too slammed, and by the time she got off work, visiting hours at the hospital were over. Still, he was glad she asked about him.

James offered a small smile. "He's okay. He's chomping at the bit, ready to come home tomorrow."

"That's tomorrow?"

"Yes." James frowned. "I told you to put it on your calendar. The whole family is welcoming him home. Please, Sam. I need you there with all of us."

The waitress reappeared with their drinks and Sam's crab cake. Her attention was immediately diverted to the food, and she dug in with her fork, moaning after the first bite. James watched, perplexed by her behavior. She was more interested in eating than hearing about his father's homecoming.

"It's so good. You want a bite?" She took a quick sip from her champagne flute and licked her lips.

"No, thank you."

"Suit yourself." She chewed another mouthful, the silence between them deafening.

James held up his hand when the waitress came by to take their order. "Could you please give us a few more minutes?"

"No problem."

Samantha watched the waitress walk away before she shot James a look of confusion. "Aren't you hungry? Don't you want to order?"

James sat upright in his chair, his jaw clenched with determination. "I want to know what's going on between us. You've been… distant."

Samantha exhaled steadily through her nose and laid her fork next to her half-eaten appetizer. "I guess now's as good a time as ever to tell you."

"Tell me what?" James steeled himself in his chair, ready to hear about her latest work frustrations.

"I'm leaving Langston Falls."

Her comment wasn't what he expected, and he stared back at her, puzzled. "Say again?"

"I said, I'm leaving Langston Falls."

James blinked. "When? Where are you going? Do you have another court case in Atlanta? Are you vacationing with your family again?"

Sam bided some time before she answered and drained the pink bubbly in her glass. Wiping her lips with the napkin, she finally stared right at him, her expression giving nothing away. No remorse. No emotion. No love.

"I'm leaving Langston Falls tomorrow for Quantico, Virginia, to begin training at the FBI Academy."

All the color drained from James's face. Sam had mentioned her interest in working with the FBI when they first started dating, but that was well over a year ago. For her to make such a drastic decision without him felt like a sucker punch in the gut.

"You passed the preliminary tests?" His throat felt dry, and he reached for his beer to take a sip.

"Of course."

James swallowed hard and carefully set his glass on the table. "Why didn't you tell me?"

Samantha tilted her head and shrugged. "Because I knew you wouldn't like it. You've never been a fan of my work."

Her comment struck a nerve. "Now, hold on, Samantha. That's not fair. I'm not a fan when you get *hurt*, okay? When you get punched in the face or slapped and ridiculed by a bunch of convicts. You said it yourself: it's a tough career, especially for a woman."

"I know what I said. And that's part of the reason I'm turning the page. James...," She paused, pressing her lips together for a beat.

"James, I can't be tied down to Langston Falls anymore. I need a fresh start. I've always thought about a career in the FBI, and the timing feels right. The intensive training is for twenty weeks while I live on campus."

"I'll come visit you."

Sam shook her head. "I need to concentrate on my training. It'll be taxing on so many levels—academically, physically, and mentally—and success is far from guaranteed. I... I don't need any distractions."

"Then I'll wait for you to finish—"

"You're not listening to me," she interrupted curtly. "I'm ready to level up in my career. I'm looking forward to the intense training regimen necessary to prepare me as a new agent to carry out the FBI's complex mission to... to..."

"To what?" He could tell she was flustered, but so was he.

Sam stared at him with unmistakable determination in her eyes, her knowledge of the FBI impressive. "To carry out complex missions protecting the nation from criminal threats from terrorists, spies, hackers, gangs, and more—while upholding civil rights and the Constitution of the United States. This is serious business, James."

She leaned back in her chair and sighed. "I'm not ready to commit to a relationship with you and settle in a small town like Langston Falls. There's no future for me here."

He was stunned, his voice croaking with emotion. "You mean no future with *me*. Ouch, that hurts."

"James, please see this from a career perspective. Don't take it personally."

He was flabbergasted she felt so little for him. Looking back, it all made sense now. He had always been the instigator in their relationship. She was just biding her time.

"So that's it, then? We're through?"

She nodded, undeterred. "I'm sorry. Please believe me when I say this: I didn't want what we had to end this way. Everything happened so fast."

"Well, you should go. If that's what you want, you should go and do it. I won't try to stop you." He pulled several twenties from his wallet and threw them on the table. "I'm not hungry anymore. I'll follow you home and help you pack the rest of your things."

Sam pursed her lips together and shook her head. Right then, he saw goodbye in her eyes.

"No need. I already got everything."

James pinned her with his stare as the finality of her words closed the door on their relationship.

"That's why I was late."

Fearless Love: Chapter Two

SARA LARSON

"Are we there yet?" Noah asked.

A cheeky grin was plastered across her son's face, his eyes lighting up from behind his glasses. Sara shook her head and offered him an exaggerated eyeroll in the rearview mirror.

"You've asked me that for the one-hundredth time, Mr. Snuggle-bunny. We have about another thirty miles to go."

"Thirty miles?" he whined.

"Yes, sir. But it'll go by in a flash if you read one more book from your bag. You don't want to be behind when you start school next week, do you?"

Her empty threat seemed to do the trick. Her smart little boy was a regular book nerd, and devoured books on all their road trips, including this one.

Sara was a travel nurse by trade, and her next assignment was in the small town of Langston Falls. She'd never traveled this far north, the mountainous area of Georgia bordering the North Carolina state line a refreshing change of scenery.

She was to care for a man by the name of Roy Bennett, who'd suffered cardiac arrest a few weeks prior. His prognosis was good, but only with ongoing at-home care and physical therapy. She was commissioned for the job, happy for another clean slate and adventure with Noah.

The winter scenery in Georgia's northeast corner whizzed by in hues of forest evergreen and gray clouds. But the dreary weather wasn't about to tamper her excitement, the anticipation for what lay ahead filling her with hope.

Noah had always been a trooper the times they'd packed up and moved before. How many was it now? She'd lost count. At least a dozen. But this particular move had left him agitated and grumpy. He wasn't his usual fun-loving self, often mopey and depressed. She knew it was because he was getting older and had become opinionated and vocal about things.

He'd grown up on her in the blink of an eye. He was on the cusp of his eighth birthday and had finally made friends in his second-grade class at the local school, classmates he didn't want to leave behind. Sara assured him he'd make new friends at their destination, promising him a festive birthday party where he could invite his entire class to celebrate.

Still, he wasn't convinced, begging her to reconsider and wait to move at least until his birthday was over. She knew he was ready to settle down and plant roots. Her, not so much. But she couldn't wait; the ink on her next contract already dried, and her new patient was about to be discharged from the hospital. She'd have to make it up to Noah with an over-the-top birthday bash to cheer him up during the transition.

The two-lane highway circled the mountain, her car climbing to a higher elevation, the dramatic overlooks from the Blue Ridge Parkway breathtaking. Her last assignment had been in suburban Atlanta, the congested traffic and never-ending road construction something she wouldn't miss. Some might consider Sara a vagabond, never staying in one place for more than a year. Her nomadic lifestyle suited her.

Peaks and valleys punctuated the landscape, the stretch of small towns so charming, they seemed like they came straight out of the pages of one of Noah's storybooks. She was tempted to wander the picturesque downtown districts and explore the rolling countryside. From her investigation into the new area she and Noah were to call home, she imagined romanticized weekends picking apples, riding the scenic railway, or strolling through the changing seasons.

She'd lived her fair share in plenty of Georgia towns, the Southern hospitality warm and friendly. But to live in this particular stretch of the Peach State mountain region where most folks trekked for a weekend getaway seemed like the perfect fit. Quiet with room to grow and a lower cost of living. No more bumper-to-bumper traffic or news of gun violence and car-jackings. Fresh, clean air and unobstructed views. She looked forward to the beckoning mountains and foliage, festivals, and the lively community of Langston Falls, the small population of less than five hundred, a nice change of pace.

Sara wanted to get them checked in at the little roadside motel she'd found online before the sun went down. But the slower speed limits up the mountain messed with her timing, especially with a small trailer hitched to the back of her car.

She took each turn slowly, the daylight slipping behind the thick foliage and elevation. Finally, her headlights illuminated a small sign in the distance that read, "Langston Falls, five miles."

Glancing in the rearview mirror at her son again, she smiled. He held a small flashlight and aimed it at the pages of his book, his little brow furrowed with concentration.

"We're almost there, sweetie. Once we check in, I'll order us a pizza for dinner."

"Hooray!"

The exterior of the two-story Langston Falls Economy Motel held a classic roadside motel vibe, the building modest and situated along the main highway. A bright neon orange "vacancy" sign was lit up above the entrance, the communal space outside featuring a fire pit with several Adirondack chairs perfectly spaced around the perimeter.

Sara was intentional with her choice, opting for a more affordable alternative to a traditional hotel in town. And she needed to find a storage facility for everything in their packed trailer while she scoped out the perfect short-term lease. She'd learned the hard way about signing a contract for a place to live sight unseen and wasn't about to do that again. A walk-through and a thorough inspection were top priorities, and she wanted to find someplace cozy to hang her scrubs, at least through the end of the school year.

"Cool!" Noah exclaimed. The orange neon made his glasses glow over his eyes.

Sara parked near a big rig, her car and trailer dwarfed by the giant machine. Breathing in the crisp mountain air, she stretched her back and sighed, ready to call it a night after their long travel day.

"Come on. Let's go check this place out. I'll bet they have a stocked soda and snack machine."

"Can I get a soda to go with my pizza?" His warm little

hand slipped into hers as they approached the large lobby doors.

"I don't see why not. We can make a toast to our new town."

They laughed and entered the building, a doorbell chime announcing their arrival. A tiny dog with a blinged-out collar yipped and stood guard, the front desk vacant.

"Hey, little doggie," Noah said in a high-pitched tone. He'd wanted a dog since he could speak and immediately kneeled, gently holding out his hand. "Come here. I won't hurt you."

"Careful, son. I don't want it to bite you."

"Tinkerbelle won't bite."

Sara and Noah flicked their heads in unison to see a middle-aged blonde coming toward them. Her hair was in a bouffant style, and her breasts were pushed up to expose her extraordinary cleavage from under her tight pink tee. Skin-tight jeans and sky-high heels finished off the woman's outfit.

But Sara wasn't looking at her clothes or boobs. Nope. She was fascinated by her pretty face adorned with false eyelashes and shiny ruby-red lips.

The woman scooped up her little dog and held out her hand, her bright fuchsia nails looking like they could fillet a fish caught from the local pond.

"Hey there. I'm Crystal Cavanaugh, the proprietor of this lovely establishment. But everybody around here calls me CC. And you've already met Tink. Say hello to our new guests, princess." The little dog yipped as if she understood every word Crystal said.

Sara shook her hand and smiled. She was usually a good judge of character and knew right away she and Crystal would get along just fine.

"Happy to meet you, CC. This here is my son, Noah." She palmed his shoulders and presented him with pride.

Crystal beveled her stance in her impressive heels and rested one hand on her hip while holding her dog in the other. "Well, hi there, handsome. How old are you?"

Noah didn't miss a beat, his voice confident with self-assurance. "I'm seven, but my birthday's coming up, and I'll be eight."

"Eight years old. Oh my. What a great age."

Sara and Noah followed her to the front desk, where she deposited Tinkerbelle on a small bed right on top. They were definitely not in Atlanta anymore.

"Go ahead and pet her. She won't bite, though she might fall asleep on ya. It's been Grand Central Station here all evening with some regulars coming in for the weekend."

Noah stood on his tiptoes and happily patted Tinkerbelle on the head. Crystal's long nails tapped away on a keyboard as she continued talking.

"You're Sara Larson, correct?"

"Yes, ma'am."

Crystal waved her off. "Please. No one around here calls me 'ma'am.' Makes me feel like I need to be knittin' baby booties or rockin' in a chair." She laughed, her Southern accent oddly comforting. "I've got you upstairs, away from the ice machine, per your request. Room number twelve."

"Twelve's my favorite number," Noah admitted. He continued petting Tink on the head, the little dog nodding off.

"Mine too!" Crystal grinned. She handed Sara a keycard and a piece of paper. "I need you to fill out this form, and I'll need a credit card on file for incidentals."

Sara frowned, looking at the printed form with blank

spaces for her information. "I, uh, thought I filled this out online already?"

"Oh, honey, everyone who comes here says the same thing. But the internet in these parts is spotty, and I'm lucky to get those completed forms in my inbox. Unfortunately, yours didn't make it. But I did get your reservation, so there's that."

"Oh."

"Here you go." Crystal plucked a pen from a mason jar that looked like it held a bouquet of flowers. But upon further inspection, Sara realized they were all pens with bright plastic flowers taped to the ends.

"Y'all are welcome to sit here in the lobby and watch television anytime you want to. I've got satellite TV with over one hundred channels, including Disney." She leaned forward with glee assessing Noah's reaction, her boobs dangerously close to spilling out of her top.

"Did you hear that, Mom? She's got the Disney Channel!"

"Super." Sara concentrated on filling out the form. She wrote in the space for her current address, "undetermined." Clearing her throat, she asked, "Do y'all get the local paper? We're currently between houses, and I'll be looking for local leasing options before I start my new job this week."

Crystal didn't press her for details, her sweet nature underneath all her hair and makeup endearing. "Honey, I'm friends with everybody in this town, including a few realtors. We'll get you hooked up in no time."

"Thank you." She signed the form before handing off her credit card. "And one more thing. Are there any pizza places that deliver around here?"

Crystal ran her card through a machine and handed it

back to her. "This is a tourist town. Of course, we have pizza."

She leaned forward again with intention, motioning for Sara to come closer. "And I've got a stash of hard seltzers in the back if you ever need a cold one after a hard day's work. You just holler, and I'm your gal. Happy time is my favorite time of the day if you know what I mean." She winked.

Sara knew right then she'd made her first official friend in Langston Falls.

Fearless Love: Chapter Three

JAMES

The pickup truck headlights highlighted the wraparound front porch of the main house at Bennett Farms as James accelerated up the hill, eager to call it a night. Knowing the home was vacant while his father recovered in the hospital, he was determined to go straight to bed.

With the engine turned off, he gripped the steering wheel and thought about his final moments with Samantha.

There was no romantic dinner. In fact, there'd been no dinner at all. No hug goodbye. No kiss. She shook his hand before getting into her car and driving off. He'd stood in the parking lot of the fancy restaurant and watched until her taillights disappeared into the dark woods of the surrounding mountains.

She was gone.

Jaxson barked a greeting from inside as James fumbled with the key into the front door lock. Being alone on the property felt odd, his siblings off living or playing house with their better halves. James was by himself for the first time in his life, the feeling peculiar and foreign to him. Thank goodness for his black and yellow labs, Jaxson and Delia.

"Hey, boy," he greeted, stroking Jaxson's sable fur. The excited animal's entire body moved to the rhythm of his wagging tail as Delia stood nearby. She was a few years older than Jaxson and waited patiently for her turn.

"Come here, D," he requested. He knelt and allowed the yellow Labrador to lick his face, making him smile.

That's the thing about having dogs. Jaxson and Delia were pleased with nothing more than a treat, a scratch behind their ears, or a pat on the head. James wasn't sure where his love of dogs came from, but he found himself calmer around his companions, and his stress and anxiety alleviated, at least for a little while.

The more he loved on his canines, the more they paid him back in ways nobody else could. He felt it deep down, the term "man's best friend" hitting him in the feels. He knew he was melancholy from his break-up with Samantha and could swear his dogs knew instinctively something was up. Still wearing his coat, he sat silently on the floor and spent time with the animals, showering them with love.

Delia laid her head in his lap, enjoying the belly rubs, while Jaxson got the zoomies and repeatedly fetched a tattered toy James tossed across the expansive great room. He knew he was a more disciplined person because of his adorable and loyal dogs. They made him fully appreciate unconditional love, commitment, and life itself. Like clock-work, they let him know when they needed to go outside or be fed.

And they were his trusty sidekicks when it came to working on the farm; his favorite times spent hiking through the pinewood forest with them following obediently from behind at the end of a long workday. Their excitement and boundless energy reminded him how important freedom was, even to them.

And wasn't that what he was now? Free? He wasn't all that surprised. It seemed like he and Samantha had been going that direction for a while. Still, the sting of rejection filled him with melancholy

James hoisted his tired body up from the floor. "Come on. Time to get home."

On his way to the back door through the kitchen, he noticed a note left behind on the island. It was from his sister, Becky.

I'll have a big breakfast for everyone in the morning before we get Daddy from the hospital. Eight sharp. Love you!

James smiled, knowing his sister was excited about bringing their father home after all this time. The big house and farm weren't the same without his presence. But he knew his dad had a long road of recovery ahead. They'd already made plans to bring in a nurse to help him through the transition and to make sure he kept up with his meds and physical therapy.

Roy Bennett's cardiac arrest rocked everyone to their core, especially James. His dad was the patriarch and their only parent since their mother died years ago. He was James's confidant and best friend. Just the thought of losing him left him shaking in his cowboy boots.

But they hadn't lost him. The man had been given a second chance, and he was grateful.

James locked up the main house and trudged across the chilly path with his big dogs by his side toward the carriage house where he resided full-time on the property. He once shared the space with his brother, Walt, until he and his new wife, Elyse, made their own home a few miles down the road on the same land as Teddy and Robyn.

But James hadn't been alone for long. Samantha changed all that. She'd stayed with him at Bennett Farms for much of their relationship while working in and around the Langston Falls area. Her career often took her to other cities, including Atlanta. And the more he thought about it, he realized she hadn't spent much time with him on the farm since before the holidays. That should've been the first warning.

The interior of his home was cold, like his heart. The dogs stopped by their food bowls and cocked their heads in confusion as James ignored them and continued toward his bedroom. Not bothering to take off his coat, he flicked on the lights to see the evidence of his relationship's demise for himself.

The dresser drawers Sam once occupied were wide open as if she'd been in a rush to clean them out. A few wire hangers hung empty in the closet space they shared, and the vanity in the adjoining bathroom was bare, the faint scent of her shampoo lingering in the air.

James swallowed a lump the size of a wine barrel in his throat, determined to keep his emotions in check. The realization she'd packed up and exited his life for good left him heartbroken. Closing his eyes, he breathed in the last traces of Sam's femininity and resolved he'd have to man up and work harder and smarter from here on out, determined to get over her.

"Screw relationships," he muttered to himself.

Digging his hand into his coat, he retrieved the red velvet ring box burning a hole in his pocket all evening.

Flicking it open, blood roared in his ears as he stared at the small, solitary Princess-cut diamond set in a gold band.

His dad helped him pick it out a few months ago, and he'd planned on giving it to Samantha at dinner, preferably during a decadent dessert served with a bottle of expensive champagne. He was ready to take their relationship to the next level. Little did he know, she'd already decided to pack up and move on, leaving him standing there with his heart in his hands.

Shrugging off his coat, James gave himself an inner pep talk. He didn't need a woman to make his life complete. He had everything a guy could ever ask for. A thriving family winery and Christmas tree farm working alongside his siblings. His father's miraculous recovery and homecoming to look forward to. Two big, loyal dogs who loved him unconditionally.

Speaking of dogs...

James whipped his head around at the sound of canine nails clicking against the hardwood floors. Jaxson and Delia obediently sat in the doorway as if trying to figure him out. Squeezing the back of his neck, he realized he hadn't fed them before he rushed off to the restaurant to meet Sam.

He settled the ring box into one of the empty dresser drawers, shoved it closed, and snapped his fingers, realizing he hadn't eaten either.

"Come on, Jax. Come on, D. I'm starved. Let's eat."

———

The following day, James leaned against a porch post outside the main house and pressed his chin into the warm fabric of his winter coat. He lifted a steaming mug of coffee to his lips and stared out across the expanse of family land spread out before him in the cold, golden morning, the winery trellises barren, and the green carpet of Christmas pines rolling up the hills as far as the eye could see. Jaxson and Delia cantered through the vineyard, their hot breath noticeable in clouds of vapor coming from their muzzles.

"James?" Becky hollered.

He turned at the sound of his name and plastered a smile on his face.

"Yeah?"

"It's freezing out there. Why don't you come back inside? I just took the monkey bread out of the oven."

James nodded. "I'll come in a sec."

The back door closed with a thump, giving James a few more seconds to sulk. He wasn't ready to face his family, especially after a fitful night's sleep. He'd tossed and turned all night, rechecking his phone for a text message or call from Samantha—anything to let him know she might've changed her mind and wanted him to wait for her.

But there was nothing but radio silence.

Flinging the last dregs of his coffee into the yard, he headed inside with his dogs, thankful for the warm interior. Setting his mug on the counter, he shrugged off his coat, smiled, and nodded at everyone before hanging it up in the mudroom.

"Do we know how long Dad needs a nurse?" Walt asked.

His brothers Walt and Teddy, their wives, and his sister Becky were gathered around the island, filling their plates with an assortment of breakfast choices. Hank and Ella Mae were in Nashville but planned on welcoming their dad home later over FaceTime.

Even Glen Kirby was in attendance, the former nemesis

of the family helping Becky with the spread. And why wouldn't he be here? The man was in a full-blown relationship with his little sister now, and she'd practically moved in with him down the road at his apple farm.

And James would *never* forget how Glen was the reason their father was still alive. He'd resuscitated his dad after he collapsed near the barn two weeks ago. He would forever be indebted to Glen and his heroic behavior, just like the rest of the family.

"It will depend on how well he does with his physical therapy," Teddy replied. He tossed a blueberry into his mouth and chewed.

James plopped a large spoonful of scrambled eggs and a few sausage links onto his plate while he listened to the conversation.

"I heard it can take several months before he's given the all-clear," Robyn added.

"Knowing Roy, he'll totally beat the odds and be up and at it in a few weeks, flirting with his nurse and cracking dad jokes," Elyse said. This induced a few hopeful chuckles and giggles throughout the kitchen.

James kept quiet and grabbed a gooey bite of Becky's famous monkey bread. Shoving it into his mouth, he almost choked when Walt asked him a question point blank.

"Where's Sam?"

All eyes were on him as he chewed slowly and finally swallowed. "She's, uh, not here."

"No shit, Sherlock," Walt laughed. "Is she on her way?"

James set his full plate of food on the island, suddenly not hungry anymore. "I guess you could say that."

"Well? When will she be here? We need to leave in the next thirty minutes," Becky said, glancing at her wristwatch.

He ran a hand across his stubbly jaw, knowing he looked

like crap this morning. His usually combed hair was mussed, and he hadn't felt like shaving. Even his shirt was untucked, which was very unlike him.

"You okay, brother?" Teddy asked. He came up beside James and palmed his shoulder.

Clearing his throat, he tried to sound nonchalant and said the words fast. "We broke up last night. She already packed up and moved out. Hey, Becks, you got any more coffee?"

His family appeared stunned, his sister going into fix-it mode. "Um, sure, Jimmy. Coming right up."

"Bro? What happened?" Walt asked.

James scanned the faces in the room and shook his head. "She's on her way to Quantico, Virginia, to begin training at the FBI Academy. She's starting a whole new life —without me."

Becky handed off a mug of fresh coffee and squeezed his bicep. "I'm sorry, Jimmy. It's her loss." She looked around the room. "Right, y'all?"

The room interrupted in unison.

"Of course."

"She's a fool."

"Big mistake, James. She didn't know what she had."

"I'm so sorry. You'll find someone else."

He waved them all off. "I'm fine. Really. It's no big deal. Please don't make a fuss. And please don't tell Dad on his first day home. I'll get around to telling him at some point. Let's make sure today is a *good* day." He brought the mug to his lips and took a big gulp, the hot coffee scalding his mouth.

"Damn!" he sputtered.

"Sorry, Jimmy," Becky lamented. "Here, eat this."

She quickly offered him another gooey piece of monkey

bread. The cinnamon sugar, butter, and dough melted in his mouth, easing the pain.

If only he could find something delicious to ease the ache in his heart.

Grab your copy...
vinci-books.com/fearlesslove

Playlist

The Bennetts of Langston Falls

Seven Days – Kenny Chesney
Just a Kiss – Lady A
Son Of A Sinner – Jelly Roll
Pick Me Up – Gabby Barrett
Homemade – Jake Owen
You Didn't – Brett Young
American Honey – Lady A
Half of my Hometown – Kelsea Ballerini
Rich Man – Little Big Town
Those Eyes – New West
Tin Man – Miranda Lambert
Hard To Love – Lee Brice
Dancin' Away With My Heart – Lady A
But You Can't Have Mine – Dylan Scott
More Than My Hometown – Morgan Wallen
One Of Them Girls – Lee Brice

About the Author

"The Singing Author," KG Fletcher, lives in her very own frat house in Atlanta, GA, with her husband Ladd and three sons. As a singer/songwriter, she became a recipient of the "Airplay International Award" for "Best New Artist," showcasing original songs at The Bluebird Café in Nashville, TN. She earned her BFA in theater at Valdosta State University and has traveled the world professionally as a singer/actress. She is a two-time Georgia Maggie Award Nominee and currently gets to play rock star as a backup singer in the "Remember When Rock Was Young – the Elton John Experience."

KG is a hopeless romantic. When she's not on the road singing, she's probably at home daydreaming about her swoony book boyfriends or arranging a yummy charcuterie board while sipping red wine and listening to Frank Sinatra. She's also a conference speaker and loves to interact with readers on social media and share about her writing and singing journey.

Acknowledgments

This story was originally supposed to be a surprise pregnancy trope. Are you shocked?? But thanks to a deep dive conversation on a road trip to Myrtle Beach for a show with my friend and mentor, Craig A. Meyer, Becky's story ended up even better than I could have ever imagined. And when he sent me a text saying Chapter 32 was the best chapter I'd ever written, I was floored! So thank you, Craig, for your amazing feedback. Thank you for putting up those guardrails and keeping me on track. Thank you for helping me realize Glen needed to earn the respect and love he always wanted from Becky and her family in the right ways, not the cliché ways. You are a treasure to me!

To my Atlanta bestie, Anne, to whom this book is dedicated, thank you for introducing me to Linville Falls (the inspiration for Langston Falls) and accompanying me on a second EPIC book research trip where we met ninety-two-year-old patriarch Jack Wiseman's granddaughter, Lindsay, at the Linville Falls Winery. I was in hog heaven taking all the pretty pictures with physical books in my hands. What a dream! I can't wait to go back when the series is complete. I may have to do a professional photo shoot next time (me, sprawled in the vineyard surrounded by my book babies. HA!) And how could I forget our floating sessions on Lake Appalachia brainstorming James's story? Seriously, you are the BEST!

As always, I must thank my awesome husband and sons

who are my biggest supporters and believe in me when I struggle to believe in myself. To my Insta-author friends for sharing the love and answering all my direct messages about reels and TikToks, Book Funnel, Sticker Mule, and bloggers (oh my!). To the best beta readers on the planet, Heather, Ladd, Blair, and Craig, for putting up with me talking nonstop about the Bennett Family this last year and how much I love them.

To Vicky Burkholder, my long-time editor and friend, for putting the finishing touches on my story. And to Gigi Blume, you are and always will be my author bestie. (She's also a USA Today Bestselling Author and writes phenomenal rom-coms! Seriously, y'all need to check her out!)

For my awesome team of ARC readers and all the fantastic bloggers who came on board with this series— THANK YOU for your continued support. Your gorgeous posts, teasers, and comments make my heart sing!

For my critique partner, Carrie, who has supported me since day ONE. (Our writing retreats are my favorite.) And to all of my readers, thank you for the positive reviews and feedback. You have no idea what it means to me.

I hope you will continue the Bennett Family's journey in the last book of the series featuring James in *Fearless Love*. I can't believe we're almost to the end!

xoxo
Kelly